M-Force

Destiny Discovered

Christopher Timm

PublishAmerica
Baltimore

First printing

ISBN:1-4241-8538-6
PUBLISHED BY PUBLISHAMERICA, LLLP
www.publishamerica.com
Baltimore

Printed in the United States of America

To my wonderful wife and awesome children —because they've been there every step of the way helping me discover my own destiny!

Chapter 1
A Change of Direction

Oblivious to existence around it, the chunk of shiny black rock had hurtled through space for longer than anyone would know. Indeed, time, as man knows it, is relative to the vastness of that which surrounds earth. Origin, composition, purpose, all are a great mystery. Into that mystery traveled this insignificant piece of the puzzle. That is until the insignificant item found itself within the remnant of man's attempt to conquer, understand and exploit the great mystery.

The symmetry of the two worlds colliding suddenly became a tangible thing when it happened in reality. The collision of a simple rock and a piece of forgotten space debris would soon have an impact on changing the course of history. But that was for later. For now, the explosion, if it had been anywhere else but in the vacuum of space, would have been deafening. The force of the blast caused the small meteorite to change its trajectory to a new point of destiny.

The consequences of this change of destiny seemed evident to those who studied space almost instantaneously. But the deeper results would be some time in becoming evident.

The alarm horn, along with a series of flashing warning lights erupted on a radar console in the firing room at Cape Canaveral, Florida.

The unexpected warning startled Eric Brunner, program manager in charge of the impending space shuttle takeoff. His voice rising to show his growing concern, he called out, "What have you got?"

The slender female operator at the panel replied, "We have a NEO trajectory change. Computers now place it on Atlantis' direct flight path."

Brunner called back, voice rising, "How can that be? There were no Near Earth Objects anywhere close to our trace."

Seeing the woman answer with a shrug, he abruptly shoved the junior data processing engineer out of the way to see what had set off the systems. Bleary eyed already from a day that began at 3:00 a.m., the head of the launch team paused to ensure what he was seeing was correct. Brunner caught the breath he'd just lost at what was showing on the monitor. For a moment the key member of the launch team hesitated to do what he knew he must.

Eric Brunner had always seemed out of place among the scientists and technicians on his team. Though middle-aged, the man was overtly muscular with a hard as steel personality. He ran daily, competing in marathons, but that wasn't what caused others to wonder about him. Brunner had an intensity about him that shone through his calm exterior facade. He also possessed dark eyes that when giving a penetrating look would cause others to avert their eyes.

Prematurely balding, the program manager had shaved his head. Now a single bead of sweat ran down from his crown to forehead. A quick mental calculation confirmed for him what the man was loath to do. Snatching a red telephone sitting beside the main computer screen, he demanded, "Get me the director."

In less than two minutes something that had been in preparation for six months was scrubbed.

"Launch sequence halted...launch sequence halted," the loudspeaker blared throughout the complex, signaling that what was to happen in less than ten minutes would not.

Everywhere people were wondering what the delay of the space shuttle launch was caused by this time.

Minutes later, in the luxuriously appointed office of the director of Kennedy Space Center, the program manager stood along with the other members of the launch team.

The group was paid to be cautious. It was their job to not only get the shuttle off the ground, but also to look for things that could cause disasters. Disasters like the ones that had been broadcast around the world, live and in color in the past. Yet, to cancel a launch had serious financial costs and consequences. Thus this group nervously fidgeted, though secretly the others were happy to not be Eric Brunner at this particular point in time.

It was one thing to call it off, it was another to be able to justify to those outside this office.

An irritated Edward G. Ware made his presence felt as he entered the office. Sitting down, the darkly tanned director, who would rather be on his ocean fishing boat right now, ran a hand over his slicked back, gray hair to signal the discussion would begin. Ensured he had everyone's undivided attention, the man in charge of all operations at the Kennedy Space Center asked, "So tell me again what happened?"

Brunner appeared calm on the outside. But inside the senior member of the launch team was involuntarily nervous. The emotion bugged him; it was something he thought should be under control. Yet, it was his call to abort the launch, costing NASA millions of dollars, in addition to the bad publicity and embarrassment it caused. Nonetheless, he knew the threat and knew his decision was the correct one.

Licking dry lips, the program manager reported, "A NEO meteor, classified M13, just entered into our launch trajectory minutes ago. It threatened the flight path of the shuttle. We had no choice but to stand down."

Ware sighed in exasperation, knowing the conversations he would be having within the hour. "It was your call to make, Eric." the Director confirmed, but each held their breath waiting for his assessment. "That was gutsy, but it was the right call. Good job."

The audible sound of breath being released showed the release of tension.

Then, in frustration, Ware pounded the lacquered mahogany desk, regaining everyone's attention. "I don't get it, there was no threat," he said in exasperation. "We were tracking this thing, how did it get into our atmosphere?"

"I'm not entirely sure, sir, but our radar picked up a subspace collision." Brunner was still calm on the outside, but within he sighed with relief that his decision had been supported.

Although Ware's reputation was for pushing the envelope, he never compromised on safety, regardless of pressure. But the pressure on this particular mission had been huge due to previous failures.

"So what? There was a collision, that's happened before." Ware let his growing irritation show. "You told me M13 was no threat to our launch. What changed that?"

"It wasn't a threat, sir, when we gave our last report. Somehow its trajectory was altered by the collision."

The declaration gave the Director a start. "Altered? How could that be?" he exclaimed, genuinely puzzled. "What did it hit?"

"How it changed, that we don't know yet," Brunner honestly answered.

"But we do know there was some sort of explosion in space. My team is checking the data feeds and satellite imagery now. In terms of what it hit, we know from our records it seemed to be an old '70s grade Russian satellite."

"And it had enough firepower to blow an M class meteor off course?" the NASA Director asked quietly, as if confirming something he was already aware of.

"It seemed to be, sir."

There was a long, uncomfortable pause in the room. It became so quiet the hum of the lights could be heard.

Ware's eyes narrowed, his look like granite, as if some new realization was taking over. A former military officer, he had earned his reputation in the "Star Wars" missile defense program. With the end of the Cold War, his skills did not seem to be as useful in that arena, so he had been tapped first as a Senior Program Manager, then quickly rising through the ranks to become director of the facility and its operations. If anyone would know what was up, it would be Edward G. Ware.

Turning to an aide, the director barked out, "Get me the Russian Federal Space Agency in Moscow now. I have a few questions for the head of the RKA."

The assistant scurried off to make the necessary connection and also to get out of the way of the foul mood of their boss. This news was not going to be received well by the head of NASA, or the Senate Committee that oversaw the country's space program.

Already the wall-mounted television showed CNN reporting live from outside the facility of the aborted mission. The only question now was who would call first from Washington.

"There's another thing you should do," Brunner added.

The head of Cape Kennedy shook his head as if to get rid of the rising migraine. "What else?" he asked.

"The collision not only put the meteor into the path of the shuttle. It's also now going to hit the earth. In fact it'll land in our Midwest."

"You're just full of good news, aren't you," Ware responded sarcastically. Catching himself, he asked, "So how big a collision was there in space?"

"A big one."

The Director's tone changed, as if the news changed something. "All right. We need to lock down the area and retrieve this item," he ordered. "I want you to personally go there and take charge of the operation. Bring in the closest FBI Field Office, get the National Guard too, and take whomever you want from your team. But that area needs to be secure."

"Is there something you want to tell me about this space rock, boss?" Brunner asked warily, his curiosity twigged.

"Not yet, it's just a hunch. After I have the official conversation with their headquarters in Moscow, I'll be talking to a couple of contacts I still have in their ops center at Star City. Better to be safe than sorry." Leaning his elbows on the desk, the distinguished looking man rubbed his temples with his fingers as if to relieve the mounting stress he felt. "So where's it going to land?"

The doors of the yellow school buses opened, disgorging their occupants. Students piled out, chatting among themselves, carrying on only as teenagers can. It was warmer than usual; the sun was shining. Several meadowlarks could be heard singing from within the expanse of lush green forest a short distance from the parking lot they were gathering in.

The merriment continued until a stern looking adult barked out, "Listen up, everyone. There's no time for fun and games here. I want you all to get yourselves organized by class and ready to move out in five minutes."

Obediently the high school students shuffled about, trying to sort themselves out. A few mumbled complaints rose up, but none would risk incurring the wrath of the crewcut wearing leader of the expedition.

"This is SO boring!" lamented Talitha Beck to her group of friends. "I can't believe that while everyone else in the senior class gets to go to Adventure Experience we get stuck on a geography field trip to 'nowhere's ville' park. It's not fair!" the petite, pretty high school senior fumed.

Wearing stylish jeans and a black cotton sweater, the girl crinkled her nose in disgust. The thought of other classes having fun on her last mid-June day in high school caused her frustration. Instead, they were at Great Pine State Park, observing terrain features and the effects of erosion on soil in a heavily forested area.

The group's teacher had pointedly remarked that anyone skipping the trip would automatically fail the course, which meant summer school. Knowing the man was serious, the combined group represented by classes of freshman, sophomore and senior high students had set out for the great outdoors while the other classes went to the popular theme park a short distance away.

Gathering near the edge of the forest, a male student, overhearing Beck's comment, philosophically observed, "Hey, they don't call him 'the Hammer' for nothing.

Another piped up, "Yea, it's bad enough that we have to go. But going with the freshman and sophomore classes too? Man, that's so lame. What are we, free babysitting for the school?"

Ulysses Hammerman, their teacher, seemed to appear from behind a pine bush. Though saying nothing, the school wrestling coach's withering gaze caused all to stop speaking. The stern-faced man's reputation for being tougher than nails was reinforced by his outdated flattop haircut and thick neck. In addition, he wore a crisp white shirt and tie with dress slacks possessing a razor sharp crease, putting him at odds with other teachers that dressed more casual. Despite the outmoded look, he had rugged good looks and dark brown eyes. His attractiveness was lost, though, by his disposition. An ex-Marine, people wondered why he was a teacher.

Certain that he had everyone's attention, Hammerman gave instructions on what was expected. Several parents were along as chaperons, though they seemed to shrink under the man's intense look. No one questioned his authority, nor his control over this day.

With a quick, "Let's move," the group shuffled off as if they were going on a forced march rather than a field trip.

The next two hours were wholly uneventful for the students, moving from clump of trees to clump of trees while their teacher explained to them the finer points of geographic import.

Though the man had eyes like a hawk, the group was large enough that he could not see everything going on. He seemed to miss a group of bored students beginning to torment a number of those who were actually interested in what was going on. Then again he may not have cared, since the group causing the problem was made up largely of his wrestlers.

Star athlete Keith Ramsey led the charge. The senior was a state champion, who didn't seem able, or willing, to leave his aggression on the mat. The object of his amusement was a tall, thin classmate wearing Dockers and a checked madras shirt. The senior had just answered a complex question the teacher had thrown out to show their lack of knowledge.

George Alexander seemed to have knowledge about everything. A straight "A" student, he was heading to State University in the fall to study computer engineering. His confidence irritated the muscular Ramsey, who decided to vent it on his classmate.

"Hey, brain," Ramsey called out, throwing a pinecone hard at the gangly youth, "what's this?"

Turning too late, the projectile hit Alexander on the face just below his round, wire glasses. The force of the projectile thrown left a mark. The people around him fled in fear of further attack, as the remainder laughed in delight at the misfortune of the intelligent senior. The teen didn't move. He neither advanced, nor retreated. Though knowing he was outmatched, George Alexander would not back down either.

Hammerman had a small grin on his face as he tardily rebuked the handsome, black-haired athlete. His victim's face reddened in embarrassment, but he did not shy away, standing his ground.

A loud, ripping sound in the air caused all conversations to stop instantly. Instinctively, the students looked up in the clear blue sky. They were rewarded by the sight of a flaming ball plummeting toward them. Like the sound of a falling artillery shell, it passed their view, hitting the ground with an audible thud close to where they stood.

"Cool! Let's check it out," someone yelled.

The declaration seemed to cause a stampede of the school kids seeking to find the object. Ignoring the yells of their teacher and chaperons, they ran off after it.

Crashing through the woods in the general direction of where the flame in the sky had traveled, the group lost all form of order. Yells and calls echoed throughout the formerly quiet forest as the quest carried on. Finally, one of the searchers, finding something, called out, "Over here."

Trees were broken from the impact and a long skid mark was visible in the turf. Resting at the end of the track, dirt piled up as a buffer at the back, was what looked like a large boulder. Jet-black in color, it was smooth and shiny. The surface, though, was an irregular texture.

"That's the weirdest looking rock I've ever seen," a red-haired girl with braces declared, voicing the other's thoughts.

"It's not a rock," declared George Alexander excitedly. "It's a meteorite." In addition to being president of the school's computer club, he also led the astronomy club as well. Though his appearance seemed overly slender and somewhat gangly for his age, it misrepresented the truth of George's character. The youth was a leader among his peers. With evident excitement he adjusted his wire glasses framing a head of blondish-brown, close-cropped hair. Grey blue eyes stared intently at the item from space, another of his fascinations.

Even from a distance it was obvious that the item was extremely hot. The heat pulsated from it, causing a number to step back to a more comfortable distance. George, though, unconsciously inched closer, drawn to the thing he had only read about. Totally engrossed, he was unaware of the searing heat on his face as he bent over. No one noticed the mark from his earlier attack disappear as he stared at the meteorite.

Meanwhile, Keith Ramsey was bored again after the discovery. The aggressive teen decided to liven things up. Grabbing two unsuspecting younger students by the straps of their backpacks, he suddenly flung them toward the meteorite. They both spasmodically contorted to keep from hitting the rock, landing heavily on the ground instead.

Ramsey's crowd roared with laughter, high-fiving each other. The younger students instinctively shrunk away in hopes of not becoming victims themselves.

The pair lay there, only feet away from the object of attention, seemingly transfixed. The June day was already warm, so the heat radiating off the meteorite caused each to begin to sweat.

Then, as if coming out of a spell, one of the victims of Ramsey's bad joke, sophomore student Beau Joseph sheepishly got to his feet, brushing himself off.

The other teen, though, was furious. Jumping up, with fists cocked, he went after the bigger student. Only a freshman, Tim David was not intimidated by the gargantuan form before him. He was not about to let this slide. Tim charged at the wrestler, running into him. But the laughing bully tossed the smaller boy aside like a rag doll. Adding insult to injury, the tormenter's friends and the others around him joined in the merriment. Tim knew he was bested. The blond, spiky haired teen slunk back into his crowd of classmates.

Talitha Beck observed the scene with disgust. The senior broke away from her own friends. Walking to where the unfortunate pair had been tossed, she recovered the knapsack that Beau Joseph had forgotten. Stooping to pick it up, she glared at Keith Ramsey the whole time with piercing sky blue eyes. Still outraged by the previous scene, the pulsating meteorite only feet away was oblivious to her. She was focused, not on the object of curiosity for her class, but rather on defying the one who others were intimidated by. The dark-haired wrestler held up meaty hands in mock surrender while his friends continued to laugh.

Joseph, for his part, made his way back to the anonymity of the crowd. Of average build and height, with a conventional haircut and ordinary looks, he blended into the scene around him. Only his eyes, as blue and piercing as Talitha Beck's, stood out. Face reddening with embarrassment, he watched the pretty senior come through the crowd to hand him his knapsack.

"Thank you," he stuttered, grateful for her kindness.

She smiled in return, but said nothing. Instead, she returned to her own friends after giving the wrestler one last defiant look.

"All right, that's enough fooling around," declared Mr. Hammerman, pushing his way through the crowd.

He had watched the antics from a distance, amusing himself. But something about the meteorite concerned him. His sense of responsibility was taking over. He couldn't articulate it, but the man trusted his instincts, honed during his time in the Marines. Right now they were telling him danger was about.

The teacher commanded, "Everyone move back and get away from that." Seeing the students hesitate, his voice boomed, "NOW!"

As others scurried away, Ramsey decided to show the others he was no wimp. Moving over to the meteorite, the solidly built teen made as if to touch it. To his surprise he felt the vise-like grip of Ulysses Hammerman on his arm.

"This is no joke, Keith. I said get away, and I meant it," the teacher ordered.

As if to add to the sense of urgency, in the distance the wail of sirens could be heard heading toward where they stood.

Chapter 2
Getting Our Bearings

Eric Brunner sat in the front passenger seat of a black FBI SUV pondering what was ahead. A report had come to the NASA leader that the state police had located and isolated the meteorite. The column of government vehicles he led was en route to the location.

The space rock had apparently landed in Great Pine Forest State Park, located less than a two-hour drive from the major city in the area. Laptop computer in hand, Brunner's GPS locator told him the region's significant urban center was Kilings-Welch. Though seeming to be one city on the map, it was, in fact, two municipal entities. The man had heard of the place from the news, so was aware that the two had grown together over time.

Despite the physical symmetry, the cities possessed unique identities. Yet, if it were not for the signs at various locations between the two, you would not even know they were distinct municipal entities. The awkward name had been shortened, so now people in the area know it as simply KW. What the man wasn't aware of yet was that though visually inseparable, in commerce and temperament they were worlds apart.

As if reminding him that geography wasn't the only thing that impacted the character of a municipality, his SUV passed a sign that declared: "Kilings-Welch: A Region on the Move!"

Changing to a different screen on his computer, the government agent downloaded a dossier of information to familiarize himself with the cities and surrounding area. Reading quickly, the man discovered that Jacob Kilings and

Zebediah Welch founded the area straddling the Majestic River in the 1850s. Initially a major waterway at the time, it now was more of an irritant for cross-town commuters trying to navigate the cities inadequate bridges. Perhaps not as grand as the Mississippi, the river was nonetheless significant and a major terrain feature. The remainder of the area was flat, surrounded by an ever-shrinking agricultural base. The insatiable demand for development had caused an unrelenting erosion of the pastoral land in the area. Unfortunately, it seemed only now people were beginning to question the wisdom of unchecked development. But the engine of progress was humming along, making this one of the fastest growing areas in the country.

Kilings was the larger of the two and had a heavy industrial base. Auto parts, along with other manufacturing plants, dotted the horizon. Ethnically centered neighborhoods built up around the factories that generations had worked at were prominent as well.

Welch was the complete opposite. A white-collar town, it proudly possessed the main campus of State University. From the school had grown a high-tech industry rivaled by few other cities in the country. Software development, biotechnology and advanced engineering firms with exotic sounding names and big payrolls made this a place of prosperity. Reflecting this, large houses on lush lots made up much of the residential community of this town.

Brunner switched from historical and economic data to a sociological assessment. He found a place whose reality was quite different from the appearance on the surface.

The two cities had become uncomfortable with each other in many ways it was reported. One was jealous of the other's prosperity, while the other resented the simplicity of the larger community. Though harmonious on the surface, like a swift flowing ocean current, underneath there was a steady undertow starting to pull the two communities into a dark abyss. Already there were some seeking ways to exploit this yet unknown fact.

In the broader context, with a combined population of over a million citizens, it was a significant regional center within the state, yet, in many ways, still retained a degree of intimacy that drew others to it. High rises dotted the downtown areas of each, reflecting the businesses that flocked to such locations. Banks, lawyers, accountants and other such professionals filled this prime real estate. But the real influence and power lay in the commercial centers ringing the two towns where the most prominent enterprises resided. Finally, all form of entertainment and shopping known to the country was available to the residents of this region.

Kilings-Welch was a place looked upon with growing envy for its prosperity by other places. Yet, for some strange reason, all the things money could buy didn't seem to satisfy. There was a higher than average divorce rate in the area, while psychiatrists and counselors were in high demand. The small town charm seemed to be giving way to big city grit. Again, another sign of the deadly undertow in this idyllic picture.

The warbling of his cell phone broke the bald-headed, tough looking man's concentration.

"Brunner."

"This is Lieutenant MacMillan of the state police sir. We've located the package, but there's a complication."

"Yes, what is it?"

"There was a fairly large field trip from Kilings-Welch High School in the park," the police officer reported. "Apparently, they also were around the meteorite after it landed."

Brunner rubbed his eyes in frustration at the additional complication. "All right. Keep them contained and keep everyone else out of the park. We'll be on the ground in approximately twenty minutes."

Ending the conversation with the police, the NASA manager thought through this new complication. Brunner was glad he'd thought to order a National Guard hazardous materials unit to deploy from the closest field medical battalion. They were only about half an hour behind him from their last report.

Tabbing the file he'd been looking at before the call, the man downloaded the information they had on Kilings-Welch High School. As he waited for the material to appear on the screen, the philosophically minded agent pondered this new development. It seemed that again youth were being haphazardly thrown into the fray, as they always have been throughout history. They were the ones with such pressure upon them to fix the errors of their parents, though not being taught the lessons to overcome them.

Mistakes were inevitable, and just as inevitably followed the criticism of the "younger generation" by those who created the problems with their own greedy indifference in the first place.

The file came up and Brunner saw that reflecting the area's prosperity, the schools in both Killings and Welch were top rate. Academically, the GPA of the students in this region was in the top 10% nationally.

The man who had seen and done much over his years saw that, despite all the learning, there seemed to be little common sense. For just as the adults of the area negatively reflected some of the poorer character traits of the day, so too do the children. Drugs, gangs, immorality and self-centeredness were in ample supply among the youth at the expense, it seemed, of compassion and honor.

From the report, it appeared that Killings-Welch High School sat on the interior border of the two towns drawing students from each. This created a diverse mosaic reflecting the sometime lack of harmony between the two communities. Although a place where people could discover their gifts, distinct cultures did exist within the school, rarely interacting with each other.

While proficient in many areas, the school was a place that prided itself on athletics. Those who excelled in this arena were revered, often treated like gods, a dangerous position for teenagers to be placed into. The nature of the community it drew from also meant there was a significant academic structure with some truly gifted students.

Of course, as with any other school, there were those who crossed the boundary of labels and those who did not fit into any. There were the students only marking time until they could leave and strike out on their own along with those who were trying to fit in. The faculty was dedicated, priding themselves on having the best high school in the country, which, of course, many believed of themselves.

Eric Brunner closed his laptop. He knew all that was needed to fulfill this mission. A sign at the entrance to a large deciduous forest announced Great Pines State Park. They were there; it was time to get to work.

Yellow caution tape ringed the area near downtown Kilings that had been the scene of a dangerous gun battle earlier in the day. The disturbingly common occurrence in the community was playing itself out again it seemed.

Lieutenant Nate DeBeer, commander of the tactical unit of the K-W Police Service shook his head at the scene of carnage before him. By the time his team had deployed it was too late.

The two municipalities cooperated on certain administrative tasks, including policing for the past twenty years. The idea had been to rationalize to cut costs and lower taxes. While that had been successful, the region-wide efforts hadn't seemed to be making any difference in terms of crime lately.

Three bodies lay dead on the ground, chalk outlines around them, numerous bullet casings, and other pieces of evidence littering the location. With the area cordoned off, uniformed officers kept the curious, or morbid, away. Plain-clothes detectives talked to several witnesses or examined the crime scene.

A heavyset, older man in a stylish suit with a badge hanging around his neck sauntered over to the SWAT leader. "What do you think Nate?" asked Commander Don Austen, the ranking officer in this particular district.

Rubbing his square jaw thoughtfully, DeBeer shrugged, replying, "I haven't talked to the guys from the Major Crimes Unit, but I'd say it's gang related."

"Bloods?"

"It looks like it to me," the tactical officer said. "This sure is their MO anyway."

The commander was called away by one of the detectives, leaving the man in black tactical coveralls to his own contemplation. With close-cropped hair and muscular features, the police officer appeared aggressive, but that did not truly reflect his nature. Nate DeBeer was a spiritual man and a deep thinker. Now alone, he was able to ponder anew something that had been eating away at him for months.

With prosperity came a rise in crime, as some that were increasingly falling behind the ideal talked about on television advertising took what they could not earn. The police, though trying their best, were underfunded and outmatched.

The politicians didn't wish to believe the truth of what was happening, blaming outsiders for the troubles. Instead of action, they launched "cultural diversity" and "Let's all get along" campaigns.

All the while the place began to seethe. Most didn't want to admit that there was any problem in the utopian-like place they had created. It all came down to dialogue and talking; working to better understand each other.

Nate DeBeer kicked the ground in frustration. They weren't the ones having to tell that to the surviving family of yesterday's shooting victim who had pleaded for his life. Nor did they have to face the hospitalized business owner who was beaten AFTER giving the robbers what they wanted.

The answer from those who didn't want to admit the problem was that they needed another mega mall or another tract of industrial land. More jobs, better infrastructure, that's what the region required

All the while the cauldron boiled even more.

The cop on the street, who usually has a better feel for the pulse of the city than the politician on the 30th floor looking down, feared what was coming. DeBeer had talked with many of his colleagues and they all thought the same thing. With summer about to begin, teenagers would be free from any restraint. If things were bad now, what would they be like in a few weeks? They knew how few of them there were. Already many of the police were afraid to go into certain areas of Kilings during the daytime. At night? Forget it. They had families to go home to and protect as well. “Free zone,” “Wild Wild West,” that was some of the nicknames already being given.

Parents seemed content to continue to build their own personal empires with hopes of being able to move into one of the gated communities beginning to grow like weeds in the suburbs. They figured that if they could segment their children everything would be fine. Unfortunately, they seemed to forget the fact that, statistically speaking, it was their children that others needed to be protected from. But no, that was not the case. It was other kids who caused the troubles. Wasn’t that why they worked so hard? To give them everything they wanted? To give every advantage? Nate DeBeer pondered the same questions. He had two small kids of his own at home. He loved them dearly and would do anything for them.

Unfortunately, that prosperity came at the expense of the one commodity that most of the children wanted most—time and attention. Attention they were finding outside the home, sometimes with tragic results.

The thoughts depressing him, Nate DeBeer gathered his team to head back to their headquarters. There was nothing for them to do here but be in the way.

Nearly a dozen green, multi-wheeled military vehicles representing the haz-mat unit and field hospital of the 137th Medical Battalion rumbled past a sign reading: *Killings-Welch—A Region on the Move* on their way to the now quarantined area at Great Pine Forest State Park. The Economic Development committee was particularly pleased with the catchy slogan. None doubted it to be true. The question was—where was it moving?

Chapter 3
Checkup

A makeshift camp had sprung up in Great Pine Forest State Park. State Police had sealed it off, while government agents crawled all over the place. NASA technicians in futuristic looking hazardous materials suits moved back and forth throughout the area that not to long ago had been occupied by the students of Killings-Welch High School.

A quarantine area was set up, with military medical personnel examining the students. For the most part the teens stood around speaking quietly with each other, impressed by the activity around them. Overall, though, most were bored by the lack of action. They still didn't understand what all the fuss was about. Those who were examining the space relic said little to the teens, intent on doing their job.

Many of the students wondered what harm could come from some black rock? Besides, the day was getting late, which meant when they didn't arrive home their parents would worry. There was no need for this fear. Already the families of those affected had been informed of what had gone on. They would be called to meet the bus when the examinations were done.

Eric Brunner watched the bored teens as he waited to be connected with the director at the Kennedy Space Center. The area had been locked down. The military haz-mat people had secured the meteorite, then his people had moved in. There had been no contact with the item that he was aware of. But despite all his efforts, this little complication irritated the man who wanted a clean recovery. The students were an unneeded inconvenience.

"Eric?" the familiar voice on the other end asked.

"Yes, sir," Brunner replied.

"What have you got for me?"

"The area is secure and no one's getting in," the head of the recovery effort confirmed. "There were a bunch of kids from a high school field trip in the area when the NEO hit, though. The Army medics are looking at them now. As for the meteorite, on first blush our people figure it's an achondrite, maybe a type A or S, which is pretty rare."

"But?" the Director prodded.

"Well, we're getting some pretty odd readings off it. The weird thing is, they're not stable. They come and go, though, and we can't get a lock. This is definitely no ordinary space rock. You got anything that can help us out?"

Edward Ware got right to the point. "Okay, I had to yell and scream a bit, but I finally was able to get some information out of our friends in Moscow. There's a complication with the satellite, which could impact the recovery operation. It was a weapon's platform. The Russians were vague about the content, but I expect you can read between the lines. This was no ordinary space collision." Ware paused on the other end of the line, as if he was considering his words carefully. He then instructed, "I need you to be thorough in your analysis on the ground before anything moves. Let's be sure we know what we're dealing with."

George Alexander watched intently from the lineup of students, a man who looked like a government agent. The bald man who was on a cell phone suddenly got a sour look on his face as if receiving bad information. At least his day didn't seem to be going any better than theirs was George thought to himself.

The teens were lined up outside a tent in order to be checked over. As if to reinforce the importance of this exercise, a cordon of military personnel made sure none left the queue.

When it was his turn, George walked inside, hopping up on the examination table. "Hey, that's a spectrometer," he correctly pointed out to the surprised technician.

"You know what this is?" the slightly overweight middle-aged woman replied.

"Yes, I've read about them," George answered matter of factly. "Aren't they used to measure chemical composition though? I thought you'd be looking for radiation. Why do you have them here?"

The NASA technician had wondered the same thing herself, but knew better than to ask questions of Eric Brunner, who had ordered the tests. The man had ordered the equipment load for this mission and gave specific terms of reference for what was to be done. The woman adjusted her glasses, responding, "Routine check. For exposure and the like."

George pressed her. "But that doesn't make sense. A meteorite shouldn't carry anything that instrument would pick up."

"Listen, kid," the technician replied testily. "Let me decide how to do my job, okay? Besides, we've still got a lot more of your classmates to check, so no more questions."

An Army medical officer walked in. With one look he silenced the conversation. George still wondered why such an out of place piece of equipment would be there for, but held his tongue.

The technician had a curious look on her face, adjusting the machine but saying nothing.

Suddenly interested the officer asked, "What is it?"

The woman didn't respond immediately, staring intently at the screen. "It's nothing, Major," she hesitantly said. "Something seemed a bit odd at first, but everything's fine." Another pause, then with greater confidence affirmed, "Everything checks out."

The Army officer spread his hands apart as if gesturing that he wanted more information. George's ears perked up, intently listening in on the conversation, his natural curiosity peaked.

The technician tried to explain. "Well, I'm not sure what to say. The reading spiked when I first turned the machine on. I readjusted it and everything came out normal. The calibration must have been off."

The uniformed man pressed, "That seems a bit strange, doesn't it? How could that happen?"

The woman shrugged, becoming a bit frustrated at the questioning. "I don't know, but everything's fine now."

"Well, I guess I'd just note it and move on," the officer suggested to the civilian. "Besides, it's you NASA guys show anyway. We don't have all day to spend here, and there's still a lot more kids to examine."

The technician shrugged her shoulders, continuing on with the examination, which went routinely. Alexander was given a clean bill of health by her, then the doctor as well. He was quickly released so the next student could be examined.

Talitha Beck stood with a group of her friends listening to them complaining about what was going on. She really wasn't listening, still being angry at Keith

Ramsey's antics. It bothered her as well that he seemed to be indulged, regardless of what he did, simply because of his athletic skills. The more she thought, the more agitated she became. The pretty girl didn't realize she was beginning to feel unwell. Others noticed though.

"Are you okay, Talitha?" one of her friends asked.

"Sure, why?"

"You look like a lobster. Here, check it out." The girl handed Talitha a mirror from her purse.

Sure enough, the girl's face was flushed beet red, though it didn't feel hot. Instead, an overall sense of discomfort hit her. This concerned the girl, but she wasn't about to bring anyone's attention to the matter. She sloughed it off with her friends, blaming it on the sun, quickly changing the topic.

When it was her time to be examined, the condition was gone and she felt better. Talitha Beck was given a clean bill of health as well and sent on her way, vindicating her earlier decision to not bring any attention to the matter.

Tim David flexed his hand open and shut. It had a strange sensation, like all the muscles inside of him were being stimulated. Doing it again, he noticed the veins in his forearm pop up like those in the bodybuilding magazines he had looked at did. He repeated the action and they seemed to bulge even further. *Cool,* he thought.

But then his mind got back onto the topic of obsession for him, making the summer football team. He'd been cut from the freshman squad in the fall, being told he was too small for it. The team he now pondered was a combined squad, even harder to make. But Tim was convinced he could do it this time. The tryouts would happen soon; he'd be ready.

Yellow caution tape surrounded the area where the meteorite had hit. NASA technicians with all form of equipment were sweeping the area in an organized fashion. Beau Joseph watched intently, though no one seemed to notice him. Dressed in nondescript jeans and tee shirt, he blended into the surroundings. His main interest lay in the large military truck with crane that had moved into the cordoned off area. It looked like the vehicle was going to be used to move the space rock. *That makes sense,* he thought. *It's not like they were going to leave it there.*

Walking back to the parking lot, Beau could see the hustle and bustle of activity continuing. The sophomore had been checked and cleared already, so there was nothing to do but kill time until they were allowed to leave. He noticed state police cars blocking the entrance to the park. It was also obvious that this had already attracted attention. Several news agencies were outside the perimeter, but none were let in. In addition, dozens of curious people were straining to get a look at what was happening. Not only were the state troopers carrying shotguns, but also men in dark glasses with radio earphones were visible patrolling the perimeter. No unauthorized people were getting in. Beau wondered what the big deal was. So a rock had fallen to the earth. So what? He just wanted to get home and play on his Xbox.

After what seemed like an eternity, the order was given for the students and adults to get on the bus and leave. No one gave any explanation, nor told what would happen next. Several official-looking men with short hair had huddled with Ulysses Hammerman, but beyond that nothing else was shared. This irritated many of the teens, whose natural curiosity had been peaked by the events that had gone on over the course of the day. After getting onto the bus, there still was no movement. It was as if they wanted the group rounded up and out of the way.

George Alexander sat quietly with several of his friends, mind churning as to what was going on. He knew that while meteorites were not common, they also were not worth the fuss that was being caused. While the students may be preparing to leave, those examining the space rock were not. Already powerful lights had been brought into illuminate the area when darkness descended. *No*, he thought, *this didn't add up. There was more to this story than what they had been told.* Unfortunately for them, he was smart enough to figure out they'd likely never find out. Agitated, his leg bounced up and down, expending nervous energy.

Outside the bus, several of the government agents could feel a pulsation emanating from the ground, yet none could figure out where it had come from. Others were called in, affirming the sensation. Seismic equipment was quickly broken out from the equipment trucks to examine this phenomenon. Strangely, none could locate the source. Then, just as it had begun, just as quickly it ended. Another mystery for them to try to solve. It was going to be a long night.

The sun was hanging just above the pine trees when the geography field trip from KW High School was finally given permission to leave the park. They had been fed from a field kitchen, so hunger was not an issue for the teenagers. The novelty of the situation had worn off hours ago, and the group was happy to be finally leaving.

Eric Brunner stood and watched the buses leave. He was happy to have the students gone. They were getting some strange readings emanating from the meteorite, so he didn't need anyone else around to complicate things. All had supposedly checked out, but he wasn't sure what that meant. He knew he'd have a long couple of days reviewing the data.

Though a program manager by title, Brunner was a man with a darker past. Something was happening at this place, he could feel it. His instincts had never let him down before. Yet, what was it? Sure, there were some anomalies with the rock, but that was no big deal. Maybe he'd spent too much time in the Florida sun and was getting soft. This was a long way from Baghdad.

Anxious parents waited for the geography field trip at the school. Though all had been called again to inform them of the estimated arrival time, many were early, nervously awaiting their children. A collective sigh of relief was audible when the buses pulled in.

Quickly the yellow vehicles emptied, students were collected and the parking lot became deserted. Rather it was empty, save for one.

Ulysses Hammerman stood looking up in the sky, quietly reflecting. Night had fallen and the stars were out. He stood staring for the longest time, thinking. Thoughts were rolling around in his mind, strange feelings beginning to stir. The stars seemed brighter than usual, his vision sharper. Finally, he walked to the teacher's parking lot, found his car, then left as well.

The day had unfolded much differently than everyone had anticipated.

In the end, while it may not have been the trip to Adventure Experience some would have preferred, the students did have something to share with the others when they were back at school the next day.

Chapter 4
School's Out!

News of the meteorite crash was all over the media the next day. But then, as things tend to do in big cities, something else superceded it for the attention of the people. The government said little, not helping the situation for those trying to profit from the event. Meanwhile, the camp that had sprung up around the space rock disappeared the next day just as fast as it had been set up. In the end if proved to be another novel diversion, lasting a few days then disappearing from the news.

At KW High School the talk lasted about as long. Summer holidays were coming and that was the entire buzz around campus. School was winding down with the last big order of business being the prom.

Tim David was in the school weight room, working out as he had diligently tried to do over the course of the year. Usually, he would be pushed aside by the upper classmen, laughing at the scrawny freshman's "exercise in futility." But now, with muscles stretching the tight white tee shirt he wore, they had taken notice. In the past few weeks the amount of weight he was lifting had grown significantly. His bench press now rivaled any in the gym. Some were being to whisper that the spiky-haired youth was using steroids, or some other performance-enhancing drug. Tim ignored them as he continued to move the "big iron" as it was called.

Despite the fact he knew this to be untrue, there was something different about him. The sudden gaining of strength and muscularity was one thing. But he'd also put on ten pounds of muscle during this period. Stranger still was the fact that the strength was inconsistent. Some days he felt super strong, then others it was like he'd been earlier in the month. It was weird. Luckily, whenever he was in the weight room he had the strength and was able to show off.

He didn't know how this happened at these key times, but didn't care. Tim was afraid, though, that it would leave him permanently sometime and he'd be back to the same old weakling. For now, he couldn't wait for football tryouts coming the week after school got out. He'd show them.

The contraption in front of Beau Joseph was certainly strange looking. At the beginning of class it had been a cardboard box filled with the odds and ends of parts left over from other experiments. Most of the students in the introductory robotics class had finished their assignments and were content to just mark time until school ended the following week. But the slender youth had quietly come in this clear afternoon, silently getting to work on a project that had popped into his mind. During the course of the class he had built what now stood on his desk. This suddenly caught the attention of not only his classmates, but the teacher as well.

"What is that?" Vic Highway, the class' heavyset instructor asked curiously, though with a note of derision.

Beau face's reddened slightly with the attention. He replied in a soft voice, "Oh, nothing really. It's just something I thought up." Then, suddenly getting excited, he blurted out, "Actually, Mr. Highway, it's a remote gyro robot."

"Oh really?" the teacher challenged, while the other students laughed at the bold claim. Though impressed with the intent, his natural cynicism got the better of him. "Where is your design sketch?"

"Um, I didn't do one," the sophomore replied, nervous with the attention he was receiving. "I was just playing around with some of the spare parts and came up with this."

"No design and you built it in this class?" Highway rubbed a meaty hand over his face in frustration. This kid just didn't seem to get it. He decided to make a lesson out of this to the broader group. "Class, gather round," he ordered. Beau suddenly wished he were anywhere else but here right now. "Mr. Joseph is going to demonstrate his latest invention for us," the teacher announced, sarcasm dripping off each word.

A snicker went up from the other students, looking for a diversion during the humid afternoon.

"How does it work?" the man asked, preparing to dissect the metal encased object before him.

Beau, knowing there was no place to hide, decided to press on. "Well, sir, it's solar powered. May I use one of the charged power packs?" he asked with growing confidence. He'd put it together and somehow knew it would work. This, despite the fact the class had never been taught anything about this type of robot.

Vic Highway was incredulous at the audacity of a student he barely even remembered, though the youth had been in his class all year. The teacher threw up his hands dramatically, "Go ahead. I want to see how you even CONNECT this thing together, let alone get it to work."

Beau blocked out the implication of this statement. Quickly he retrieved the power source, then slipped it into a built-in receptacle within the sleek unit. This simple action caused a buzz of excitement within the group who had not even recognized the port. Flipping a switch, the blue-eyed youth took a breath and stepped back.

Suddenly the machine whirred, coming to life, and then four arms came out from within. They rotated, setting themselves into position and the unit hummed as if waiting for instruction. Beau grabbed a small control unit, then began to move levers around, causing it to move in step.

Mr. Highway stood frozen, mouth open, eyes wide as saucers. The other students were transfixed as well, not realizing the significance of what had just happened. Beau Joseph, sophomore high school student, had just accomplished something in less than an hour from spare parts that it took many advanced robotics students at the university level weeks to accomplish. The bell rang to signal the end of class, yet no one moved, as if frozen by the scene.

Finally regaining his composure, the teacher announced, "Okay, class dismissed. But, Beau, please stay behind for a few minutes. I'd like to speak to you."

George Alexander sat in the school lounge chewing the end of his glasses absent-mindedly, oblivious to the buzz of activity around him. He did this when thinking hard, and right now he was deep into it. Something wasn't right and he wanted to figure it out. His mind felt stimulated. This was no unusual thing for the thoughtful teen, but it seemed even more so now than before. Questions he had been pondering for months suddenly had become clear the last week. Unfortunately, they led to even more questions.

Yet, throughout it all, he worked through them, as if his intellect were growing exponentially. A process of logic that he'd never even considered now drove his thought patterns. But why? How had it developed so suddenly? Nothing had changed; he had acquired no new knowledge. Yet something was different in him. Though calm on the outside, within he was churning. The only visible sign of what lay within was his rapidly bobbing foot.

I'll figure this out, George thought, *I just know it.*

The main campus of State University in the city of Welch was known for many things, particularly its computer science department. But the broader sciences were well represented also. One of the many active areas was geology. To train the students in real world skills, the school had set up a seismographic station on the campus. Though nowhere near any fault lines, it was interesting still to work the equipment and monitor the readings. As part of one of the classes, the students were assigned to spend one period in that environment. On this particular day, Aaron Nelson and Tom Card, from the sophomore class, were working the equipment when suddenly everything spiked.

"Is that what I think it is?" Tom asked his friend nervously, suddenly forgetting the night at the pub they had been discussing earlier.

"Man, it sure looks like it, but how can that be?" the other replied, not believing what he was seeing.

"Think we should call Dr. Field?" Aaron asked.

"I think we better," Tom replied. "Maybe something's wrong with the equipment. I don't want to get blamed for busting it."

Picking up a phone in the office, it connected them directly with the head of the project, Dr. Emerson Field, professor of geology. Fortunately, he was in his office, so in less than five minutes the two students and the eminent scholar were together.

"You're sure of this?" the professor questioned skeptically. "It was a tremor?"

"Yes, sir. Look at the chart yourself and tell me if we're wrong," the students replied uncertainly.

Before saying anything the gray-haired professor looked at the data. Shaking his head, he looked at it again to see if his eyes were deceiving him. Reluctantly, he had to agree. "It's hard to believe, but it sure looks like it."

"But how can that be? We're nowhere close to a fault line," Aaron Nelson correctly surmised.

The geologist checked some readings on the machine, adjusted a few settings, but could find nothing wrong.

“There it is again!” Card called out.

The needles jumped again, denoting another tremor was taking place.

“This is incredible!” Dr. Field exclaimed, still not able to believe it. “I wouldn’t believe it if I wasn’t seeing it with my own eyes. Turn on the recorder so we can capture this information.”

Then, just as suddenly as it began, the tremor stopped.

Back at KW High School, the bell rang for the next class and students scurried to get to where they needed to be.

Talitha Beck had a problem. His name was Keith Ramsey. The star athlete kept asking her to go with him to the prom. She still didn’t have a date, but was determined to not go at all rather than go with him. The petite attractive girl had not forgotten the incident on the geography trip, nor the other times she had watched him torment weaker students. While the whole school seemed impressed with his success, she was not. He was nothing more than a bully.

The blondish-brown haired senior had more determination than people gave her credit for. She was an excellent scholar, getting mostly A’s, but was also a top athlete in her own right. Talitha was captain of the girl’s soccer team, while also running track and cross-country. Besides that, there was also an artistic, sensitive side to her. While the girl was a talented artist and singer, she also had a kind heart, so volunteered in many programs dealing with children.

As if inviting trouble, her thoughts transformed into the reality of the presence of Keith Ramsey. She noticed him glide into the school cafeteria, looking around. For someone of his size the young man moved remarkably quickly. Spying Talitha sitting alone, he immediately moved to her, trapping the girl.

“So, Talitha, is today going to be your lucky day?” the wrestler asked lightly.

She feigned ignorance. “What do you mean, Keith?”

Ramsey confidently pressed the point, “The day your year is made complete by me taking you to the prom.”

There were a dozen replies that came to mind. Talitha Beck desperately wanted to put the big lout in his place, but that wasn’t the type of girl she was.

“No thank you, Keith. My attitude toward going out with you hasn’t changed since yesterday,” she replied. Though calm on the surface her heart raced.

“You can’t be serious,” he responded with growing irritation. This was an often-repeated exchange between them since he had asked her out that was beginning to seriously bug him. There were other girls, lots of others, he had gone out with. Talitha Beck was the only one to refuse his advances.

In his mind, this one was no more special than the rest. The difference was she said no. That made her more desirable, a match yet to win. She was going from a fancy to an obsession. He was Keith Ramsey, lord of this school. Therefore, she couldn't genuinely not want to go out with him. This had to be some game and he won everything he played. "Give me a break, Talitha. There's a dozen girls who would kill to be in your position."

"Well, then take one of them," the petite girl replied coldly.

Something snapped within the mind of Keith Ramsey, surprising even him. Face contorting with rage, he snarled, "Fine. If you don't go with me, you don't go with anyone!" Stomping off, he called back, "You'll be sorry for this."

Talitha was frozen to her seat, unable to move. Something about his look frightened her. For the remainder of the day she was disturbed by the image in her mind, those of interest turning to hate.

In the end, no one invited her to the prom. Keith Ramsey saw to that. The strong wrestler scared off any male student showing interest in inviting the girl out. Despite this, she was determined to go to the dance. In the end, she rallied several friends who were without dates as well, planning a gala evening for the lot. Talitha would not allow her happiness to be dictated by another.

So the school year steadily came to a conclusion. For most, it was as if time stood still, tantalizingly close, yet still not here. Plans for the summer were being made for some, plans for the fall and even for the rest of their lives, made by others.

While this was going on, one with very different intentions was making plans of another sort. They were plans, really only idle thoughts in the past. Then they had laid in the mind for some time more as an exercise in theory. Now, like a seed bursting forth from its shell, suddenly they came to life, vivid and tangible in the mind of the creator. The thoughts had passed from theory to reality. An idea was becoming a plan. Formulation was beginning; the clock was ticking.

The late June evening was windy and foreboding. A storm was rolling into Killings-Welch this particular night. The wind buffeted the cities, howling at times. Trees swayed, litter swirled around in the current. Yet, one stood unmoving in the face of the storm. A shrouded figure in a dark cloak watched from a perch on top of one of the biggest buildings in the area.

The opportunity to fulfill a bold vision was perfect. It was ripe, like fall apples hanging heavy on a tree waiting to be picked. All that was needed for the whole thing to fall into his lap was a little push. That could be arranged so easily.

Opportunity. That's what the shadowy character saw looking over the city. From the highest tower the view commanded the whole area. There was much that could be accomplished for the ambitious. Threads that, if knit together, would create not only a profitable business venture for the one who could pull it off, but also reorder society. Who was the one with the capability of making this bold vision come to life? The one pondering this question knew the answer.

Chapter 5
An Eventful Evening

The bell rang at 3:30 p.m. on the last Friday in June, finally signaling the end of the school year. Marks were already in so it was a nothing day that many chose to skip. This was particularly the case for those wanting to prepare for the prom. Girls had appointments at hair salons, rented tuxedos were picked up, limo's ordered and cars washed and polished. This was going to be a night to remember for so many, one that some had looked forward to for four years. While the Senior Prom was the highlight of the school's social calendar, it also seemed to stand as the gateway to adulthood for many of the participants past and present.

The ballroom of the Hilton Hotel in downtown Killings was breathtaking. The decorating committee had outdone themselves turning the cavernous hall into a place of wonder. Balloon arches, trellises, fountains, silk streamers and other visual delights were placed strategically throughout. Uniform-clad caterers were ready to serve a wide variety of tasty h'oer derves and punch while a band, along with a DJ, had been hired to provide the entertainment. Everything was going to be perfect.

Talitha Beck was not feeling well. She sat at the vanity in her colorfully decorated bedroom holding her head. It was as if waves were relentlessly crashing inside. Pulse after pulse hit with a resounding thud. Eyes tightly closed in discomfort she extended her hands as if to push the distress away. Opening her eyes, the sight was shocking. It was as if a hurricane had gone through her previously neat room, everything was topsy-turvy.

She looked around, disturbed by the change, wondering if this was some form of hallucination. Yet, there were no pink bunnies or other freakish sights. Closing her eyes and opening them again nothing had changed. She was tempted to pinch herself to see if this was some sort of bad dream. But no, she was very much alive.

"What happened?" Talitha said to herself with a quivering voice. She remembered the strange feelings, almost like pulse waves, but couldn't connect them with what she was seeing.

Weird, Talitha thought. There was no opportunity to linger on what had just happened. It was time to get ready for the prom. Cleaning up her room the best she could in the time remaining, the teen tried to distract herself with thoughts of the night ahead.

Wearing a dark blue suit and tie George Alexander walked into the decorated room of the Hilton shortly after the event began, wondering anew why he'd come. The youth came with no date, though he'd had several opportunities. Yet, he still came. George knew that this was an important social event and so he needed to be there.

Though the thoughtful youth was not interested in decorations and such frivolous things, he could appreciate the creative efforts of others. What George saw truly impressed him. The already attractive room had been turned into a breathtaking fantasy. He smiled despite himself, a warm feeling coming over him. George was glad that he'd come. Almost immediately, several couples who were friends of his from the computer club greeted the youth, inviting him to join them at their table.

With the graduates gathered, on cue the band began to play. Couples made there way to the dance floor, others took pictures of each other or sat at tables along the edge of the parquet wood dance floor.

Talitha had been on the floor dancing several times despite the glares of Keith Ramsey. Wearing a black silk and organza gown that set off her blue eyes the girl definitely stood out. She guessed those who had asked figured it was the last time they would ever see the brute, so they decided to take the chance for an opportunity to be with her for a few minutes. Thus the girl and her friends were having a great time. Standing at a crystal punch bowl she poured herself a glass.

At the same time, George Alexander came over for the some refreshments. The pair was familiar with each other, acquaintances really, having been in several classes together over the years. After exchanging greetings they chatted together.

"So what are your plans for the summer?" Talitha asked him.

He replied, "I'm working in one of the research labs at the university. I'll find out where next week. It doesn't really matter to me which one. All of them are interesting projects." Then he asked her, "How about you?"

The teen brushed a wisp of hair out of her eyes, answering, "I'm going to be a leader at a kid's summer day camp program in town."

"You'll do great at that, Talitha. You've always seemed to be good with kids."

"Thanks, George. Hey, did you hear about the kid that built the robot in Mr. Highway's class?"

"Yes, I did," the tall senior replied. "I never got to see it, but I heard the unit was pretty advanced. I think it was the guy you stood up for on the geography trip a few weeks ago."

Talitha winced at the reminder, but said nothing. Instead, she commented, "Well, I'm sure you'll be developing all kinds of advanced things some day. You'll become famous and we'll all say, 'I went to school with him.'"

The girl noticed that he wasn't paying attention. Irritated at first by the perceived rudeness, she was about to speak until the realization hit her that the intelligent youth's mind suddenly had become preoccupied. It was as if he were intensely concentrating on something. The look on his face showed that whatever the subject matter, it wasn't good.

"Is everything okay?" Talitha asked.

"No, actually it's not," George responded gravely. "Something bad's about to happen."

"How do you know?"

"I'm not sure, I just do," the intelligent youth answered with conviction.

While that conversation was going on, for the rest the mood of the evening was light and cheerful. People were happy, filled with joy.

No one at first recognized the arrival of several out of place visitors. Much earlier, the ticket takers had moved from their post since the night was well advanced. For some reason the hotel security people were not around. Several new arrivers soon grew into a dozen and some of the partygoers began to take notice. They were not dressed in finery, but rather street wear. That in and of itself was not remarkable. Instead, it was the bright red bandanas the young men wore tied around their heads, arms or legs that distinguished them. Already a whisper of fear was circulating around the room—Bloods.

These were members of the most feared street gang in the area. The Bloods home turf was downtown Kilings, but their activities spread throughout the area. Over the past few years the group had perpetrated crimes of all form, often viciously executed. The Bloods were a force to be reckoned with. Most people steered clear and prayed their paths never crossed. For the participants of the KW High School prom that prayer was not being answered this night.

The tough looking gangsters began to move around the room like locusts, eating food, drinking lustily, laughing loudly. In general, doing what was needed to draw attention to themselves.

Something needed to be done, though no one acted. The teachers and parents who were acting as chaperones were strangely absent. Finally, the "security" for the evening arrived. Two university students in white dress shirts and dark slacks showed up in the room. They nervously approached the group who watched the pair's less than forceful arrival.

Everything had stopped by now. The band had even quit playing to watch this drama unfold. The tallest of the pair was the one who spoke. Clearing his throat, he announced with as much authority as he could muster, "This is a private party. I'm going to have to ask you to leave."

The leader of the group of Bloods opened his eyes wide in mock surprise. "Yo dude, we was invited to this party. It just took the posse a bit o time to get over here, you know?"

The student swallowed hard, then asked, "If that's the case I'm going to need to see your tickets."

The dark complexioned youth, who had his bandana jauntily tied low over his forehead, threw up his hands as if exasperated. Then, in false sincerity, answered, "See, that's the problem, dude. We forgot our tickets."

Standing his ground, never had ten dollars an hour ever been more sorely earned, the hotel employee announced, "You don't belong here. I'm going to have to ask you to please leave."

"Oh PLEASE. Look at this educated white bread talking up in my face. He don't believe me," the gang's leader said with a sly grin. "Ain't that just the way? No one ever believes us. Well, boys, what are we to do? If we're not wanted, I guess we'll just have to leave."

Turning to leave, the young street hoodlum suddenly sprung back like a snake, striking the young man who had confronted them. The victim went down hard, lying motionless on the floor. His partner froze and was soon set up by a pair of the gang members. Other began overturning tables and destroying decorations. Several screams rang out as people began to scramble to get out of the path of destruction.

Finally, a number of students, including several members of the football team, rallied to try to stop the destruction. It had become a matter of honor for them. By now a 911 call had gone out to police, and within minutes several squad cars had rolled up to the Hilton, sirens announcing another typical night in downtown Kilings.

The nightstick wielding police officers waded into the pandemonium that greeted them. Already many of the prom guests had fled the scene, leaving the hotel. Others though milled around the periphery watching the spectacle with perverse delight. Another group still had taken this as an opportunity to participate in the carnage. They now ran throughout the hotel, causing destruction and all form of mischief. To add to the problem, several fire alarms were pulled in the pandemonium. So now fire trucks were racing to the scene as groggy hotel guests were being woken up for evacuation.

The police concentrated their attack on the distinctly dressed gang members, ignoring the crimes of those more properly dressed. Later, some community activists who said local law enforcement discriminated based on socioeconomic conditions would use this incident as fodder for debate. But this was no time for a discussion on sociology. This was a battle.

More units arrived, including members of the black clad police tactical unit. Several members of the Bloods were seized. But, like rats fleeing a sinking ship, by the time sufficient police were on the scene to restore order the others were nowhere to be found. Now those arrested were people whose crisp tuxedo and frilly dresses no longer displayed any form of order or innocence. After well over an hour, calm was finally restored. The room was a shambles, a fraction of the original party goers remained. The night had been ruined and there was nothing left for it but to call of the rest of the prom.

By this point, many of the students who were not interested in sticking around to either watch, or participate in the carnage, had, by an unstated mutual agreement, retired to a quiet nightclub to continue their celebration. It was close enough to the site of the original party that everyone could get there yet far enough removed that the whirlwind that had consumed the first gala would have no further impact.

Among those were the groups made up of the friends of Talitha Beck and George Alexander. The people talked excitedly about what had happened, sharing and retelling their own perspective or acts of heroics. The adrenaline was flowing and this would be a night talked about for a long time. As the music played, conversations continued and people danced.

Talitha looked over at the young man she had been conversing with before the carnage broke out. She remembered his comments right before things happened and wanted to know how he knew. George was uncharacteristically reserved, sticking to himself in a dark corner. He was talking little, as if trying to work through some mathematical equation. It was a conversation they would have at some point she determined. This night had truly become unforgettable in many ways.

Well after the destruction of the senior prom, the remaining members of the Bloods moved through the dark, quiet streets of the "hood" that acted as their base of operations. This was home turf for them. Cutting through a littered alley, they laughed boisterously at the antics of the evening, well pleased with the lesson they had given out. The ones arrested would be charged and released, as they did other times, adding to their rep.

Out of the shadows came a strange clipped voice. "I would have a word with you."

No one dared talk to a member of the Bloods, let alone one who was traveling with his pack. Sensing some more sport, but slightly irritated at the tone of the confident voice, the leader retorted, "What do you want?"

The voice became a figure illuminated in the moonlight as the one who had spoken took a step out of the shadows. The gangsters saw it was a tall, unrecognizable person shrouded in a cloak. "I want your allegiance. Follow me and you can profit from giving it. Turn away and be destroyed."

"Are you on drugs?" the young tough spat out. "Do you have any idea who you're talking to?"

The rest of the Bloods instinctively fanned out in a semi-circle, trapping the bold character that had moved no further, against the wall. There was no avenue of escape, yet the figure didn't seem to wilt at all. Instead, the odd voice replied, "You are sadly mistaken, my young simpleton. It is you who do not know whom you speak with."

"Man, you're nuts. You in no position to bargain." Tiring of the dialogue, the leader decided it was time to move on. "Gimme everything you've got and I might let you live."

As the young gangster advanced a few steps, a weird chuckling sound gave the thug a shiver, involuntarily causing him to stop. Rather than continue his advance to the supposed victim, he found himself frozen in his tracks. None were moving now. The chuckling stopped and the strange voice said instead, "Let me live? You are again mistaken, my foolish young friend. It is you who have forfeited that claim."

Suddenly a crushing energy force emanated from the mysterious figure. The gangster was struck in the head by the blast, pushing his face in. The thug fell, dead before he hit the ground.

The unrecognizable person with strange power said, without emotion, "There, now that's done. Are there any more questions?"

The other members of the gang, stunned by what they had just witnessed, looked down at the twisted form of their former leader. None said a word. Instead, they were captured by the moment. The remaining Bloods now listened to the instructions of the one who held their attention.

Chapter 6
Shifting Focus

Tweet!

The whistle blew to announce the commencement of practice. Everyone had been kited out and so summer football tryouts could begin. This was elite level ball, since there were only two teams in the area, one for Killings and the other for Welch. This Monday morning was reserved for tryouts for the Killings team, the better of the two. Their coach was Tom Jeffries, head coach at KW High School, the reigning county champions. Being this was a citywide team, the best of each school were coming out to attempt to secure a place on the squad.

Coach Jeffries was making the rounds of the hopefuls while several of his assistants led players in a series of warm-up drills, greeting those he knew and finding out more about those he didn't. He loved this coaching, since there was little pressure. Being only two months long, the summer league was designed to tune up the players for fall. There were teams in several other cities, so the competition was quite good.

Jeffries, though he loved to teach, also hoped one day to coach at the college level. Already he'd had some discussion with several schools about the move up, but the right opportunity had not come along. He was viewed as the best coach in the region, so more were beginning to take notice of him. The sight of a totally unfamiliar player going through the drills interrupted his thoughts. Smaller than most, he looked younger than the others, who were mostly seniors and juniors.

"What's your name, son?" Jeffries asked.

"Tim David, sir."

What school do you go to, Tim?"

"KW, sir."

"KW?" the coach responded in surprise. "Sorry, I don't recognize you. What squad did you play on last year?"

Suddenly Tim was very nervous. Other players were beginning to notice the conversation. He replied timidly, "I was cut from the freshman team, Coach." Seeing the look on coach's face, he quickly added, voice cracking, "I did play minor football instead, and I've been working out all year."

Jeffries shook his head in amazement at the earnest face looking up at him through the cage of his helmet. "This is not minor ball, son. This is city league. Are you sure you know what you're getting yourself into?"

Tim nodded his head vigorously in agreement.

Jeffries chuckled, then said, "All right, Tim. I'll give you a chance to show what you've got."

Being such a short season, the cuts would be made the first three days with the squad determined and practicing by the end of the week. Their first game was in two weeks, so there was little time to get fancy. Dealing with seasoned players made the job easier, but it also made the task of making the elite squad that much tougher.

By the end of the morning the first cut list was posted before the young men were out of the showers and changed. Tim's heart leapt to see his on it. He'd made it so far!

"You had a good morning, Tim. I was impressed by your hustle and how quick you followed instructions." Tim was surprised to see Coach Jeffries standing behind him. The sun-weathered man added, "That was good. But tomorrow you're going to have to show me something to make it to day three. I like your spunk, but it takes more than that to make my squad."

Tim couldn't wait until the next day. He'd show the coach he could play.

Already the kids were wound up and it wasn't even 10:00 a.m. Many of the other councilors were getting stressed by now, but Talitha Beck only smiled. She loved kids, the more enthusiastic the better. But Talitha also knew that she would end up with those deemed to be problem children. That was okay with her, she was up to the challenge. Her philosophy was to look beyond the surface to the character within the child. She'd never been disappointed in the past by doing this.

So many children labeled as a problem simply were misunderstood or neglected. They were sedated with mind-altering pharmaceuticals, causing them to move through life like glassy-eyed zombies. Yet, all they needed, and desperately desired, was some positive attention. With the right opportunity and encouragement they could soar. The teen instinctively knew this, even if society didn't. That was what motivated her.

By lunchtime the groups were assigned and the six children Talitha would be responsible for were all ones no others wanted. This was the Killings Summer Playground program, run by the city. Thus it attracted a large number of inner city children, all of which were in her group. She could have easily gotten a job at one of the privately run camps. In fact, many had asked her to join their staff, but Talitha, in the end, stayed with the less prestigious group. Yet, there was something about those who didn't have the same privileges she did that kept calling her back. She wanted to help them have a chance for a future.

The particular group Talitha had this year would challenge her desires to help though. Already they were testing her, seeing if she would hold them in check and keep them focused. One of them in particular, a boy named Tommy, seemed to be the worst. He was a cute boy with mischievous brown eyes, a ready smile, and messy blond hair. Appearancewise, his clothes were dirty and tattered, while his shoes were worn out. The six-year-old boy's face was dirty with caked on food.

Tommy was hyperactive, which got the other kids whipped up, causing Talitha to have to give him a time out already. He was going to try her patience, but she would have the rest of the summer to try to help him since he was signed up for all four of the two week sessions. Fortunately, she liked challenges.

Beau Joseph sat on his bed staring at the wall. Silence filled the room as he tried to comprehend what has just happened. The bed was still the same, four short, wooden posts covered with a thick blue comforter, same posters on the wall, same desk. But it was the object on his desk that caused the questions.

Earlier in the day he had absentmindedly begun to tinker with his computer. It was an older model, since his parents couldn't afford the latest for him. But it got the job done. As if in a dream, the machine was apart before him and the slender, dark blond-haired sophomore was putting it back together. This time he didn't do it the same way it had been disassembled. The youth had taken parts, changed them, than started to put it back together.

Realizing what he'd done, yet not knowing how to put it back into the original condition, he smacked his forehead with the palm of his hand in exasperation, thinking he'd wrecked it. This would get him in trouble with his parents, something he didn't want to be this early in the summer. Yet, something in his mind told him to turn the machine on.

Pushing the power button, the computer booted up faster than it had ever done before. He opened a few programs and they too responded with a swiftness he'd never known. On impulse, he grabbed a software program that had been given to him recently with a game on he'd wanted to play. Unfortunately, it was configured for the highest system going right now, about five steps ahead of his machine. Yet, it loaded up right away and he was able to play it. Better still, the graphics ran better than even the pictures on the package and it handled smooth as glass.

Now really confused, Beau opened up the computer's hardware performance program. The diagnostic showed a memory, power and performance level above anything that was on the market. But how could that be? What had happened to change the machine in such a dramatic way?

Beau sat dazed in his room, wondering if he was having some sort of weird dream. First there had been the robot he built in school. He couldn't explain that, which made his teacher mad at him in the end. Then the quiet teen had tinkered around with his dad's Chevy Cavalier and now it was running like something on the NASCAR circuit. Now there was this thing with the computer. The weirdest part was he didn't even think about what he was doing, he just did it.

Beau now felt like he was in some sort of a trance when building. It was a new sensation for him. When building, he could see nothing other than the components of the creation. He seemed to have tunnel vision, yet what went through his mind when he was working on the particular innovation was way beyond his comprehension. Then he would snap out of the trance-like state and he'd see the finished product. Every time what sat before him was way beyond his abilities.

Beau didn't know what to do and didn't know who to talk to about it. This was getting pretty weird.

George Alexander stared at the whiteboard again as he'd done every afternoon for the past three days. His job was to assist with experiments in the Particle Physics lab this week, but he kept being drawn back to the focal point in the room. The formula on it was incomplete, but that was part of science, seeking to discover the solution. Dr. Harvey Grey and his team had been working on this complex problem, seeking to develop better particle accelerators, but couldn't find the answer. They had tried dozens of scenarios, but all of them came up short.

George's job was to assist with experiments, keep records and generally help out where asked. This was the second assignment of the science department internship he'd gotten. Over the course of the summer the student was to receive a broad exposure to the various working areas of the science department at State University. This would help him to determine his area of specialty, since he was entering into that particular area of academic study in the fall. It was a good job, though fairly routine. But the strangest thing had happened at this particular one.

The bespectacled youth kept being drawn back to the formula dealing with quarks on the board. Something wasn't right. He'd watched the best minds in the university tackle it. George was impressed by their dedication, coming back again and again to something they were blocked on. The second day, an idea flashed in his mind, but it was too outlandish to even consider, so he went about his work. Today though, as he watched them again, the idea grew stronger, but he didn't know how to approach it.

There was an error in the formula early in its development stages. If that were corrected the equation could continue. Not only had George discovered the error, but he also knew the entire formula. But how could that be? These were trained scientists and he was a high school graduate. Surely he must be wrong. But as the day wore on he became more confident his thoughts were correct, as improbable as it seemed.

Several times Dr. Grey had caught him staring at the board and reminded him to get back to work. Grey was not known as a patient man to start with. Now he was getting surly due to his inability to solve the mathematical puzzle.

Finally, toward the end of the day, the head of the project caught the young lab assistant fixated on the equation again. There was something in the pale blue eyes of the youth that made him ask, "You've been staring at that board all day, Mr. Alexander. What are you doing?"

George took a deep breath, deciding to do something that would likely get him fired. "I think there's an error in the initial equation, sir," he stated matter of factly. "That's why you're stuck."

Face turning red, Grey's voice boomed, "There's a what?" Calming down, but totally irritated with the tall, slender youth, he decided to vent his frustration on him. "So you think you've discovered an error in my work, huh? I didn't know you were an expert in particle physics."

George could hear the sarcasm in the distinguished man's voice and see the smiles on the faces of the two assistant professors who worked with the learned man. But, instead of backing down, something inside caused him to stand his ground. "I've been looking at the quark equation for the last three days and I'm sure there's a miscalculation." Already out on a limb, he decided to go one step further. "I also think I can finish the formula by correcting the error."

The professor's face turned from red to white at the outlandish comment the youth had made. Incredulous at the nerve, all he could say was, "Do it," handing George a marker and eraser for the white board.

George swallowed again, a bead of perspiration appearing on his high smooth forehead. He walked to the board, acutely aware that the three scholars, plus everyone else in the room, were now staring at him. He couldn't back down; the humiliation would be too great. He wiped his eyes with the fingers on his right hand, then began to write. First he rubbed out then changed the formula in the early stages. Then he went to the end of the equation, continuing where it had left off. Fifteen minutes later he was done, filling most of the board in the process.

Turning around, he saw Dr. Grey staring at him, mouth ajar in wonder. All George could say was, "What do you think?"

The Professor of Particle Physics reply was curt. "Get out."

George Alexander hung his head and slunk from the room, figuring tomorrow morning he'd be looking for a job at McDonalds.

The attractive woman sighed heavily, allowing the letter she held in her hand to flutter to the floor. Yet again she'd been rejected. Lola Karan could not believe the turn of bad luck she was having. It was becoming her life story. After graduating first in her class from the prestigious New York School of Fashion Design she could have gone to any design house in the world. Instead, she had chosen to live the high life, staying in the Big Apple.

Lola had grown up in a small town in Ohio. Rejecting the simple pace of rural America early in life, she had developed a taste for the bright lights and fast pace of the big city. Even while still in school she'd fallen into the party scene. But the brilliance of her work and natural gifting had gotten her through. Unfortunately, her first assignment for one of the top firms in New York had fizzled out with a lack of ability to control herself. Missed assignments and sloppy work due to overindulgence overrode her talents. Before the year was out she'd been fired from the position. Several other jobs had fallen through the same pattern of destructive behavior to the point where no one in the business would touch her anymore. The risk was too high.

She'd ended up in Killings-Welch following a boyfriend. This, she reflected, was another bad choice on her part. That relationship had ended like all the others, in disappointment. As much as she hated the place, there was nowhere else to go, so she stayed.

Now the talented designer had her own dress business and was able to scratch out a living by making wedding gowns and selling some clothes from her shop. It was a far cry from where she had once been.

Lola had matured over the years, with some of her wild ways falling away. Now the woman wanted to prove she was as gifted as her famous cousin with the same last name.

Though age and the fast pace she'd lived over the years showed, Lola Karan was still striking in her looks. Dark brown hair framed an olive-hued complexion. But it was her eyes that set her off. Blue, deep as the ocean, that would flash when she let her passion fly, could still catch people's attentions. Some they drew, others they intimidated.

The note that had fallen was another rejection letter from a design house. Lola had hoped to rebuild her reputation through freelance work. She would submit designs and hope they would be picked up. Thus far the reaction had been less than encouraging.

Business was slow as usual. She had little to do and hadn't seen anyone in the shop all day. With a growing sense of depression, Lola decided to close up for the day and take a walk in the park. With the shop cleaned up, the woman prepared to leave when the bell attached to the front door rang, announcing someone had entered. Her hope of a customer faded quickly as an unwelcome form stood before her worktable.

"Hello, Lola," said a familiar voice with a hint of arrogance.

"Hello, Ulysses," she replied without emotion.

"What are you up to?" the man asked with no particular interest.

Lola tried to keep her emotions in check, though her heart was beating fast. "I was about to close the shop for the day and head out."

"Why don't you let me take you out for a drink?" the barrel-chested man standing before her asked. "I've missed you and thought about you a lot lately."

Lola had dated Ulysses Hammerman earlier in the year. It had been a short relationship, one Lola hardly even counted. But, to the ex-Marine, it had been like they were practically married. Theirs was a relationship born out of a lonely desire for company on her part. He, on the other hand, had become smitten with the woman and didn't want to let her go. His possessiveness was an irritant to her, so now his not infrequent visits were unwelcome.

"I don't think so, Ulysses."

"You don't know what you're missing, Lola," Hammerman pressed. "Something big is about to happen in my life and you'll want to be a part of it."

Her eyes crinkled as she tried to keep calm. "We've been through this before," she stated. Her own bad mood and frustration at the rejection letter caused the woman's usually cheerful demeanor to crack. "There is absolutely nothing you can give me that would be of interest. We have no relationship anymore. I'm not interested in restarting one with you. Leave me alone."

Lola was shocked at the cruel statement she'd just made to the high school teacher. Although the man was a bit of pest, he wasn't a bad guy. She opened her mouth to apologize, but the cold, deadly look on his face caused Lola to freeze. There was an eerie intensity in her former boyfriend's eyes that burned into her very soul. With a shiver running up her spine, the woman found herself frightened.

The man stared at Lola, his glare saying more than any words could. After an uncomfortably long silence, he finally spoke, "Alone is what you want to be is it? We'll see."

Without saying another word, the stocky man turned about, storming from the dress shop. The door almost burst from its hinges due to the force with which he slammed it closed.

The dark-haired woman was shaken by the experience. While the conclusion of their brief meeting was disturbing, the look Hammerman had given her frightened Lola even more. She couldn't identify it, but it almost seemed evil.

As was the norm with the woman, when her emotions were up, she would sketch. Grabbing a sketchbook, instead of leaving, she began to draw. Lola became lost in the exercise and the hours flew by. When she finally finished, it was dark. The mood of dread had passed. Feeling better after looking at what she'd accomplished, the designer decided to do what she had tried to do earlier and call it a day.

Attempting to bolster her confidence, she observed that the creativity in her work was coming back. The woman continued to believe that a break would come soon. A bit more cheerfully, she left the shop. Locking up, Lola walked down the street to where her car was parked. She didn't know that a cloaked figure standing in the shadows was watching her the whole way.

Chapter 7
Discoveries

George walked with trepidation into the main science building at State University. His heart was beating hard in anticipation of what was going to happen. The bright sunshine and warmth of the day did nothing to alleviate the somber mood of the youth as he reported for work.

He'd thought more about what he'd done the day before and the reaction of Dr. Grey. "Why do I do these things?" he murmured to himself. "Why couldn't I just keep my big mouth shut?"

Yet, despite the self-chiding, he also knew he was right. The reaction of the science professor had shown that as well. The man was shocked by what he'd seen, responding with anger at George's discovery. The teen's thoughts grew darker. Grey would likely steal the formula for his own use, claiming credit and fire him in the process to keep it quiet. Who would believe a summer intern?

To make a discovery this big was just too much to comprehend. He hadn't told his parents, they wouldn't believe him. Who would? He didn't believe it himself. Rather than go into the lab right away and face the dismissal, he sat down in the hallway to ponder what had happened.

When he was honest with himself, he wondered too how he could have made such a discovery. How could he, with no particle physics background, solve a puzzle eminent scholars hadn't been able to in months of study? Could he have gotten lucky? That was unlikely, this was no guess. No, he KNEW the answer, but how?

There was something going on with him, he could feel it. Things that had been questions before in his mind were now being answered. Complex problems seemed like grade six math now. What was happening to him?

As George's mind processed everything, his leg began to bob up and down with nervous energy. Suddenly the youth could feel a significant tremor underneath.

Earthquake! he thought to himself in panic. But then just as quickly he realized that was impossible in this particular region. Before he could figure out what was happening the movement was over.

Beginning to ponder his dilemma, the teen's anxiety increased. Just as had happened before the same seismic movement could be felt. Focusing on trying to determine the source, once again the tremor ended.

Then George had a thought enter his mind that nearly caused his heart to stop. On a hunch, but more on intuition, he began to bob his leg up and down nervously. Again, the floor began to shake. Stopping the movement, then calming himself, it stopped.

Whatever force was being manifested it seemed to be connected to him!

George decided to try an experiment. Mind churning, he tried to concentrate and focus his thoughts. Staring at a garbage can across the hall, this became his focal point. Suddenly, for no apparent reason, it moved slightly to the side. He looked hard at it again. Once more it moved, but this time further.

Startled at the implications of what he'd just seen, the teen banged his head on the wall behind while sitting up suddenly. The can slid down the hallway.

"What's happening?" George whispered to himself. "Did I really do that?" Could all this strange stuff be connected? That was hard to believe. He didn't want to believe it. The implications of the connection that was beginning to form in the young man's mind was more than he wanted to consider.

"Mr. Alexander."

George's impromptu experiment was interrupted by the presence of Dr. Grey. The man, whose hair matched his named, looked inquisitively at him. "Why haven't you reported to the lab yet?" he asked.

George replied, "After yesterday I thought I was going to get fired, so I wanted to prolong the inevitable."

Grey chuckled, "Fired? Oh no, my good man. That's the last thing on my mind. But you're right, I must apologize for my reaction yesterday. I was tired from my work and didn't properly acknowledge the aid you had given us."

George was uncertain where the professor was heading, but it seemed different from what he'd expected. In fact, an idea was entering his mind that he didn't think was possible.

The reality was confirmed in the youth's mind when Grey continued. "That was a good piece of observation, Mr. Alexander. You watched us work and your perspective obviously allowed you to see what we had been missing. Your help was appreciated. In fact, I'll even add your name to the research team when the paper is published to acknowledge your contribution."

Help? George thought to himself. *I made the discovery on my own. The credit belongs to me.* While his mind was screaming, his face was like stone. Grey had been nowhere close to discovering the formula when he'd taken over. What was the man up to?

That was revealed right away.

"I like your work, George. So I've asked to have you permanently placed in my lab for the remainder of the summer. The other professors have agreed. What do you think of that?"

"Great," George replied, with as much enthusiasm as he could muster. Not only was the professor going to steal his idea, he was going to make sure that no one else had the opportunity to be "assisted" by him as well. This was worse than being fired.

From now on the youth determined to mirror the self-serving attitude just demonstrated to him. He'd simply do his job and keep any discoveries to himself.

"Well, let's get to work," Dr. Grey stated cheerfully.

George nodded his head in agreement, saying nothing. It was going to be work from now on.

Keith Ramsey was having a miserable day. He sat alone at the mall feeling sorry for himself. No one other than his mother knew the senior had lost his scholarship due to the poor marks he'd gotten over the course of the year. The thought that this could happen to a state champion had never entered into the mind of the successful wrestler. The sense of injustice and wrong committed on him continued to grow. It wasn't his fault. No one helped him with his school, but, in truth, he'd shown little interest in learning. His mother had called him a loser when she found out, but what was she? A two-bit waitress at a no-good diner in town. She was going nowhere. Not like him, things were going to happen for Keith Ramsey.

The youth's handsome features were distorted as he began to brood again over the course of his life. Keith didn't remember his father and had never seen him since the man left their home when he was just a toddler. His mother never talked about the man and the young man learned to never mention his name.

That error of judgement would earn him a cuff on the side of the head. When she wasn't working, she was off at bingo or some bar, leaving him to fend for himself.

No, he had made something for himself. He had earned his shot. No one was going to deny him what he deserved. If what he sought wasn't going to be given, then it would have to be taken.

With a new determination, Ramsey stood up to leave the food court. Walking past a table with three male high school students, he grabbed a can of pop and container of fries right off the table.

"Hey, what do you think you're doing?" one of the youths called out, standing up in protest.

Ramsey, muscle rippling through his white tee shirt and denim shorts, stared at the slender boy defiantly. "Are you going to do anything about it?"

The slender student saw the angry look and clenched fists of the hulking form before him. A half-finished meal was not worth the trouble, so he sat down.

Ramsey felt a sense of elation, the same feeling he had when he won a wrestling match, savoring the look on the faces of the three defeated boys. "I didn't think so. Smart choice, boys."

Draining the remnants of the pop, he casually threw the can back onto the table, then walked away with the fries, happily munching the prize. *I'm going to win,* he thought, *and it's going to be fun.*

Tim David lined up for his turn at the tackling drill. This was day three and he was still there. But the intense youth also knew it was due to the kindness of the coach. If he hadn't gone to KW High he wasn't sure he'd still be on the squad. Tim had become a bit of a sentimental favorite, a bit of a modern day Rudy, which kind of bugged him. Today, though, the freshman needed to show something. He wanted to earn a spot on the squad. But what did he have?

This particular drill showed the coaches not only strength and speed, but also aggression. One player was the ball carrier, the other the tackler. The idea was that both would lie on their back ten yards apart between a set of orange cones. When the coach blew the whistle both would get up as quickly as they could and see who would come out on top.

Tim stood in the tackling lane. He counted those opposite him and his heart sank. He was to face off against Tyrell Waters, the all-district running back. *This is going to be embarrassing*, he thought. *The guy is going to run over me, sending another useless victim packing.*

As the young blond-haired youth thought of this, he also felt a growing surge of energy. The thumping of his heart was distinctive, resonating through his whole body. It was as if he could feel the blood coursing through every vein, pumping power into every fiber of muscle. Tim looked at his forearms and they seemed to be growing with each beat. A new confidence began to grow, a transformation of timid freshman to savage lion took place in the line. Tim David was not going to be intimidated by anything anymore. Suddenly he felt different and looked forward to the challenge.

Now his turn came up. Waters got the ball, about to lay down in the ready position, with Tim doing the same thing.

Coach Jeffries stepped in, asking, "You up for this, Tim?"

"Yes, sir," he confidently replied through his mouth guard.

Waters looked at Tim with compassion, then to the coach. Both finally lined up. Finally the coach nodded his head in agreement.

The whistle blasted and both started the round. Tim leapt to his feet, beating Waters up. The freshman charged through the ten-yard gap separating them. The running back tried to dodge the charging player wasn't able to, so turned into him. Tim hit him, dropping the powerful ball carrier easily.

The whistle blew. Coach Jeffries stomped into the center of the tackling area in irritation.

"That was AWFUL! If you float through these drills, Tyrell, I'm going to cut you. Bring it on. Show me something. Both of you, line up and do it again."

Tyrell Waters had not gone as hard as he could have on Tim David, but now was being challenged on it. Adjusting his helmet, he lay down once more to do what needed to be done. Tim did the same thing.

The whistle blew again, both players were up at the same time, but Tim charged forward. Waters didn't deviate, deciding to run over the smaller player. Tim held his ground, gaining speed.

Crack!

The sound of the collision echoed throughout the complex, causing others to stop and look at what had just happened. What they saw was Tim David laying on the top running back in the county, who was flat on his back. He'd put him down! The coaches and the others who had just witnessed it stood in stunned silence at what had happened. Waters jumped up in anger and embarrassment. No one had ever pancaked him before, and he wasn't going to let some little freshman do it.

"Line up again," he yelled. "I wasn't ready. I want another rep."

Tim was standing on his feet, hands on his hips, with a great feeling of elation. His confidence was starting to surge. The coaches nodded in agreement, not believing what they'd seen either.

The pair got down into their familiar positions, Waters pawing the grass in anticipation. The other drills had stopped as players drifted over to witness the spectacle. Once more the whistle blew. Waters was up in a flash, charging straightforward, his powerful legs giving him momentum. Tim, though, didn't back down, but at the moment of collision lowered his head and shoulder, catching the star player in mid stride. Picking the sturdy running back up right off his feet, he drove him to the ground. The force of collision again echoed through the complex.

Those watching saw an unknown freshman hit the star player, taking him right off his feet and knocking him hard to the turf. Tyrell Waters lay still for the moment, the wind knocked out of him from the force of the collision. Tim David stood up, a look of triumph on his face.

Gary Jeffries lifted the hat from his head, wiping his brow in amazement. Never had he witnessed such a scene. Whoever Tim David was, he sure had shown them all what he could do. Freshman or not, he had just made the team.

Breathing hard, Beau Joseph lay on the lush green grass in his back yard staring up at the sky. He gazed at the fluffy white clouds seeming to fall from the blue sky. The heat of mid-day warmed his face, adding to the beads of perspiration already glistening in the afternoon sun.

The sophomore was beginning to wonder if something was wrong with him. It seemed like more than just hormones were changing. He'd just finished a series of Kung Fu moves that were impossible for one who was less than an experienced black belt. The thing was, he'd never even taken a lesson before. The teen had watched a martial arts movie, then began copying what the fighters had been doing. Once he'd started to spin and kick about the room, Beau decided to go outside to see what he could really do. There he really let go, moving about with ease like a seasoned expert. He felt like Neo in the Matrix and decided to watch some more movies later. *Who knows how good I could get?* Beau thought to himself.

Then there was his newfound building ability. He'd always liked to construct things. As a child, he'd constantly be making Lego creations. In fact, he still liked to build with the plastic blocks, but what had been happening of late was unsettling. The stuff he'd been building and the repairs he had been making in the last month were way above what he could have ever thought of. He couldn't chalk it up to luck anymore; this kind of thing was happening all too frequently. What was wrong with him? But then, unwilling to go through the stress of wondering why, he began to rationalize it in his mind.

He lay there, unconsciously pondering this puzzle, unaware that his younger sister Lucy was calling for him. Not responding, the ponytail haired nine-year-old began to search for him. She looked first in the front yard, but remembered last seeing her brother go out back. Next, looking through the screen door into the back yard, she searched around, but couldn't see anything. Thinking perhaps he had climbed a tree, which he still liked to do, she went out to get a closer look. Scanning the yard, she still couldn't see anything. Next, the determined girl began to walk around in the grass, gazing up at the large elm trees that framed the property. Suddenly she tripped on a fair sized, soft object, falling hard to the ground.

"Ow, what are you doing Lucy!" Beau exclaimed, irritated that his sister had tumbled over him. "Watch where you're going!"

Lucy's innocent eyes went wide with surprise. She could feel the object and could hear her brother's voice, but she couldn't see where it was coming from, or what she had stumbled over. "B-B-Beau?" she stammered, somewhat frightened by what was going on. The next moment she could see her brother right beside her. It was as if he'd appeared out of thin air.

"Pay attention to where you're going," he retorted, rubbing the side she had tripped on.

"You're playing tricks on me!" Lucy cried, angry at what her brother had done. "I'm telling Mom," she added, running into the house.

No I hadn't, the teen thought.

Instead, he'd been lying there in the middle of the yard, minding his own business when she had tripped over him. Looking down from his sitting position, the boy's heart almost stopped. He couldn't see his legs! They were still there, he could feel them, but he couldn't see them.

Staring at the point where they would be, he could see a light shimmer, but all that he could see was grass. Startled by this spectacle, suddenly his legs appeared, as if by magic. He went over to their redwood shed and put his hand up against it. This time his hand seemed to disappear, though the outline could faintly be seen. Pulling the appendage closer to his body, it again seemed to reappear. He did this with the other hand. Same results. It was like he was some sort of chameleon. Okay, there was definitely something wrong with him.

The field trip for the Killings Day Camp program had gone well so far. By well, that meant no one had gotten lost or hurt themselves yet. A visit to the

Children's Museum was supposed to be a fun, cultural experience. But this close to the end of the school year had made it feel like work for the campers, so they ended up running a little wild. The university student who was acting as coordinator of the program had misjudged this in her planning. Now her staff was suffering for the lack of insight into the nature of children.

The morning had been a disaster, with kids scampering all over the place. Too large a number had been guilty of not listening to the program and generally misbehaving. Lunch had been chaotic, with a food fight breaking out in the concourse of the three-story building. Now the campers had some free time with their leaders, so were exploring the whole place.

For the most part, Talitha Beck's kids had behaved well. It could be argued they were the best behaved so far. It was true that they were equally rambunctious. Yet, the young woman had built up a strong enough relationship with them that they would listen to her.

While they listened, that didn't mean they didn't get distracted. This was especially the case with Talitha's favorite troublemaker, Tommy. The mop-haired boy would get involved with some activity and start to show some real effort. But then he would become distracted by the actions of someone else around him. His problem was not intellect; it was rather concentration. He had not learned the discipline yet, especially in his chaotic home life, to block these things out. This afternoon, like a top getting wound tighter and tighter, he was about to spin out of control with Talitha determined to keep him focused.

The group was on the third floor looking around the museum. They were the only ones in this particular area at the time, since the others were mainly racing around the first floor. The building was fairly new and had been designed in a contemporary fashion with lots of steel and glass. Circular in design, with a center atrium, it was open on all three floors. A tree was growing on the main floor that would eventually reach the whole height. Right now the kids were looking over the raised edge down below.

Talitha was keeping close tabs on them, mainly to ensure they didn't throw anything over the rail. She had noticed Tommy and another boy whispering and giggling with each other, but didn't know their conversation. Little did she know that the other was betting the hyperactive boy that he wouldn't run around the ring that formed the perimeter of the open drop. Before she could do anything about it, he had climbed up onto the ledge and began to walk away from the group.

"Tommy!" Talitha yelled too late, as the boy began to run.

She ran after the adventurous camper, desperately trying to catch him on the narrow ledge. He looked back with his mischievous grin and kept going, unaware of the danger. But, as his momentum got going, he lost coordination. Trying to negotiate the curve at top speed, he lost his balance and fell over the edge. Tommy screamed as he began to tumble the three stories to certain death.

In futility, Talitha tried to reach for him, but she was too far away. All she could do was watch him drop like a stone. In a reflex action, she stretched out to the falling boy, when suddenly a shaft of light emanated from her hand, reaching him.

Tommy had already plummeted the ten feet to the second floor, but now was suspended in midair as if on some sort of platform. His dark eyes were wide as saucers in terror, so he had no clue what was going on.

Talitha was stunned as well, but more focused on helping the boy. He was falling no more, but rather was lying on this shield of light. The girl moved her arm, pointing to the ledge of the second floor. Incredibly, the shaft of light and light platform protecting the boy moved in the direction she did. It was as if she were controlling this force projecting from her fingers. In this way Tommy moved through the air until he was safe on the floor. By now he was crying, so Talitha ran to the stairs behind her, the other children following along. Reaching the lower level, she grabbed the sobbing boy, clutching him tight in an attempt to bring comfort.

The yells and commotion above had gotten the attention of the others in the building. The result was people had moved to the center of the structure and looked up to see what was happening. It was a sunny day and the atrium was built with a large glass skylight at the top. So, when they looked up, the noon sun was shining directly down, obscuring the vision of those that tried to see what was going on. They could only hear the cries of the boy. Museum staff and other leaders raced up the stairs to assist. By the time they got to the scene of the commotion, they found Talitha sitting on the floor holding the scared boy and the others huddled around the pair.

"What happened?" the camp director demanded, out of breath.

Talitha's heart was racing, feeling as if it were going to burst out of her chest. The girl's anxiety was due, not only to the frightening experience, but also at what she'd done. "Tommy got up on the ledge and fell," she mumbled, still in a daze.

"But she caught him, but she caught him," the other children were saying in excitement.

The camp director was smart enough not to press the point at this moment.

She would talk to Talitha about what happened later. "Do you need to call it a day?" she asked.

Talitha took a deep breath, calming herself down, then replied, "No, we're all okay. It might be good to have some activity to get them refocused."

The director nodded in agreement, calling the others to begin the afternoon activities.

For the rest of the day Talitha Beck looked at her hand and wondered what had happened. Something had caught the boy in midair, saving his life.

Tommy was well aware of this, though he still hadn't said a word. The fright he'd felt was so real it changed him. The mop-headed boy followed her around the rest of the day. She was afraid to point her finger anywhere for fear that the strange beam of light might come from it again, but, in a way, was hopeful that it might.

But then, as is the case with many teenage girls who are desperate not to be different, she began to feel as if something weird may have taken over her body. The more Talitha tried to understand, the more she became certain there was something wrong with her. The heroic teen fell victim to a disease of confidence so common among girls her age. Different was definitely not good.

By the end of the day the group leader's mood was somber. Not only did the kids pick up her heavy spirit, but it was reflected back in the form of lifeless silence. Nothing was said about the incident and no one mentioned it.

But by the time they returned to the rec center where the camp was held, the kids had long forgotten it. The incident became ancient history since mid-day was a lifetime ago in a child's mind. Talitha still couldn't shake the feeling of dread she had though. She feared being alone with her thoughts, since the kids were being picked up.

But Tommy turned back, ran to the young woman and gave her a big hug, holding on tight. "Thank you, Miss Talitha," was all he said, tears in his eyes.

His expression gripped the girl's heart, causing her expressive blue eyes to well up also. Suddenly the teenager didn't feel so strange. Whatever change that was going on within her that had caused this to happen was worth it.

Chapter 8
Choices

Who does she think she is? Ulysses Hammerman thought to himself, anger rising. He was still steamed that Lola seemed uninterested in him. *How could that be? He was a good catch. She was lucky to have a guy like him interested. There had to be something wrong with her. That was the only explanation. He was in good shape, looked good and also was well known for his coaching abilities.*

The more the teacher thought about it, the more his dark mood intensified. There were lots of other women interested in him. That was the point of his interest though, wasn't it? It wasn't that Hammerman didn't have other opportunities. He did. It was bad enough the dress designer had turned him down. But her continued rebuffs of his displays of interest were too much. That grated on his nerves. All his life he was used to getting what he wanted.

His narrow set eyes darkened as he thought about the situation. She would change her mind, or regret it in the end. That gave Hammerman a certain sense of satisfaction.

Then another thought entered into focus. He couldn't allow this to be the cause of distraction from what was at hand. Things were about to change for him. The breakthrough was coming. When he made a name for himself he'd remember who his friends were and those who were not. A smile of satisfaction chased away the dark look that previously had clouded the confident man's face.

Bulldozer. That's what the guys on the team were starting to call Tim David after the spectacle of his pummeling Tyrell Waters the previous week. But the player was not resting on that incident. He continued to make a name for himself with his ferocious hitting.

Though the blond-haired youth played with aggression, his skills were not yet up to the level of his power. Nonetheless, he was slotted to play middle linebacker. Tim liked that; there would be lots of hard contact. He knew that his skills were not at the level of the others, so he'd have to play more aggressively. That wasn't a problem now for him. It was as if a boiling volcano was inside ready to spill over at any time. No, aggression was no problem for the still immature youth. He liked it.

That was not the only change recognizable in the young football player from the previous fall. He also found that his endurance had increased almost ten-fold it seemed. No matter how hard the team practiced, no matter how hard they ran, he never felt tired. His energy level was amazing. The week had been hot and dry. While the other players wilted, needing frequent trips to the water buckets, he didn't. Throughout, Tim stayed fresh as when he started. He'd never felt better in his life, strong and vibrant.

The team had a game coming up and he knew that there would be some playing time for him. This was a dream come true, not only to perform at this level, but now he looked forward to fall as well. Coach Jeffries had already been hinting that there might be a place for him on the championship squad, allowing him to do what few could, skip the junior circuit. He was playing in the big leagues. College ball, then the pros, could they be far off? On the way home from practice Tim liked to dream about the future, and he had a big imagination.

That was the positive side. On the negative, the whispers started up again about where the freshman student's power had come from. Though his hair was short, he had the good looks and light summer tan of a California surfer. With neck muscle bulging, there was no mistaking the youth had power.

Rumors swirled, fueled by speculation and jealousy. But, considering he hadn't even made the junior team the previous year, it was not an illogical progression of thought. Tim had risen to this level quickly, so it was natural that there would be some that were talking about the blond-haired youth taking performance-enhancing drugs.

Tim didn't let that bother him; he knew he wasn't doing anything wrong. People could ask all the questions they wanted to, there was nothing to hide. Everything that had been accomplished was his. He had made it happen through his hard work and efforts. Those that questioned this were just envious because of how he'd grown of late. There was nothing wrong with him.

Never did it enter into the aggressive youth's mind that the growth and strength had come in less than a month and a half. That was a breakthrough for him, as far as he was concerned. No, this was all his and he was going to enjoy it.

"Now where has Beau gotten to?" the teen's mother asked herself in exasperation. "It seems like every time there's work to be done he's gone and disappeared." The frustrated woman walked down the upstairs hall of the family's comfortable home, taking the carpeted stairs to the main floor, then crossing to the kitchen.

As if coming out of the wall, Beau, with a lopsided grin on his slightly freckled face, appeared undetected in the same hallway his mother had just traveled moments earlier. His new talent had gotten him out of more work this week than he could remember. At first the unexpected discovery of the ability to disappear had upset him. But, after a little bit of practice, he realized whatever condition this was could be turned off and on by simply concentrating. From that point on it became fun.

Not only had the blue-eyed youth used it to get out of work around the house, but he'd found other exciting opportunities for the skill. One of the first tests had been to spy on his neighbors. He'd heard a most interesting conversation, so now knew their marriage was in trouble despite the image the seemingly perfect couple projected. That could be useful. Then Beau found he was able to walk right into people's unlocked homes and not only listen in, but also observe what they were doing. That had been pretty interesting.

Once he knew what was possible, a darker side of the boy had surfaced. Something inside of Beau kept telling him it would be a great way to not only find out whatever he wanted, like personal information and test answers, but it could also be used to get whatever he wanted. He could simply "disappear," enter into some store or home, grab whatever he wanted then "reappear" when far away. He would only take from those who had a lot, never from those in need. After all, he did have a set of values.

Beau was tempted, but his core morality would not allow him to seriously entertain such a thought. At least not at this point, though. The challenge for the immature boy was that the temptation seemed to grow each day. For now it sufficed to think of all the neat stuff he could get.

The thought never occurred to him that his lack of satisfaction with all the things he already did have would cause the problem to grow like a snowball rolling down a hill, gaining momentum the more he got. No, there were things he wanted, lots of things. Unfortunately, he didn't have a job and his allowance only went so far.

Every time he turned on the TV or opened one of his favorite magazines or comic books he saw something he wanted. There was something growing inside of him that he didn't understand, but would have to deal with at some point.

For the meantime, he used this newfound talent to shirk duties. Whenever his mother asked where he'd gone, the boy merely replied that he was in another part of the home and didn't know she'd been looking for him. Because he could appear anywhere he wanted, his story had never been seriously challenged as of yet. His summer had been more exciting already than he had thought it would be.

Talitha checked the elapsed time after finishing her regular Saturday morning run. She was unable to believe what her watch's digital readout showed. There was no way she could have just run that route in half the regular time. Despite her athleticism, Talitha had delicate, fine features. Her expressive face was soft and pretty. The girl was a bit of a creature of habit as well, so she consistently ran the same course, always finishing in about the same length of time.

The usual purpose of the regular jog was to not only stay in shape, but also help to clear her mind. On this particular run, though, Talitha had been thinking about the strange beam of light that had come from her fingers earlier in the week. Since then the petite girl had avoided pointing her fingers at anything, which had been hard. The fear of discovery, then exposure of how different she was, was more than the youth could handle. As a result, there had been little thought of anything else, such as the elapsed time while she was out.

Unable to believe the reading, the only logical conclusion was that there obviously had to be something wrong with the watch. But then a strange feeling, a sense of dread that there wasn't, that this was yet another change, came over her. She went in, checked it against another timepiece and went back outside. There didn't seem to be problem with the watch, yet the reading just couldn't be true.

Though perspiring and tired from the run, she wanted to know for sure. Hitting the start button, Talitha began to jog the familiar course once again. In spite of her excellent physical condition it was tough the second time, so fatigue rose quickly. Despite this, it appeared as though she was making good time. The urge was there to check her watch, but for some strange reason she couldn't bear to look at the time until the journey was completed. Finally, getting back to her own home, Talitha hit the stop button, then looked down. Perspiration beading on her arm, again the watch registered that she had completed the course in about half the regular time, even with the near exhaustion felt throughout.

There was only one conclusion that could be reached, something was definitely wrong with her. Despite the good it had accomplished earlier in the week with the saving of Tommy, whatever had happened to her was a terrible thing. Worse still, there was no explanation for it. Though she felt fine, there were these strange things going on. Talitha was looking forward to entering State University as a freshman in the fall, yet all these changes were happening to her. Would it have an impact on that experience?

Sitting alone on the front step of her home, the popular girl felt alone for the first time in her life. *What's wrong with me?* she thought. *Why is this happening to me?*

The more Talitha thought about what was happening, the more she felt as if there was no one to talk to about it. If she did tell someone, it might get out. Then people would want to do experiments and poke into her life. She would die of embarrassment if any kind of focus were put on her. All she wanted to do was be a normal teen and be left alone to do her own thing. If this got out, there was no saying what could happen.

Talitha also was scared. How could she even control when these weird occurrences happened and what was going to happen next? First the beam of light, now the speed. What was next? Was her head going to be able to spin around? The thoughts and their connected emotions began to flood into her mind faster than she could push them out or try to understand them. It was an overwhelming tidal wave that consumed the sensitive girl.

Before Talitha knew it, hot tears were streaming down her face and she was crying. "I don't want to be different. I want to be normal," she wept to herself, stamping her foot on the concrete for emphasis. "I want my old life back."

"Wash only in lukewarm water, no bleach, tumble dry, iron on low." Adjusting his wire rim glasses, George read to himself the label on the shirt that had been sitting in a laundry basket. But this was no Napoleon Dynamite-like exercise in boredom. No, what distinguished this exercise was the fact that he was doing it while the shirt hung suspended in the air before him. Satisfied with the accuracy of what he'd read, the tall, wiry youth sought another target. He then turned and looked at a box of cereal left out in the breakfast nook. Like the socks, it too rose in the air unaided, then floated over toward the couch where the blue-gray eyed youth sat.

Remarkable, George thought, *I'm sitting in my living room moving these things from twenty and thirty feet away. Cool.*

That wasn't the only source of amusement this Saturday morning. He not only was able to move the items, but he could maneuver them as well. Proving the point, he refocused on the socks located in the same laundry basket. One pair rose out of the basket, then a second pair, then a third. After circling in the air, the white sport socks changed direction. Next they went up and down.

I'm sure Mom would be more impressed if I could match and fold them, George thought to himself.

He'd become reconciled to the fact that some sort of strange power pulsed through his body. The teen would cause slight tremors when nervous, but, by concentrating, seemed to be able to direct the energy. With practice he became pretty good at moving objects around with his mind. What started as the ability to reposition had quickly evolved into the capacity to manipulate small objects.

Reading on the Internet the last few days about telekinesis, it was pretty obvious this was what he had. Even more interesting, by all estimates, his was likely the best case ever recorded. The ability seemed to grow daily. In conjunction with his new higher intelligence, the possibilities were endless. Who knows what level these things might rise to?

Yes, George thought, *this had some incredible possibilities.*

He'd not revealed yet to anyone, especially Dr. Grey, the special powers he seemed to have. Instead, George kept on as normal, honing his skills, trying to learn more about them and pondering their best use. The research possibilities were huge, the commercial applications many.

"Think of how many places work with dangerous substances," George pondered. Surely they would be interested in the services of someone who could move such materials with dexterity without having to touch them.

Not only that, his mind was processing more and more difficult information, while retaining even greater amounts of data. More interesting still, there was even a sense of intuition and anticipation within the intellect that seemed to be growing. It was like his brain was now some sort of supercomputer.

Yet, the increase in intuitive intelligence didn't seem to increase the youth's humility. Instead, the opposite effect was occurring. Pride in his accomplishments, though he'd done little other than discover them, began to dictate not only his attitudes, but now his actions as well. Dr. Grey had already been trumpeted for his great physics discovery. Well, that truth would come out soon enough. He would get his due. It was no matter; there would be no more freebees. From now on people would have to pay for his services. He would get what was coming to him.

George was surprised by the ambition that was surfacing within him. The youth had never really thought this hard about money or success before. But then, he'd never had something this valuable either. He was getting smarter, surely his brain could figure out a way to cash in on these new powers.

Chapter 9
Dog Days of Summer

Crime Spree! read the headline of *The Recorder*, the dominant newspaper in the region. It was perhaps too early to make such a contention, but there definitely was something happening. Banks were brazenly being robbed in daylight, jewelry stores were being held up, home invasions, car jackings; all form of crime was soaring. The police seemed unable to explain what had caused this spike in crime, let along do anything about it. They did pinpoint the majority of it to the street gang called "The Bloods."

Although this group had been the source of difficulty in the past, it was way beyond anything the Bloods had ever previously attempted, let along accomplished. They suddenly seemed better organized and led than before. Doubly strange was the fact that the criminals seemed to have disappeared. Raids on the familiar haunts for the gangsters turned up nothing. No one seemed to be able to find a single member. Yet, they seemed to appear where the opportunity to score was the biggest. But then they were gone, vanishing after their criminal activities.

T.T. Tomlinson, editor and publisher of *The Recorder*, sat content in his high-back leather chair, hands folded behind his head. With a look of satisfaction on his ruddy face, the newspaperman pondered the recent events in his sumptuous office located on the top floor of The Recorder Building.

The feature on crime in Killings-Welch had sold well. Plus, his scathing editorial on the police had been rewarded by howls of protest from the chief and commissioner. That only made it sweeter for the man. Tomlinson didn't make the news. He only reported it. Besides, he had cut out the point about them being like keystone cops. That was a concession.

This story would play for another week at least, two if he was lucky. Chomping on an unlit cigar the heavyset man ran a hand through his wavy salt and pepper hair. He thanked good fortune for the action, since the news traditionally slowed down during the summer. Yet, what was happening had nothing to do with luck. No, it had everything to do with yet unrevealed ambition.

Regardless, to T.T. Tomlinson, if luck were on his side the police would fumble their way through this all summer. That would help his circulation numbers.

"Chambers," he barked at his assistant. The beleaguered aide to the publisher came promptly into the office. "Run another thousand copies of today's edition and tell printing to prepare an extra two thousand for tomorrow's edition." *Yes, it was going to be a good summer*, he thought to himself.

Destinies. Four young teens, George Alexander, Talitha Beck, Beau Joseph and Tim David, each from different backgrounds, each with different hopes and dreams, continued to travel the path of a mutually inclusive destiny. The meteorite had altered them physically. None, as of yet, had taken the changes that were happening to them and made the connection.

But the space rock had only changed them physically. Emotionally, they were still the same people. But, based on what was happening to them physically, not only that could be claimed anymore. As with any hugely altering event, such as a big lottery win or signing a NFL contract, one is, by result, changed. The question is then raised: what does one do when they reach the point of realization? It can be a gift or a curse. The ability is a tool, to be used or misused by the holder.

In our particular case, the tools have the potential to be used for the greater good, personal gain, or even evil. Not only for these four mentioned, but for all who go through a change, questions naturally arise. Are destinies in our control, or some divine being? Are we puppets on the stage of life, or do we chart our own course? What do we do with the cards dealt to us? There are many practical questions when things beyond our control happen to us requiring an answer.

In the lives of our four anonymous teens that point of destiny is about to come to an intersection, to a choice, that will shape the rest of their lives. But it doesn't end there. The decisions they make, as ours do too, will shape the lives of those around us like the ripples caused by a stone being thrown into a lake.

The day was steamy hot even for summer, causing a number of the modern day knights clad in armor to complain about the conditions. This was the opening game of summer football season. Despite the temperatures, it was like a dream come true for Tim David. He was participating in his first big time game. As an added bonus, he was even able to wear his favorite number 25 jersey.

Standing on the sidelines was a thrill at first. But late in the first half the impatient youth began to itch for a chance to get in and show the world what he could do. That chance came minutes later.

Coach Jeffries called him over. "Tim, get in there and sub for Greg at middle linebacker. Pay attention to the motion and don't get trapped. Go!"

The freshman listened intently to the instructions from his coach, adjusted his helmet, then ran onto the field. He was entering the game for the first time for the red jersey clad Killings Warriors. His heart pounded so hard as he took the field that Tim was sure the other players could hear it. This was a moment he'd dreamed of for a long time. They were playing the select squad from Waldenburg, and there were a lot of rivalries between the two teams.

Tim lined up, waiting to spring into action. The opposition quarterback barked out his signals and the ball was snapped. Tim was to stay in his zone, but spotting an opening, charged into the gap. He could see the ball and was ready for a big hit. But just before contact the quarterback flipped the ball to a player that had slipped into the spot he just vacated. Tim had the sinking feeling that he had been trapped. The Waldenburg Wildcat player gathered in the ball, running through the opening vacated by Tim, going hard through the gap. He was finally hauled down after a twenty-three yard gain.

"Pay attention, David!" one of the coaches yelled from the sidelines. "Play your position. Don't let yourself get trapped!" he added.

The next play he determined to hold his ground, letting no one get past. The ball was snapped again. This time, after a handoff, the running back came straight at him. The player was fast, but Tim had the angle. At the last moment, though, the ball carrier shifted position just as Tim committed. The result was the freshman was left grasping at air, falling to the ground heavily. The ball carrier kept going in the gap, resulting in an eleven-yard gain.

Tim couldn't see the face of the high school senior who had made him look foolish. But he could hear him laughing as he went back to his own huddle. The Waldenburg player also intentionally bumped into him on the way back. In the Killings huddle no one said anything to the youth, but none of the others eye contact with him either.

Lining up in position, he could see the player that had ridiculed him still smiling and laughing. Something started to boil within the blond-haired youth. Like a cauldron bubbling over, a rage was beginning to build.

By the time the ball was snapped, it seemed like Tim was in some sort of tunnel with only one inevitable conclusion. The quarterback rolled out to pass and the running backs remained in position to block for him. Tim bulled his way through the line, forgetting again that he was supposed to hold his position on this particular play, charging toward the quarterback. But that was not his objective, it was the running back. The ball was thrown before contact and fell incomplete. Tim didn't see that, rather he charged into the blocker. Knocking him off his feet, he pushed the running back five yards back before slamming the Waldenburg player hard to the ground. Tim lay on top of him, savoring the look of pain evident in the player's eyes.

"Laugh at me will you?" Tim said before getting up. The feeling of satisfaction soon sank upon seeing a yellow penalty flag beside him and one of the referees looking with disapproval at the scene.

Without emotion, the zebra striped official announced to both team benches, "Unnecessary roughness, number twenty-five red, fifteen yard penalty, first down."

A player was coming in from the Killings bench to announce a substitution. Tim didn't have to wait to see whom the new player was coming for. He was being pulled out. Three plays and he had embarrassed himself, allowing the other team to get into scoring position in the process.

Coach Jeffries grabbed him by the shoulder pads when he arrived at the sidelines saying, "Good hustle, Tim, but you've got to think out there. Don't let them use your enthusiasm against you. Use your head." With that the coach went back to the flow of the game. Tim went to the bench by himself.

The game went badly for Killings from that point on. Waldenburg scored shortly thereafter. From then on they took control and began to run up the score. If that were not bad enough, a number of the players on the other team began to taut the Warriors. Frustration was building. Tim felt like it was his fault. He had let the team down.

Finally, late in the fourth quarter, and with the game out of reach, Coach Jeffries began to freely substitute everyone on the team to give them playing time. On a defensive series, Tim was included in that batch. Still smarting from the earlier embarrassment, he wanted to prove he belonged.

Running past the Waldenburg huddle, the player Tim had the earlier run in called out, “Looking for some more, are you, boy? I thought Killings had some guys who could play.”

On his first play in, Tim was held by an offensive lineman, then tripped to the ground with no penalty called. The sound of laughter from the Wildcat players was not only getting on his nerves, but the rest of the Killings defense. Nothing was said in the huddle, but the look of frustration, not only at losing, but the taunting of the other players was starting to get them down.

Tim began to seethe inside. The volcano was beginning to boil over once more. “Someone needs to teach these clowns a lesson about respect,” he murmured to himself. Adjusting his helmet, Tim decided he was the one to do it.

The ball was snapped, then pitched to the Waldenburg running back that had been antagonizing the freshman. The ball carrier’s blocker missed Tim blitzing in, giving him a free shot. He accelerated and the running back leaned into him.

CRACK!

The sound of the collision drowned out all other noise. The linebacker picked the ball carrier right off the ground, then drove him savagely into the turf with a fury that caused all action to stop. It was a single act of violence, breathtaking, even for the aggressive game. Tim hopped to his feet and yelled out, “Let’s hear some lip now, man!” And was mobbed by his teammates for the hit.

The other player still was not moving, causing several of the Waldenburg players to wade into the mob and start shoving Tim. He fought back and soon pandemonium broke out. Other players joined in. The pent up frustration of the Killings players was unleashed. Whistles blew and referees pushed in to restore order, finally separating the players. Surrounded by concerned coaches, the ball carrier still wasn’t moving.

Tim was still be pounded on the back by his teammates and felt like a million dollars. Finally, the motionless player moved and was carried from the field on a stretcher just as an ambulance screamed into the stadium. Already the word had circulated that he’d been knocked unconscious by the blow, likely suffering a concussion, in addition to probably separating a shoulder.

The wail of an ambulance quieted his teammates down. But Tim stood defiantly, hands on his hips, staring at the opposite bench. Taunt him would they? He had showed them a little bit about respect.

The game ended shortly after. Tim saw no more playing time. He wasn't happy about that, but also wouldn't question the coach. The immature youth thought more about what had happened, not even recognizing the person that had acted with such force and violence. He felt something inside of him that he didn't understand.

Coach Jeffries interrupted Tim's thoughts. "You played with a lot of intensity today," the coach commented. "That's a good thing, but you need to learn to control it a bit. Your hit was clean, but it wasn't warranted. We go out to WIN, not to hurt people. No matter what others do on the field, never lose your respect for the ones you face." The mature teacher looked at the young man with a mixture of affection and concern. "I don't know where your power is coming from, son, but let me caution you to use it wisely. Power without self-control will only get you in trouble." Seeing Tim drop his head in shame, the wise man added to encourage him, "I think you could go places, but don't mess it up by losing control."

The coach patted him on the back, as if to say that nothing more would be mentioned about the incident, then walked away. Tim, head hanging down, was sorry for the first time for what had happened. The boy was more sensitive than others gave him credit for. The words of the coach, who he looked up to, had not only hurt, but they had also registered with him. For some strange reason he had some sort of physical power in him. It seemed to be growing. He hadn't even hit the kid as hard as he could have, or had wanted to, at the time. He needed to learn to control this rage. The alternative was beginning to scare him; it was something he couldn't even consider.

Twelve dollars. That was all the money he had to his name. It was a pitiful amount to buy a birthday gift for his mother with. Beau had begun to feel guilty for shirking his chores of late, so wanted to make it up to the beleaguered woman with an extra special gift. He noticed how tired she looked and couldn't help but think he was contributing to this worn-down state. With her birthday only three days away, there was no opportunity to make enough money to get her something nice.

He stood across the street from the jewelry store, wondering what to do. Beau had already been inside, so knew he could barely afford a gift box for twelve dollars in the place. Yet, the sparkling pieces of jewelry had caught his eye. He HAD to get something for his mother there. That would show her how much her son cared. There was only one thing to do.

In a now familiar pattern, by concentrating, Beau seemed to vanish into thin air. No one could see him, that was for sure. Crossing the street, the invisible figure waited at the entrance for someone else to enter the shop. He was rewarded less than a minute later when an older man opened the door to the store. Beau silently followed in after him. There was no one else in the expensive place other than the owner, a pale, elderly man who attended the newly arrived gentleman. Beau was free to cruise around. His conflicted heart beat in anticipation, but his mind was made up.

Spying a diamond encrusted bracelet, he decided that with so much else in the shop the owner wouldn't miss this. Besides, the gift would mean so much to his mother, who didn't have anything this nice.

Beau slipped undetected to the display case. He was about to move behind and it in order to steal the bracelet when the door opened again, announcing another visitor. Without thinking, Beau turned to look at who it was, immediately knowing the new arrival was not a shopper. Three people, with balaclava masks over their faces, entered in. One stayed at the door while the other two approached the owner and the customer.

"Let us do our thing, old man, and you won't get hurt," one of the robbers barked out, producing a handgun to emphasize the point.

Beau was riveted by the moment, but in particular was frozen by the look of terror in the eyes of the man facing the gun.

The customer tried to protest, "What are you doing? This is ..."

He didn't get to finish his thought. Instead, the older man was beaten savagely to the ground by the other thug. The owner, his look of horror deepening, sunk to his knees. With hands in the air, he pleaded for mercy from the merciless pair. They both laughed, beginning to fill sacks with whatever jewelry they wished.

Beau watched this and was cut to the core of his humanity. *How could I have ever thought of robbing this man?* he thought. He was no less guilty than these three criminals, who were now having fun tormenting the old shopkeeper, making him plead for his life.

The quiet boy had never been particularly brave before, but perhaps his invisibility helped. Maybe it was the new martial arts ability. Or perhaps, whatever had caused the new condition brought about some new form of courage. Regardless, the teen knew he had to act.

Looking around, Beau spotted a telephone in the small office just off from the showroom. Silently stealing over to it, ensuring no one was looking, he dialed 911. He didn't say anything, but left the receiver open, hoping the operator would pick up what was happening at the store and trace the line.

Beau could see that the robbers were getting close to leaving. He knew something had to be done to slow them down for the police to arrive in time to catch them. Moving from the office, he slipped past the pair, then their partner to the front door. The invisible teen was able to quietly turn the deadbolt, locking the door without anyone hearing.

A cry of fear caught his attention. The main thug was raising his gun as if to shoot the cowering shop owner. Beau transferred positions fast. Moving up to the thug, he used a judo move to shove him as hard as he could. The gun clattered to the ground, causing the robber to stumble.

"What was that for?" the thug cried out savagely to his partner.

"What do you mean? I didn't do anything," his partner retorted.

"Stop screwing around," the third one called. "Let's just get out of here."

The leader picked up his gun, following the one who held the bag of jewels. Suddenly the first stumbled and fell, the loot spilling out on the floor.

"I told you I didn't do anything! Why'd you trip me?"

"I didn't, you clumsy idiot," the other shot back. "You tripped over your own feet."

The two were about to come to blows when the third ordered them, "Cut it out! Get what you can and let's get moving."

None of them could see the lopsided grin on Beau's face as he stood beside the one he'd tripped. This was too easy.

Finally, retrieving their goods, the robbers went to the door, but found it locked. The three began cursing and shoving each other around trying to get out. The last straw was when, after unlocking the door, the trio seemed to trip on the threshold, stumbling hard to the sidewalk in front of the store. As they gathered themselves together for the getaway, the hapless criminals were greeted by the sight of a pair of 9mm pistols pointed at them. The police had arrived.

The confused trio was swiftly ordered to not move. Woodenly, they obeyed. As the robbers were being handcuffed, another officer cautiously entered the store. Finding no one other than the victims, he quickly called for an ambulance to assist the injured shopper. After the area had been secured, the police officers examined those they had arrested.

"I can't believe it!" one exclaimed. "These are Bloods."

"We'd better call this one in to the sergeant," his partner observed.

Grabbing his two-way radio, the first added, "Yea, this could be the break we've been looking for."

Several more squad cars arrived after the call went out, as did an ambulance. The sergeant began the investigation until a pair of plainclothes detectives from the Major Crimes Unit arrived and took over.

Beau, still invisible, listened with amusement as the confused store owner tried to explain what had happened. The older man knew nothing about the 911 call, nor did he understand how the dangerous thugs had begun to seemingly trip all over each other. The store owner was simply pleased to be alive and the gangsters captured.

The feeling of pride that swelled within the boy was tainted by the thought anew that he had planned to rob the man as well. While it was not going to be in the same violent fashion as the Bloods, the result would have been similar. A defenseless person would have been unable to stop the process.

Something grew in the heart of Beau Joseph, something he'd never experienced before. It was something much bigger than the amusement he'd felt at skipping chores or eavesdropping on neighbors. HE had stopped a major crime. HE had helped to thwart a group of criminals the police hadn't been able to. The sense of pride growing within was pure and lacking arrogance. The youth liked this new sensation. But then the sight of the customer who had been beaten down being taken on a stretcher to the waiting ambulance outside countered his pleasure.

The realization came instantly, like a switch being flipped. He had helped the one, but failed to protect the other. Looking again at the injured man, Beau made a solemn pledge. No more would he allow someone to be hurt like that if he were around and could do anything about it. He had great power, that was for sure, but it was to be used to help people. The way to accomplish this was still uncertain to the teen, but a plan was already beginning to form. It was no matter, from this day forward a new purpose would drive him, the desire to use what he had for the greater good.

Beau Joseph was reborn as a new man.

Chapter 10
Undertow

Blood Lord. That's what the followers of the crimson cloaked figure contemplating the last few weeks had begun to call him. The name suited his purposes and had a catchy ring to it. What he once had been was no more, a pale comparison to what his future was and, by default, that of Killings-Welch. He was the future.

The Blood Lord had taken to wearing the deep-hooded crimson cloak, not only to hide his identity, but also now as his symbol. There was an air of mystery about him and his peculiar powers that he liked. Soon the area would get to know the Blood Lord more formally. But that introduction needed to be done in a spectacular fashion. That time was soon the ambitious character thought.

After his demonstration of power to the street thugs following the prom in June, it had been easy for him to take control of the gang. A few more displays of his abilities had been necessary, since these were, in his opinion, unintelligent young men. But once that was completed, they were more than compliant. The greatest inducement now was not fear of his wrath, but rather greed. The success of their recent criminal endeavors, along with the inability of the police to stop them gave the greatest incentive.

Other criminals in the area were beginning to catch wind of the new direction through the grapevine. Thus, some were seeking to join the Bloods. At this point, though, it was their new leader who was selectively finding them. The process of education was slow, since up until the point these new followers had thought it was on the Bloods achieving the success. Little did they know.

So the Blood Lord was expanding his network slowly, incrementally, consolidating power each step of the way. Soon he would control all criminal activity of note in the region, since any resistance from within was being crushed. The next step was to take over the entire town; he had a plan for that too. The power he felt surging through his body was not only physical, it was almost emotional, and even spiritual. He would have the power of the gods and every perk that went with it. He liked this feeling of empowerment.

Sitting on a raised platform in the main room of an empty factory, the Blood Lord waited for the report of activities from his minions. The abandoned business was a pale comparison of its former self. The whole area it sat within was derelict, so no one ever paid attention to what happened there. But, inside, the crime boss was converting it into a headquarters. All things necessary to run a successful new "business" were being installed. Shortly, it would rival the facilities of the best corporation in town in terms of function and comfort.

A group of young men that the Blood Lord had appointed as leaders entered to give an account of the day's activities. The first approached.

"What was our take yesterday?" the cloaked figure asked the young street hood before him.

"Likely about ten thousand dollars in cash and goods, master"

The reporter could see the approving nod of the deep cloaked head. None had ever seen the face of the man who now directed their every step. As curious as they were, none were brave enough to try to find out. Disobedience was met with swift, deadly punishment. Thus, the part of the lieutenant's report he was loath to share came next. Involuntarily wincing in anticipation, the tattooed thug added, "A few of the guys got arrested yesterday."

"What!" the figure thundered, causing everyone in the abandoned factory to cringe in fright. The powerful force that each of his followers dreaded came from the Blood Lord. They were thankful the wave of energy that seemed to ripple through the air was directed at an abandoned piece of machinery, crushing it, not any of them. They'd seen that display too often.

Calming down, the leader of the gang asked accusingly, "Tell me what happened."

Swallowing uneasily, the speaker, who felt like a rabbit in the presence of a hungry wolf, related what he knew. "It was Diego, Anton and Terry. They were holding up a jewelry store downtown, but they got busted by the cops." No bolt of energy had crushed him, so he continued, feeling a bit more comfortable since he was only the messenger. "When they didn't meet at the rendezvous point, I thought I'd check out what was going on. I got to the store and found it crawling with cops. The guys were in the back of some cop cars. I couldn't get close enough to find out any other details."

"Very well," the Blood Lord replied, hands folded together. "I will deal with those bunglers myself," he added with a sinister tone.

Talitha sat in Victory Park, the fog of depression enveloping her. The warm, sunny day and cheerful quaking of ducks in a nearby pond did little to lift her spirits. All the changes that had gone on recently upset her. This was not like some outbreak of acne that would go away. These were strange, freakish things that had happened. So, she sat brooding, oblivious to everything around her.

The teen hadn't run lately. The inability to control the new speed she seemed to have developed scared her. In addition, she wore gloves even though it was summer. Talitha thought that might help to keep away the awful thing that came out of her fingers, which again she'd proven the inability to control.

A passionate girl, she would often wave her hands about when speaking for emphasis. In the last few days, several times, when doing this, awful pale blue, baseball size energy blasts had come out, knocking things over. She was embarrassed beyond description, so was beginning to stay by herself.

The usually bubbly, charismatic teen was sinking into a protective shell, not allowing anyone to come in. She wasn't talking to her friends, while her parents, never the best communicators before, just figured she was in some sort of "mood." They left her alone instead of trying to engage the thoughtful girl in any discussion as to what her difficulty was.

Work had been the hardest. Talitha didn't want to touch any of the kids for fear of somehow hurting them. The result was she barely played with them. A wall was being built between emotionally needy campers and their leader. The kids were perceptive, picking up that something was going on. Not knowing what it was, and instinctively figuring it was because they weren't loved, the campers acted out. The negative feelings translated into poor behavior for these children, so things were out of control there too. Her life was a shambles; everything she valued swiftly eroding.

The emotion-filled cauldron that is the spirit of a teenage girl can ebb and flow like an ocean tide. The power of the flow often comes like crashing waves, battering the fragile will of one who is sensitive like Talitha Beck. In the span of a few short weeks, she had gone from a normal, outgoing girl to a brooding, quiet caricature of her former self. The thought that she no longer wanted to live had begun to creep into her thoughts. The dark, sinister idea of how and when was becoming a reality in Talitha's tormented mind.

An attractive, college-age woman caught the distressed teen's eye. She was casually walking along the gravel path adjacent to the pond with an elderly lady supported on a cane. It was likely her grandmother.

How happy they look. They don't have a care in the world, Talitha thought bitterly to herself. The chestnut brown haired woman smiled as she passed the brooding girl on the bench. Talitha despised her for that. The woman had looks, great clothes, probably a great boyfriend, a loving grandma.

What do I have? Talitha considered. In a mind tied tight in knots, venom coursing through her veins, she could come up with nothing. She was a freak, a loser, worth nothing. Out of her own pain she began to hate the pair.

There was almost a perverse delight when a group of five young men forcibly stopped the pair on their walk, beginning to accost them. The harassers were all wearing the color and style of the street gang the Bloods. They grabbed the purse of the older lady, shoving her aside. With a cry, she fell hard to the ground. They grabbed the young woman, tossing her back and forth between them. She screamed for help, which only made them laugh.

The park had been full of people only moments earlier, but now this section was empty. Everyone else had scattered, not wanting to get involved. Spectators from a distance were sorry for the hapless pair, but glad it wasn't them chosen to be victims this day.

Like a sadistic cat tormenting trapped mice, the gangsters had their fun with the two women. What they ultimately intended to do with them was unknown. But as the younger of the pair was shoved to the ground, then held down by two of the attackers it was becoming clear.

Something snapped in the mind of Talitha Beck. The fog of self-pity lifted. Getting up off the bench that had been her prison only moments before, she suddenly found herself on the edge of the drama. Gloves off, she confronted the predators.

"Leave them alone!" Talitha demanded.

The command was met by howls of laughter as the Bloods realized another victim had willingly entered their domain.

"Fresh meat!" one of them called out.

"It's party time!" another added. Stepping menacingly toward Talitha, the gangster was instead knocked flat on his back.

"I said leave them ALONE!" Talitha screamed.

Suddenly, pale blue balls of energy seemed to be flying everywhere, originating from the hands of the petite girl. Bloods were being knocked every which way. Several tried to reach their nemesis, but none could get within five feet of her. The girl seemed to be able to direct the powerful blasts that she unleashed, sending the assailants spinning out of control to the ground.

Painfully realizing they were outmatched, the five toughs turned tail, running as fast as they could. A few parting shots encouraged them to not stop until they were out of sight of the mysterious girl with the strange powers.

The drama over, people suddenly appeared. Clambering to the scene, they wanted to lend assistance when it was no longer needed. More importantly, they wanted to know what had happened in order to gossip with those not privy to the scene. All of this was oblivious to the three women who were still gripped by the emotion of the spectacle they had just lived through.

For Talitha, it was over almost as fast as it had begun. The spectacle had unfolded as if she were watching a program on television. It was as if she could see what was happening, but not able to connect it to her. Snapping out of the moment, the girl realized for the first time her hands were shaking with emotion. Not only that, but her breathing was rapid and shallow with anxiety. It was over almost as fast as it had started. Calming her nerves, she helped the two assaulted women to their feet. Both immediately latched on to her, giving strong hugs, not wanting to let go.

"Thank you, thank you," the twenty-something woman could only say. The words tumbled from her mouth as fast as the tears of gratitude streamed down her cheeks. "You saved our lives," she choked out between sobs. Then, gaining some control over her emotions and wanting to know whom their angel of mercy was, asked, "Who are you?"

Talitha suddenly came back to the reality of the situation and what she'd done. The crowd was clambering around her, the two women still holding on as if their lives depended on it. Emotions climbed again, overwhelming the girl. She couldn't process what had happened to her and needed to think. Embarrassed by the attention, she knew she had to get away.

Saying nothing, Talitha instead carefully pulled away from the pair. Once free, she ran as fast as she could, holding nothing back. The next thing the petite young woman knew the scene of the drama was far behind her. A distance of nearly a mile had been covered in a little over a minute.

Standing with hands on hips catching her breath, Talitha realized no one was around, so she began to relax. The crisis that had unfolded played out in her mind. Suddenly there was no question about the value of the strange powers again displayed. Finally the realization of what could be done with them broke through the negative thoughts.

Twice now she had saved people from danger. Her, Talitha Beck. The thought of this shattered the darkness that had lingered within her soul, saying that something was wrong with her. Yes, she was different, but it was a gift. Purpose suddenly flooded in light, the sun breaking through clouds. The powers were something that could be used to help people who were in need. A new feeling was growing within the girl to match the glow on her cheeks. Joy. She had saved these people. A beautiful smile matching the radiance of the noon sun lit up her face.

She knew there now was something to live for. Her life had meaning and purpose. Almost like flipping on a switch, vitality returned. Talitha Beck was a new woman.

The pile of chips on the table before George Alexander continued to grow with every hand. He'd started with fifty dollars and now had hundreds before him, maybe thousands. He was taking on all comers and beating them with ease.

Every Saturday throughout the summer, at the Fairway Mall, a charity poker tournament was held. George had never even played the game before, nor done anything like it, especially where real money was concerned. He'd not liked the odds. Now though, with his newfound intuitive intellect, the thought had come to check it out.

He'd already won the day, taking first prize. With the contest completed, George was taking on all comers just for fun and some more cash. Already the slender teen had made more money in the span of a few hours than he would make in a month working at the lab. That was incentive enough, but the reaction of the crowd watching was intoxicating. It had steadily grown as he went through player after player, the excitement building with each hand.

Another challenger, a well-dressed man of about fifty had bowed out after losing everything to George, the crowd going wild. By now, though, while spectators were plenty, players were scarce. No one wanted to be taken by the slender teen.

"Any other takers?" the organizer encouraged, hoping to extend things. For him it was not about the game, but rather he got a cut of the winnings, in addition to the charity. There was incentive for all if it kept going. Besides, this was going to be the best payday of the summer, thanks to this unknown youth who'd walked up to play.

The game would fold if no one else came in to make a fourth. George was about to count his winnings to see what he would net, when a gruff voice announced, "I'm in."

There had been one in the crowd who was unimpressed with George's play, so decided it was time to teach the smug teen a lesson. Pushing his way through the crowd, he announced, "It's time someone taught this punk a lesson."

It was Keith Ramsey. The tough wrestler was a successful poker player himself, using intimidation to beat his opponents. It was a game he loved to play, not only for the financial rewards, but also for the opportunity to grind an opponent into the ground. He was going to enjoy teaching the intelligent student from K-W High a lesson.

A murmur of anticipation went through the crowd. George gulped at the sight of the hulking figure sitting down in the chair across from him after cashing some money in for chips.

Ramsey gave him a sarcastic smile, and asked, "Seen any good acorns lately, brain?" referring to the incident on the geography trip when he had embarrassed the thoughtful teen. He didn't like smart people, and he definitely didn't like this particular one.

His concentration broken, George played badly, initially losing several hands to Ramsey. The buzz from the crowd grew as people began to realize that there was something personal going on between the pair.

Finally, though, George settled down and started to take control. All day he had been able to figure out the sequence of the cards, along with what his opponents were holding. It was almost as if he could see their cards, or into their mind. He also was able to calculate the probability of certain cards coming up, which happened most of the time for him. This created an inevitability of victory, coming into play again.

Once back on track, Ramsey had no chance, getting wiped out in short order after making several aggressive bets. He'd not been able to intimidate his cool opponent. George had won the day, beating all comers.

With the sport finished, the crowd soon returned to their shopping and other distractions. The fickleness of those who chose to be spectators in life, rather than participants, showed itself in how quickly their collective attentions changed.

The tournament organizer counted up the total pot, giving George a check for the amount of his share of the winnings. He stared at it for a long time, in shock at the amount he had won. It had been so easy, so much easier than having to listen to the arrogant Dr. Gray carry on day in and day out. It was certainly easier than doing his grunt work and getting no credit for it. George had not helped with any further formulas, keeping those thoughts to himself, which irritated his boss. The work environment was not a pleasant one. But this new avenue had potential.

The organizer shook George's hand, inviting him to come back the following Saturday, then turned his attention to the maintenance men who were cleaning up the stage. The teen was left alone with his thoughts. But he wasn't alone.

"Think you're pretty smart don't you, brain?" It was Keith Ramsey, face red with agitation and fists clenched. "You may be able to scam these idiots," he accused, " but not me. You cheated."

"No I didn't. I won fair and square," George countered, though a bit nervous at the thread of truth in the accusation.

"Whatever. I want my money back and some more for you embarrassing me like that."

"Forget it, Ramsey. You chose to play and you lost. I'm not giving you anything."

The powerful young man advanced menacingly, saying, "That wasn't a request. That was an order."

George had been backed into a corner of the stage, so escape was impossible. With the angry Ramsey moving closer, George didn't know what to do. Then, spying a chair just to the side of the aggressor's path, he moved it into the way with his mind. Ramsey tripped over the object, falling hard. He got up in a rage. George had slid out of the way, but the wrestler kept coming. Again a chair got in his way and he fell down. By the third time this happened, George had relaxed, was starting to have some fun.

Keith Ramsey couldn't get to him since obstacles kept appearing in his way. A crowd had gathered at the commotion, now laughing at the spectacle going on. Ramsey was roaring in frustration, humiliated at what was happening to him, yet unable to do anything about it. For some strange reason he couldn't lay a hand on his antagonist.

The turmoil caught the attention of the mall security. A pair of guards moved in, breaking up the scene. They pushed the irritated Ramsey from the scene, but before he was removed from the mall he called out, "It isn't over, brain. You'll pay for this!"

George gave a nonchalant shrug to the people around him, then went to the food court to get something to eat. All the excitement had suddenly made him very hungry.

Sitting with two burgers and a coke, he reviewed what had happened. His brain capacity was growing. Also, his telekinesis had not only saved him a beating, but also allowed him to humiliate a brute who'd been bugging him for years. Life was good.

The brain, George recalled, rolling the words around in his mind. It was a name that had been used to taunt him and put him down for years. Now he liked it. Instead of a source of embarrassment, it would become a name to be recognized, a name that others would respect and some would even revere.

This is great! George thought to himself. *These are gifts, better than Christmas day.* In the end, he figured that they would not only be profitable, but also fun.

Finally, George Alexander was going to get what he thought he deserved. He'd worked hard all his life, had kept out of trouble, and now it was like he'd won some sort of celestial lottery. Good fortune had come to him in the form of these powers. It was time to let the good times roll and see how far it took him. He looked forward to the next poker tournament.

Chapter 11
Connections

The annual Summerfest Celebration in Killings-Welch was ready to go the end of the week. It was the biggest festival in the state, drawing thousands of people from around the country, making it the biggest tourist attraction of the year. Every hotel room in the area was booked solid, most a year ahead. The economic development committee and tourism board looked forward to the millions of dollars that it would pump into the local the economy.

The event was a week long party focusing on cultural diversity. Brightly colored tents were erected in Victory Park housing a variety of events, while halls and arena's throughout the city held other activities. Leading entertainers, a variety of talent, rich food and plenty of drink made this a topnotch event. The highlight, though, tended to be the kickoff celebration held the first Friday evening of the festival where all would gather at Victory Park. There would be fireworks, entertainment, a kid's park and a massive celebration.

But there were other fireworks being planned this Friday. They were of a different nature, though, with a more explosive impact. It would have a catastrophic effect if coming off as planned, not only on the event, but the progressive set of communities as well. The impact would effectively signal a new, darker direction. It was a bold stroke that some would call a declaration of war. But the planner preferred to consider it a change in vision.

An angry, twisted mind considered what he was planning and why. There was a veneer of gentility that had existed over this region for years, a sickening illusion of harmony and cooperation. All he was doing was stripping the layer off, allowing people to see the hypocrisy of their own lives. He would bring to the forefront the ugliness of whom they really were and profit from it. When these same broken people begged for leadership, only he would be able to provide it.

The Blood Lord sat back, hands folded calmly together, contemplating his plot. He had been going through every detail in the meticulous plan. It was amazing how swiftly everything had come together. For such a complex scheme to develop in less than two months and be ready to unfold was remarkable. With an evil smile on his hidden face, he pondered what things would look like in a year at this pace.

"Is everything in place?" the leader asked one of his lieutenants, not as a question, but rather a demand.

"Yes, my Lord," the black clad thug replied. "Everything's ready for Friday night."

The Blood Lord let rip a wicked laugh. "Good. We want to ensure we give the people a show they will never forget."

Tim sat on a metal bench outside the office of Coach Jeffries after practice. The coach had called him to discuss his play. As he waited, dreams of NFL contracts, fast cars, clothes and money went through his head. He'd be the top linebacker in the city this fall; scouts would start knocking at his door. A college scholarship would be next, meaning a free ride to a big program. *The bigger the better for me*, he thought. Then, after a few All-American performances, a first round draft into the NFL, where he'd really show them what he could do.

His body was strong and growing. Already he had the best bench press of anyone on the team, which only increased his rapport with the others. They respected him now. Yet, Tim also knew he was still getting stronger. That was the scary part. This growth spurt he was having was nothing like anyone had experienced before. By the end of the summer, who knows how powerful he would be?

Tim's second game went far better than his first. He was learning the skills of the game quickly, and also learning to control the rage within him. That was more difficult, since it seemed to boil within him like lava about to bubble over the lip of a volcano. He'd played nearly half the game, had made ten tackles, gotten two sacks and caused a fumble on a particularly crushing hit. That was the good part. The bad was that he had also received two penalties for unnecessary roughness.

He was becoming somewhat of a controversial figure too. Some loved his aggressive play, cheering him wildly, while others spoke disparagingly of his almost unchecked aggression. The coaches were even mixed on the blond, spiky-haired youth.

The six men who made up the staff of the K-W select team were reviewing their player's performance. Inevitably, though, the topic of the controversy over Tim David came up, dominating the conversation.

"Tom, this kid is dangerous," one coach cautioned. "He's going to seriously hurt someone, and that's not what this is about."

The defensive co-ordinator rebutted, "That's garbage. He plays hard. If you don't want to get hurt, go and play soccer," the stocky man added. "This kid's a tiger. He's rough around the edges, I'll grant you, but he's got potential. Besides, look how he's challenged the others to step up their own game."

"Remember, this is only summer football. It's not supposed to be that competitive," a third tried to remind the group.

"There's no such thing as ONLY football," the defense coach retorted. "If you don't play hard all the time, you shouldn't play."

Tom Jeffries finally interjected into the conversation between his increasingly agitated assistants, "All right, that's enough. I think there's middle ground here, so let's remember we're all on the same team. Leave it with me. I'll sort it out."

The coaches left the office and Tim entered in. Jeffries sighed, saying, "So what are we going to do with you?"

No more freebies, George thought to himself as he stared intently at the formula before him.

Dr. Grey waited impatiently for his intern's comments. The professor had sent the other assistants out of the lab and was now alone with him. The eminent academic needed a breakthrough. Earlier in the day, a meeting with the school's head of research funding had made it clear, that without progress his funds might be pulled. Nervous that a project he'd put so much of his life into was on the chopping block, the professor shared this with his research team. Something needed to happen fast.

So now he was expecting it from his young assistant. The man could see in the teen's eyes that he'd come up with something, but wouldn't share it. The deep thinking youth just didn't seem like a team player.

George had taken another poker tournament the past Saturday, so had enough money to quit this job. But he liked the lab; he liked being around science. He just didn't like Dr. Grey. Poker was only a means to an end, not even a diversion for him.

"So what do you think?" the silver-haired scholar finally asked impatiently.

The answer was plain as day to the teen, but thus far undetected to the learned scholar. George had figured out the complex formula earlier in the day, but had held his tongue. Instead, he'd amused himself by moving vials of chemicals and other small objects around with his mind. There was no profit in it for him to help this man. If he ticked the guy off enough he might get reassigned to someone better. George thought, *No more freebies.*

"Well?" Grey prompted him, a look of anticipation on his stress-lined face.

"Sorry, Dr. Grey," George answered with a smug look on his face, "I'm stumped."

Lola was deep in thought, not noticing that she was being followed. The last few days had been strange for the attractive designer. She couldn't shake the feeling that someone was watching her. In addition, her phone made a strange clicking sound whenever she picked it up. Even in the privacy of her own apartment Lola sometimes felt like there was someone else there. Sadly, this increasing burden was carried alone, since the discouraged woman was a bit of a loner, not really having any friends to talk to.

The day had been slow as usual at her shop. That was bad enough, but now the place of inspiration was starting to give her the creeps for some reason. So Lola decided to close up early and go for a walk in Welch Park which was nearby he uptown location. Hopefully, the fresh air might be good for her.

Walking by herself, engrossed in personal reflections, the dressmaker didn't notice the two tough looking men shadowing her every move. Traveling into a wooded section that was free of people, at first the idea of being alone with her thoughts was exhilarating.

Despite the model-like looks and career choice, Lola was a woman filled with intense thoughts. Sadly, the burdens of life lately had not allowed her to exercise her mind in the way she'd like, but at this moment that freedom had been found. A fragrant aroma of fresh cut grass coming from the soccer fields over a rise beyond the expanse of trees helped to lift her spirit.

Perhaps things aren't as bad as I think they are, the woman thought as she approached a wooden bridge straddling a small stream.

She was wrong.

Partway across the bridge, a tough looking African-American man with a shaved head and red sweatshirt appeared, blocking that end of the bridge.

Turning to go back the way she had come, that path was barred by another scary looking younger man in red as well.

Involuntarily, she moved toward the center of the bridge, trying to find a way of escape. With wicked grins on their hard faces, the pair matched her step, squeezing the designer into the center.

"What do you want?" she finally cried out in fear.

"See'n you, babe, we want a lot," the shaved head responded with a knowing look. He reached out and grabbed her arm in a vice-like grip.

Lola recoiled, screaming in terror. But the other attacker stifled the sound by putting his hand over her mouth.

The pair drew in close to the woman, pressing into her. A fear she had never experienced before filled her soul. Tears began to well up in Lola's deep blue eyes in anticipation of what was to come. She felt more alone than she'd ever been.

Suddenly, one of the attackers gave an involuntary jerk, releasing the woman in the process. The other gave a hard shudder, then pulled back as well.

Opening her eyes, Lola saw pale blue balls of light the size of baseballs hit the one who'd had his hand over her mouth. Spasms of pain registered on the thug's face with each one he seemed to absorb.

Meanwhile, the other attacker was being pulled back as if tied to some invisible rope. He was flailing about, but hitting nothing. Next, the shaved head seemed as if he were shoved, causing him to topple over the small bridge into the water.

Unable to do anything to stop this, his partner was totally disoriented by what was happening to him. But, upon seeing his partner in the water, wading to the side of the stream, he decided that it was time to retreat. Both rejoined, then ran off into the woods, never looking back.

Lola's knees began to shake with the emotion of what had just happened to her. She was disoriented first from the assault, then by how she had been delivered from it. Two tough thugs had been forced to, not only release her, but also turn tail and run. How did that happen? As if in answer to the unstated question, before her appeared a young-looking, nondescript boy in his early teens with light brown hair. On the other side was a petite, pretty teenage girl. The boy smiled at her sheepishly, but didn't say a word.

The already agitated designer was becoming baffled, wondering if her mind was playing tricks. She'd been looking in the direction the male youth stood, but hadn't seen him appear. It was as if the boy had come out of thin air. The girl had been behind her, but she didn't know what her connection had been to the incident either.

A crow shrieked unseen high in the trees, snapping the woman out of her dream-like state. The sound sent a shiver through Lola, causing the clothing designer to panic and run.

Both youths were now alone. The pair had been so focused on their individual part of the drama that they'd been unaware of the presence of the other. Each was startled by the discovery of the other, so they reacted instinctively. The male seemed to disappear right before a blue ball of energy flew at him. But then it was as if the pair came to an equally instinctive conclusion. They knew not only that there was no threat, but also each shared a similar character trait.

Prior to the attack, Talitha had been cruising through the park, feeling that something was not right. Her intuition was rewarded when she came onto the scene unfolding at the bridge. The girl could see what the toughs were doing, so she responded, taking care of the one. But when his partner seemed to fly into the creek that gave her pause to consider she might not be alone. The teenage boy with the light brown hair had come out of nowhere, startling her. The response had come automatically.

Beau, for his part, had similar thoughts. He'd heard of late that there was an increase in crime in Welch Park. So he went to see if his help could put a stop to it. Coming onto the scene of the attractive woman being accosted, Beau "went grey," as he referred to it now, then stepped in. The slender teen had easily taken care of one of the attackers with a hold-throw combination when the other was beaten off by a series of strange light balls. Once the victim had fled, he became aware of the presence of another. Thinking it was an unseen attacker, the boy's disappearance saved him from an energy sandwich. About to respond, he was surprised to see standing a short distance off a familiar face.

Lola involuntarily ran as fast as she could, leaving the scene without speaking. She didn't stop until there were people all around, attracting their attention. When finally able to compose herself, she went back to the spot of the attack after asking a helpful couple to come along.

Pieces of what had happened came back to her. The rest was a blur. Lola did know that she was helped out of a jam. The face of the teenage girl was embedded in her mind. Instinctively, though, she knew there was another, more mysterious one, who had helped too. The flash of the face of an early teen's boy entered into her mind.

The designer kicked herself for not staying long enough to thank them and find out who they were. The powers she thought she'd seen were incredible, like something out of a comic book. Yet, she had not only witnessed it with her own two eyes, but had also been saved by them as well. The woman needed to know who they were. Unfortunately, by the time she returned to the scene of the drama, neither attackers nor defenders were present.

Before Lola returned, both defenders stood staring at each other in amazement, breathing hard after the exertion. Talitha stared at the indistinct looking teen before her, realizing there was something familiar about him.

Before any connection could be made, the youth spoke, "You're Talitha Beck."

"Yes, I am" she replied. "I recognize you, but forgive me, I don't know you're name."

"That's okay." He smiled. "I'm Beau Joseph. You stood up for me on Mr. Hammerman's geography field trip. I'm only a sophomore, so I wouldn't expect you to know me."

Talitha winced at the reality, but was impressed by his honesty. "You were able to disappear and reappear, weren't you?" she asked eagerly. With anticipation, she added, "I wasn't seeing things, was I?" Suddenly she didn't feel so lonely.

The boy grinned sheepishly, lowering his head in embarrassment. "Yea, I guess I can." Then he perked up. "What about you?" he asked eagerly. "Were those balls of light from you?"

Now it was Talitha's turn to feel awkward. "Yes, it was," she confessed. "Pretty weird, huh?"

"Are you kidding? That was awesome!" he enthusiastically shot back. "I'd love to be able to shoot energy balls. Man, that's cool."

"I don't know. I think it would be better just to be able to disappear and not let anyone see me sometimes."

"Well, I don't know," Beau cautiously replied. He wasn't used to talking to girls, especially ones that were older than him. He suddenly developed a strange, awkward feeling. "I think you're pretty lucky."

Sensing the younger boy's discomfort, Talitha tried to reassure him, "You were pretty awesome yourself the way you pushed that punk off the bridge."

A thought entered into her mind, like someone entering a room and turning on the lights. A connection of some sort was brewing, an answer to the questions she'd had of late. "How long have you had your powers?" Talitha asked, changing the subject.

Beau's response was prompt. "Not long. Only about a month really. It's the weirdest thing. One day I'm just normal, then the next this stuff happens. I can also build things like you've never seen before."

"Do you know how you got them?" Talitha pressed, remembering the robot she'd heard about him building. "Was there something you did?"

"I don't know," he replied, shaking his head. "At first I was scared, but now I just accept it." Hesitantly he added, as if embarrassed by his feelings, "Now I see them as a gift."

"A gift," Talitha murmured to herself. "That's the same way I think about it." But the young man before her seemed to be dealing with it better. Suddenly a thought hit her like a lightening bolt. "You were one of the ones that Keith Ramsey shoved toward the meteorite, right?"

Beau's face lit up. "Yes! You do remember! I was wondering if you would. You stood up for me, and I really appreciated that."

"But you weren't the only one. There was another."

"Yea, I don't know him. He's a freshman. I think his name is Tim." Beau started to catch the girl's drift, "Hey, do you think there might be some kind of connection?"

"I'm not sure. The only way to find out is to ask."

Then, like someone rewinding a tape, Talitha thought back to the ruined prom. She remembered a conversation she'd intended to have with George Alexander about how he'd known the attack was coming. An idea was starting to form in her active mind. "There's another one as well who got close to the meteorite like you and I did that we should talk to."

We? Beau thought to himself. *I'm not alone in this?*

Talitha was pretty, but the freshman wasn't attracted to her in that way. It was almost like the big sister he never had. He'd love to hang out with the popular senior. Besides, it was a person who could help him figure out his powers. Two would be better than one. He wondered if there were any others. That would be cool. You don't feel so different when you have a family around you.

"Come on," Talitha said, with a light wave of the hand, "let's go see if we can figure this out."

Chapter 12
Destinies Confused

For the first time in a while George couldn't figure something out. Talitha Beck had called earlier, asking if she could come over to talk. While they were acquaintances, having been in many of the same classes for years, that didn't mean they were friends.

Of late, he'd been able to discern what was going on, but was stumped this time. Strangely, that irritated him. For some reason he thought he should be able to figure everything out.

Well, it's no matter, George thought. *The answer will reveal itself soon enough.*

Despite the little hitch, the youth was in good spirits. Though it was Thursday afternoon, he was already looking forward to the Summerfest kickoff the next night. That had always provided ample stimulus for his curious spirit, thus making it a highlight for him. More importantly, he'd been reassigned to another professor since Dr. Grey no longer needed his services. That was a relief and in some ways a source of satisfaction. As an added bonus, because the change didn't start until Monday, he had a couple of days off.

The doorbell rang, signaling the arrival of a visitor. George leapt off the overstuffed couch in the living room where he had been pondering the purpose of Talitha's visit. Opening the door, he was surprised a second time this day, seeing not only Talitha, but also another younger student, who he instinctively knew for some reason was Beau Joseph. Recently he'd gone through not only the student directory, but also the yearbook, memorizing the details of who everyone at K-W High was to see if he could do it. His power of recollection seemed pretty good.

"Hi, Talitha," he greeted the girl. Then, looking at the second visitor, said, "It's Beau, right?"

George was rewarded by a smile of appreciation at the recognition, along with the vigorous nodding of the youth before him.

Inviting the pair into the Alexander's comfortably appointed living room, the host bid them to sit down. Once everyone was comfortable, George attempted to assess the situation. He was uneasy with the fact that not only were there two people visiting, but, more obviously, they were such an unlikely pair. One was a popular senior, the other an unremarkable sophomore. This was obviously not to be a social call.

What's their purpose? he thought to himself, but was still stumped. Deciding to forgo any chitchat, the senior got right to the point. "So what's up?" he asked. "Why did you want to meet?" He could see Talitha shifting nervously in the chair she sat in, only increasing his curiosity.

For her part Talitha, was uncomfortable being there and still wasn't sure what she'd say. The plan she and Beau had come up with was not only unusual but based on a lot of assumptions. The first assumption was that George Alexander wasn't going to laugh them out of his house. Talitha had always been a proud girl. Not proud in the sense of arrogant, but protective of her reputation. Yet, what she was about to share could blow that all away.

Suddenly at a loss for words and lacking confidence, she hesitantly started to speak, "Do you remember last month when we were on the field trip and we saw that meteorite?" Seeing the look of acknowledgement on George's face encouraged her to relax a bit. "Well, we were hoping you could give us some information about it."

George's tone changed, instinctively knowing this had something to do with him as well. "What kind of information?" he asked cautiously.

The doorbell rang again, interrupting their conversation. George opened it and was surprised a third time to see another unknown, but familiar face. The yearbook study had paid off. But what was he reaping? Standing before him was a freshman named Tim David, who had even less connection to the three than the first two visitors had possessed. Inquisitiveness was giving way to irritation at the bizarre group assembled. The freshman with bulging muscles seemed as agitated being at the door as his host now was at three unconnected people dropping in on him.

For Tim David, when Beau and Talitha had shown up at his home earlier in the day every fiber of his being had said tell these two to buzz off. Yet, when an invitation to a meeting later in the day was extended, something had compelled him to accept. He didn't know either of them, nor did he want to at this stage of his life. There were new friends on the football team and that was his future. Still, something in the way the pair asked encouraged him to say yes. It was as if some strange force had intervened, causing Tim to accept. Now, here he was, unsure of why he'd accepted.

The pair had met at Talitha's house the previous day to decide what to do with their powers. It had taken each of the teens little time to decide to use them in an attempt to stem the growing wave of crime in the area. Something had to be done. Each felt convinced of the need to do what they could, regardless of their age. But, as they delved deeper into the issues, the scope of what was happening made it imperative to have others involved.

The discovery of Tim David had come quite by accident. While discussing how to approach George and find the other who had been involved with the meteor, Beau had casually glanced at the newspaper and seen a picture of Tim playing football. Despite the equipment, he recognized the youth as the one they had sought.

Regretting already his decision to attend the meeting, Tim slumped sulkily into a wing back chair with the others.

"So, is there anyone else coming?" George asked, a slight edge to his voice. Receiving Talitha's acknowledgment that the four of them were it, he pressed on, "Now what do you want to talk about?"

Talitha suddenly felt extremely awkward. In her own mind, the conversation played out simply. She would lay out what happened and everyone would agree, then they would figure out what to do with the talents each possessed. Looking at the two boys staring at her, she realized that might be overly optimistic. Her heart began to pound with growing anxiety. But there was no turning back. She had to reach deep within herself, going out on a limb the girl didn't even know was in her character.

"Okay, remember back in June, on the geography trip, when that meteor hit the ground?" So far she had their attention. "Well," suddenly she felt incredibly awkward, "did either of you notice anything different about you afterward?"

George became suspicious of her intent. Guardedly he asked, "What do you mean by different?"

"I mean, like any changes in you. Like, is there anything you can do now that you couldn't before?"

George adjusted his glasses, then replied unconvincingly, "I don't know what you mean."

She could see he was uncomfortable, so decided to come right out with the honest truth, trusting the secret would be kept. "Beau and I have developed certain powers, things that are really unusual since then."

"And you think it has to do with the meteorite?"

"It's the only answer," Talitha responded, her enthusiasm rising. "We thought that you guys might have changed as well, since you were both exposed."

To George there was a certain inescapable logic to her conclusion. But he didn't want to consider it, never having examined the how or why of what had happened to him. Instead, he preferred to ponder the rewards of the change. To deflect the line of thought, he countered, "The whole class saw the meteorite, yet no one else seems to have stepped forward with anything like this."

"Yes, but we were the only ones who got close to it," she countered.

George wouldn't give her any room to maneuver. "I've seen Keith Ramsey. He doesn't seem to have any sort of special power." Then, trying to end the conversation before it went any further, he countered, "How do you even know what you've got is that special?"

Beau disappeared and then reappeared.

"Okay, that's special all right," a shocked George agreed. "I believe you."

"What about you?" Talitha challenged, pressing him anew. "Have you had any changes?"

George was put on the defensive. Every fiber of his body screamed lie to her. But, for some strange reason, the open face of the girl before him wouldn't allow for it. Instead, he grudgingly acknowledged, "Well, yes, I have noticed a few changes, but never took the time to analyze them."

Talitha turned to Tim. Without saying anything, the inviting look on her face encouraged him to join in, sharing anything he might care to divulge.

Arms folded, Tim sat stone-faced, revealing nothing about the way he was feeling. The look of aggression in his eyes was intimidating to the sensitive girl. She lost her train of thought. Suddenly an awkward silence flooded the room.

Beau, who had been quiet thus far, came to the aid of Talitha. "Well, think about it now. What's happened to us?" Receiving no response, with a slight lisp in his soft voice, he added, "Okay then, how did it happen?"

George knew he had to say something. "I have to admit I've wondered about that. But I've been busy, so really haven't given it any thought." Hoping to deflect their curiosity and attention, he decided to offer a compromise. "I can probably help you figure this out. Leave it with me. I'll do some research and determine the probability of the occurrence. That should help."

"Probability!" Talitha spat out. "You've been changed already, I know you have! You're hedging. The WHY doesn't matter, it's the what we do with it that we're talking about. These are gifts, given to us for a purpose. We need to do something positive with them."

"Well, yes, but WHAT about the side effects, WHAT about how long it will last, WHAT about the spin-off usage," George almost taunted, countering her point.

Talitha doggedly kept up. "All the more reason to use it for good now while we have it. There are problems in the city all around us that we can help with. You can't be blind to what's going on around you. If we sit around and study it, that does no good. We need to act."

"But it will help us understand?"

"I don't want to just understand," Talitha retorted. "I want to do something to help those who can't help themselves. Are you going to be a spectator all your life?"

Suddenly irritated, George snapped back, "Listen, Talitha, don't get all high and mighty with me. We could just as easily talk about the morality of taking the law into our own hands. No one is asking us to get involved." Trying to lessen the harshness of his previous statement, he added, "Besides, are we sure there's such a big problem in the area? Sure, a couple of neighborhoods are a bit rough, but so what? Every city has its share of trouble. K-W is basically a pretty good place. Why don't we just live and let live?"

The girl would not give up. "Live and let live? It doesn't matter to you because it hasn't impacted you. Get your head out of the sand."

"Listen, we can go around and around on this exercise of futility." George was tiring of the pressure being put on him. Changing tactics, he countered with, " Say we agreed, what would you propose we do?"

Beau enthusiastically stepped in, "We would form a team, then work together to help people in need. We'd use our gifts to look after people."

"A very noble thought, Beau," George replied with a slight chuckle. "But wouldn't that bring us a lot of publicity, making it harder for the team to do what it wants?"

The young sophomore looked crestfallen at his point being countered. It was all so obvious to him he'd never considered the others wouldn't see it.

Sensing her friend's disappointment, Talitha continued for him, "You're right, George. That means we'd need to be low key and anonymous. Each of us would only be able to use our powers while fighting crime. That means we couldn't risk attention by using them for personal gain or outside those circumstances." She knew what was being asked was a lot, so added, "I know it would be a sacrifice, but we'd need to be anonymous. But think of the impact we could have if we worked together."

"No way! No way!" an aggravated Tim shouted. "I've been working hard and no dumb rock gave this to me. It's mine. I deserve it." He pounded the coffee table in front of him so hard it cracked.

Unconcerned about the damage he'd just caused, Tim shouted, "I'm not going to give up my shot just to stick my nose in other people's business." He stormed out of the room, but hurled back before the door slammed shut behind him, "If you are stupid enough to not use what you've got, fine, but count me out."

George grimaced slightly at the emotional outburst. While his opinion was similar to the freshman's, he didn't feel it was necessary to express them in such an uncontrolled way. "It's a noble idea, Talitha, it really is. But it's not reasonable. What possible difference can we make? It would be a drop in the bucket of human suffering."

"We could do our part," the girl replied, but without conviction. The writing was on the wall and she could see they were not going to get through to the pair. They hadn't even found out for sure if they'd even been changed. It had been a waste of time.

George could see the look of defeat in the girl's face. As if to sooth the pain, he tried to make her see it the correct way. "It wouldn't make any difference, Talitha. And to give up what we CAN do with these gifts, as you call them, would not be in anyone's interest. It's just not logical."

Seeing Talitha's pained expression continue, he added, "I admire your desire to help. You always did have a good heart. But you know what? It's not practical. No, this is just not for me. I have too much on the go right now to get involved. Sorry."

He walked out of the room, leaving Talitha and Beau right back where they were before.

Friday night the weather was perfect. The air was warm without any humidity, the stars shining on the clear evening. A record-breaking crowd had come out to witness the kickoff of Summerfest. A number of entertainers had already performed on the main stage, but the headliner was just starting to crank it up. Packed in front of the stage, people danced and enjoyed the electrifying atmosphere.

Beyond the central stage area, a sea of humanity went though the booths and displays set up all around the park. The children's village was filled with clowns, bounce castles, games and all forms of delight for the young. The mood was festive and the celebration in high gear.

Tim, wearing his number 25 jersey, walked along with several of his teammates, taking in the action. They had a game the next day, but the excitement of the evening was too much to keep them away. With muscles rippling under his uniform, he and the others caught the attention of a number of teenage girls there looking for another sort of excitement. Tim liked the attention, responding by showing off for the older girls. They reacted like he was some sort of hero.

But, inside, he was still irritated by the conversation he'd been part of the other day. The freshman didn't know why, but something was gnawing away at him, not allowing him to have any peace. Perhaps a blowout tonight would get him back on track.

Talitha and Beau were hanging around on the periphery of the action, watching for a different reason. They had not come to join in the festivities, rather being drawn by a sense of foreboding. Both had felt as if something was going to happen this night, drawn as if by some unseen magnet. Even if the others had rejected the vision of standing up to help the community, they weren't going to. They would do what they could to help those unable to help themselves.

Dressed in nondescript black sweatsuits, the pair blended into the scenery around them. But they also had thin balaclava masks in their pockets just in case.

There was an evident police presence in the throng, yet the pair of teenagers strangely felt the need to be at the event. Talitha and Beau tried to keep out of the way, but it was difficult with so many people in the park. But they didn't want to be noticed, instead assuming the role of silent guardians.

George found himself wandering alone through the sea of people. Though he didn't like crowds, he used to like this particular activity. But, after the previous day's conversation, his mood had soured. When friends had called, he'd said he didn't want to come. In the end, though, something drew him to the event. The senior had been having trouble concentrating all day, not knowing why.

Now, here he was, aimlessly walking along. The intelligent teen was not looking at anything in particular and finding little of interest. The noise of the band on the stage was distracting him, making it hard to think. He hadn't run into anyone he knew yet, nor did he want to. But then, as if a wish were being granted, the music suddenly stopped, apparently in mid-song.

For no obvious reason, not only did the sound die, but the stage lights went down as well. The band members were dumbfounded as to what was going on, confusion evident on their faces. They were equally uncertain when a lone figure in a long crimson cloak and shrouded face walked confidently to the center of the stage. The backstage area that only moments before had been filled with people running the show was now strangely empty.

Irritated by the disruption to their performance, the leader of the band yelled out to the approaching figure, "Hey, man, you're not supposed to be up here, this..."

The shaggy-haired singer never finished his sentence. Without being touched, he flew hard across the stage as if shot out of a rocket. Though the face was hidden, a look from the strange person caused the others to flee the stage.

A number of people at the front of the stage, thinking this was part of the show, began to cheer what was happening. Others, though, were silenced by the ominous aura the lone figure seemed to give off. Nothing else happened for several moments. The cheering died down, the void being filled with an eerie silence.

As more people became aware that something unscripted was happening, the center of attention finally spoke in a clear, yet odd, voice. "For almost a month there has been concern about a rise in crime in this area. I stand here to tell you that this was only the drizzle before the storm you are about to experience. For what you have witnessed has been the artwork, but now meet the artist."

Police and security were slowly working their way to the stage after ascertaining this was not part of the show. The figure raised a gloved hand that seemed to freeze them in their place. Satisfied he had everyone's attention, he continued in a guttural tone, "I put you all on notice. No longer will your excesses go without a toll being paid. No longer will your aimlessness come without a price tag attached. I offer you a return to peace and prosperity, but at a price. From this day forward, you will bow to a new master, the Blood Lord, or suffer my wrath."

People began to laugh, still thinking it was part of the performance.

Though outwardly calm, the strange speaker added, "To show you I do not speak idly, let me show you what I mean. What you are about to experience is only the beginning."

A few in the front rows began to hurl insults at the cloaked figure as he raised his hands. Suddenly, a tidal wave of energy broke free from him, bowling over those people who had been mocking him. As if on cue, dozens of tough men clad in red came swarming from behind the stage.

Another wave of energy hit the crowd, sending others tumbling like dominos. Screams broke out and panic ensued as people scrambled to get away from the wave of violence.

George had been caught off guard. Not paying attention, it took him several minutes to figure out what was happening. At the last moment he turned, and from where he was standing could see the cloaked figure's energy blast. The scene before him was like something out of a movie, and he was frozen by the drama. But, with Bloods surging toward him, the youth instinctively joined the other people running from harm. Heart pumping, all that ran through his mind was survival.

A middle-aged man running beside George was suddenly yanked from behind by one of the gangsters, then engulfed in a swarm of attackers. The panic-filled teen ran harder to get out of the way. But then, as if hitting an invisible wall, he was stopped dead in his tracks by what had come into view.

Moving against the flow and toward the danger at hand, two people in ski masks and sweat suits were pushing their way through the crowd. Instinctively, George knew who they were before anything happened. Setting themselves between the attackers and those trying to flee the carnage, two youthful voices yelled above the din for people to get out of the park. George's intuition was proven correct as he watched one of the would-be defenders vanish and moments later an attacker go flying through the air. The other was shooting baseball-sized balls of blue energy. Bloods began to surge toward the new battle, attracted by the action. The pair was in danger of being overwhelmed by the growing number of attackers.

For an instant George almost joined in the battle. But spying a Blood advancing toward him, his sense of self preservation took over, so he began to run. He ran hard, heart pounding, face flushed, not stopping until safely home.

Doubled over from the exertion on his front lawn, sucking air into his bursting lungs, George could hear the sounds of sirens throughout the town all heading toward the park. Despite the heat radiating from his face, the tears of shame that began to stream down it were even hotter.

Back at the park, Tim stood transfixed, taking in all the action. It was thrilling in a way, like watching some reality TV show live. The few police on the scene were quickly overwhelmed, so forced to fight for their lives rather than protect those being set upon. The volunteer security had already melted in the face of the threat, self preservation foremost in their minds. Like a whirlpool growing bigger, more were being drawn into the circle of violence.

But not Tim David. He was safe at a distance with the other masculine football players watching the drama unfold. Suddenly he saw at a distance two Bloods pull a young teenager into the vortex. What caught his attention was that the youth looked almost exactly like him, though only a lot weaker and unable to defend himself. The scene held Tim spellbound. The thought then occurred that this once could have been him.

For all his aggression, the teen was strangely passive now, unable to move due to the turmoil of indecision reigning in his spirit. So he continued to watch. Now it was no longer as an amused spectator, though, but rather as a fellow sufferer. With no one stepping forward to assist, the boy was beaten to the ground, then robbed of his wallet, watch, and even his shoes. Laughing, the attackers then threw them away.

Tim had no time to recover from the disgust of that scene. Next he saw the same group pull a screaming teenage girl into the mob. The football player's heart sank as he realized she had been one of the ones admiring his muscles earlier in the evening. Suddenly his strength didn't seem so impressive anymore. It seemed to be backed up by a heart that this night was revealed to display no courage. Without knowing the outcome of the tragedy unfolding before him, Tim, who could take it no longer, turned and ran away in shame.

Beau and Talitha were fighting for their lives. Their initial success had been significant, but now the element of surprise had been lost. Beau was finding it hard to concentrate, the adrenaline flowing hard, so he kept coming in and out of his gray zone. Plus, despite his new found martial arts prowess, being only fifteen, he was still undeveloped physically, so no match for the street thugs.

Talitha was tiring, becoming unable to control her energy balls. The cordon of evil humanity was tightening, not allowing the room she needed to use her gifts. Yet, despite the fear she would never see the next sunrise a calm filled her spirit. The teen sensed that she was doing the right thing, even if no one knew. Despite her insecurities, she had tried.

The pair of them had rescued a number of people from attack, while shielding a group of others who were all able to escape the whirlwind.

Unfortunately, the tables were now turned. The rescuers were in danger of becoming the victims.

Beau was hit by a piece of lumber broken off a booth, tumbling hard to the ground. He expected to be kicked to a pulp in no time. Talitha was struck hard as well. Stunned, she fell beside Beau. For a split second they looked into other's eyes, knowing they had done the right thing. A bond of common purpose forged earlier in the week had now been tested and would not be broken, despite what was happening. Neither would even think of leaving without the other.

Unconsciously, they reached out for each other, not in intimate affection, but rather an affection linked through service. They had experienced something together that only those who experience combat usually do. They were now brother and sister, bonded through the crucible of fire.

Holding hands as the final onslaught of violence began to rain down on them, for some reason they were not hit. Each could see the feet, hands and weapons flailing, but for some reason nothing was connecting. It was as if they were in some sort of bubble. Then, just as strangely, with quizzical looks on their faces, the attackers faded off, joining others in the carnage that continued in other parts of the park.

Once alone, Beau and Talitha realized that both were not only shielded by some force, but also were invisible. The powers of the individual had melded with the other, creating an even more powerful force. This was something to ponder another day. For now the duo was happy to be alive and happier still they had stood up against the impossible odds.

Sore from the beatings they had taken, the pair painfully stood up assessing the situation. The police riot squad was organizing and there seemed no one else around but the thugs. The strange character that had called himself Blood Lord seemed to have vanished in the action. With little else to do, Talitha and Beau limped off into the shadows.

Hours later, with Victory Park in shambles and the Summerfest kickoff ruined, the chief of police, commissioner and mayor of Killings all stood in the center of where the action had been fiercest. Ambulance crews were still tending to the injured, while merchants wandered around dejectedly, wondering how they would ever recoup their losses. Despite the reports that continued to pour in and the witness interviews, none of them had any idea of what was just unleashed upon, not only Killings, but Welch and the whole area as well.

Chapter 13
A Force to Be Reckoned With!

Terror! screamed the headline of the weekend edition of *The Recorder*. T.T. Tomlinson had ordered the presses stopped and the edition's first section redone after what had happened at Victory Park. He hated to do it because of the cost of the restart, but this story couldn't wait. In addition, another five thousand copies were ordered.

Details were sketchy, but an amateur photographer had snapped some blurry pictures of this person who called himself the Blood Lord. They would be the lead, followed by pictures of the destruction, along with interviews of people who had been there. It was a sensational story the hard-nosed editor was happy to run with. Lost on him, though, was the suffering of many who had been there. That was a mere fact of life.

The television stations were already running the same story. A brief clip from someone's camcorder had also caught the sinister figure. That had run on the 11:00 news with followup for the morning news shows. The whole region would be abuzz with this news before the end of the weekend. Summerfest had now taken on another meaning. The implications were as of yet unknown, but the excitement grew.

The big Saturday parade had suffered disruptions the next day. It was mostly acts of vandalism by street thugs out to prove that they were worthy of recognition. There had been no further appearance from the Blood Lord, but a couple of high profile robberies by the Bloods showed the previous night had not been a fluke. Already hundreds of tourists had left town prematurely due to the violence and continued threat. Hundreds more who were to arrive had chosen to cancel.

The Chief of Police and Commissioner had held a hastily called news conference to try to calm the public's fear. But when a smoke bomb had been set off right in the middle of the meeting, the panic it set off was amply captured, then broadcast throughout the state. The police had to admit they were struggling with this new wave of crime. Doggedly, they asked for patience, but the uneasiness at the situation was evident in their faces as well.

While details on what was happening were fairly clear, the reason why it happened in the first place was still up for debate. Some commentators were preparing to use it to criticize the police, others to rail against the materialism and plight of the poor. Yet, beneath all this, there was an understanding that these were no random acts of violence. They were being carefully planned and flawlessly executed. This was the work of no mere street thug.

Already some were quietly drawn to the confidence and power of this unknown person called the Blood Lord. They were not uncertain that his form of leadership would be good for the area that had grown soft in their prosperity lately.

In addition to reports on what had happened, there also were also accounts of some who had tried to stem the wave of violence that had initially crashed into the Friday evening party. In particular were accounts of two unknown people in ski masks that had singlehandedly saved a number of people from harm. Who they were, nor their fate, was known, but they were being hailed as heroes by most.

George lay on his bed pondering what had taken place Friday night. Articles on what had happened at the Summerfest kickoff were piled on the desk in his room. The last few days something had been eating away at him. He'd skipped the poker tournament, not feeling like going, then called in sick to work on Monday. It was as if the very ambition and purpose that had been so certain only a week ago had evaporated.

Could I have done something to help on Friday night? he thought. *How could I? I'm only one man.*

Yet, George knew in his heart he was more than just one man. He had special powers. Was there a higher calling then for him, a higher obligation? Was this offered to him because of what he'd do with it? The questions pounded him relentlessly, offering the troubled teen no rest.

Reports of the unknown pair who had waded into the action to try to help were etched in his mind. He knew who they were and felt ashamed. This was exactly what Talitha had been speaking about.

He remembered the look of terror on the face of the man that had been pulled into the vortex of violence. It could have been him. Would his powers have helped if he'd been set upon? Would anyone have come to his aid? The dots were connected and a new train of thought emerged. If he were not willing to help those in need, then who would? He'd already seen the answer lived out in the pair who days before had been mocked for their naïve ideas.

This threat to the community was real. Though the media had seemed to miss the point, the Blood Lord's act was a declaration of war against the peace of the community he lived in and valued. Could he sit back, allowing this to happen? More to the point, could he take the powers he possessed and use them for any other purpose than the common good?

George's skull pounded as he closed his eyes and rested his head on the wall behind him. For once his superior intellect seemed to be a detriment. There was no escaping the reality of what he must do.

With a new resolution, he reached for the phone beside his bed in order to place a call.

Guilt. That's what Tim David was feeling. He found himself distracted, so unable to concentrate on the game being played around him. Not performing well, the usually aggressive linebacker was benched for the second half. In truth, after what had happened the evening before at Summerfest, few players or fans were really paying attention to the match that was going on.

Sitting on the bench, he looked around at the world that was so important to him. He noticed for the first time a pair of police officers standing at the entrance to the field. That had never happened before.

More had changed in Victory Park for the community then first thought. Their innocence had been lost. A level of violence that most had never considered was now here in their own hometown. This sort of thing was supposed to only happen as a byproduct of unstable foreign countries, not their land of prosperity.

It couldn't be ignored, but yet that's what people already were attempting to do. They would take extra precautions, review their home security features and stay away from downtown. This was not going to be their problem, they had enough to contend with. Life was too complicated already. But it was an illusion. The shark was still swimming at the beach.

Tim, though, couldn't so easily shake the feeling of dread for Killings-Welch like others had. Perhaps it was because he was naïve, or a deeper thinker than he gave himself credit for.

Regardless, as he sat blankly watching the flow of the game that overcast summer day, it suddenly didn't seem important. The eternal consequence was gone. The expression of fear he'd seen on people's faces ate away at him. His inability to do anything about what had happened right before his eyes condemned him. He'd had no fear and also the ability to intervene in the situation. Yet he stood around watching.

What does this make me? Tim thought to himself. *A coward? I don't think so. I'm not afraid of anything.*

Then what was it? Finally the answer struck him like a fullback going off tackle at full speed. A plan was missing. He was a football player, trained to react to a series of plays in a set pattern of responses. There was no ability to act because there was no playbook. The youth lacked a plan or vision for the use of what he possessed. Tim knew he needed to respond to this new revelation, that his talents needed the direction only focus could provide.

Determination also filled his spirit. Never again would he stand on the sidelines watching others suffer if there was anything that could be done about it. But how could he accomplish this? Who was to be the coach? Then, like a burr that wouldn't go away, the answer came to him. It made the muscular teen shudder at first, but then a sense of resolution for what needed to be done chased the dread away. Honor compelled nothing less.

The four teens quietly gathered in the same living room that less than a week earlier had been so animated. Now there was a muted calm, as if each silently knew a monumental decision was about to be considered.

Talitha was still a bit stiff from the beating she'd taken Friday night. Emboldened by the experience, she broke the ice, "Okay, George. You called us here again. What do you want? If it's to tell us how foolish we are, you can save it. Beau and I will leave."

"No," George replied, swallowing his pride, "you were right about the threats that are out there. You were also right about trying to help." As if to add experience to the comment, he added, "I saw what you did that night."

A look of appreciation lit up the pretty face of the girl at the compliment.

Suddenly wary, the thoughtful boy cautioned, "Just because I admire what you did doesn't mean I'm sold on the idea of acting with you."

Talitha knew he was close. "Listen, George, you can't have it both ways. If you agree with me, then you need to step up and do something about it." Then she restated her previous offer. "Join Beau and I. You too, Tim. We need you both. Help us stop this criminal and his gang."

George was scared by what he was contemplating. Trying to find some breathing room, he responded, "This is not some comic book adventure, you know. This is real life!"

With growing conviction, Tim waded in, "What you're asking us to do is crazy!" Unconvinced of the previous statement before it had left his lips, instead the powerful freshman had a growing sense of excitement. "How can we make a difference? We're a bunch of kids."

The question was asked in a way that begged for a convincing response.

Talitha took the challenge, going on the offensive, "Look at what we've done as individuals so far. Tim, I've read about you. I know how strong you've become. And, George, I know there's something inside of you that you've not shared. Beau and I have done a lot so far. But we now know we can't do it alone. We need your help."

Sensing a shift in the attitude of the pair that had previously refused her, the girl declared, "Think of what could happen if we worked together. The four of us could make a real difference in so many ways. But if we don't, if we just leave it as a good idea and walk away, who's going to stop this Blood Lord and his gang?"

"That's the job of the police. We shouldn't get involved," George tried to counter weakly.

Beau interjected, "The police can't handle them. They've admitted it themselves already."

"That may be good in theory. If we decided to do this, how do you think it should be done? There needs to be a plan." George cautiously advised, having to admit the truth in the statement of the younger boy.

Excited, Beau blurted out in a staccato tone, "We work together, set up some sort of meeting place and a communications system. Then we stand together to stop what's been happening."

Talitha was impressed by the passion of her partner. Adding to what he'd said, she added, "I'll say it again. We need to work together, with each contributing what we have to offer. Every one of us has powers. Let's use them! Alone, it's like trying to stop a swarm of bees with a flyswatter. But together I truly believe we can end this." Her tone then changed from excitement to somber. "I don't know why this has happened to us. I don't even think it's fair in a lot of ways. But I believe our powers used together will be even greater than what they are alone. Who knows what we'd be able to do."

The sensitive girl watched the response of the other two boys. There was still something missing. She and Beau had laid out a plan. But what was the purpose? It was the why that needed answering. That question had pounded her like a hammer for so many days. But did she even have the answer? Then, as if the revelation was coming for the whole group through her, she concluded, "I didn't ask for this and don't really want it. It's unfair in a lot of ways, but something needs to be done. I can't sit back and watch others suffer when I can do something about it."

George had been silent, pondering the challenge Talitha had given, moved by her conviction, as well as Beau's. Finally he spoke, "I think you're right."

The brainy teen looked over at Tim. There was no disagreement on the expressive face, rather what seemed for the explosive freshman like a look of determination. Taking a deep breath, George Alexander decided it was time to get off the fence and get involved in something bigger than his own ambitions. With that in mind, he knew instinctively that it was time also for a plan. "If we were to do something like this, and I say IF," George added with caution, "we'd need tight discipline. We couldn't draw attention to ourselves. Our strength will be in not only working together, but also anonymity. We would need to blend into the culture around us." Though perhaps directed at Tim, the statement was for him as well. It signaled the death knell of his own material ambitions. No longer could he play poker for money, or dazzle people in the lab. Selflessness was about to come at a cost.

The young football player had still not reacted negatively, and in George's own mind the idea was even becoming appealing. Already the logistics were clear. "The communications system would be easy," George stated confidently. "We could set up cell phone equipped Blackberries. That would give us text messaging and instant access. Of course, they'd need some special encryption to keep anyone from hacking in." Seeing a smile light up the face of Beau, he knew that likely wouldn't be a problem.

Next on his mental checklist was a place to call headquarters. "We'd need some central location to work from equipped with GPS and information gathering equipment."

"That sounds expensive," Talitha declared. Though excited by the plan, she'd never really given any thought to how it would come together. Her reactions had been purely emotional so far. Now the grim reality of how was coming to the forefront.

George thought about everything he had intended to do with his poker winnings, the things he was going to buy, the trips he would take, then responded with a slight sigh, "Money won't be a problem."

"It sounds to me like we've got a leader for our group!" Beau said enthusiastically.

George had not thought of this, but the idea sounded good to him. He liked to lead, and now this project mattered to him. But would the others agree? In the brief moment of silence, he desperately hoped there would be no opposition. It was as if this were becoming more important to him than anything else.

"So what should we call ourselves?" Talitha asked, signaling no opposition to the senior's leadership.

"What do you mean?" a confused George asked.

"We have to have something to refer to ourselves by," the girl responded simply.

George had to agree to the logic of the statement. "You're right. So what's it going to be?"

"How about the Fantastic Four?" Beau chimed up.

"I think that's been done before," George reminded the enthusiastic youth.

A number of ideas were kicked around, but none seemed to capture the essence of what they thought they were.

Tim had yet to speak, other than his initial comments. Now, with a new look of purpose, he said quietly, "What about M-Force? We were changed by the meteorite, and we'll be a force to deal with."

"M-Force…I like it," Talitha agreed.

The others quickly concurred, excited about the name. Then, solemnly, they all shook hands. No words were spoken; none needed to be. Each had looked within themselves for the answer they sought. No contract was signed; no agreement was needed. The four that moment formed a covenant with a hold greater than any legal document. Theirs was a pledge forged out of common purpose. None needed to speak, all knew. M-Force had been born.

Chapter 14
Baby Steps

Talitha was alone with her thoughts for the first time since her new destiny had come to light. She contemplated how a girl who had successfully avoided getting involved with anything bigger than herself ended up right in that place. The path had never been a conscious decision, rather it was something she'd almost morphed into. Now, though, it was here and it was real.

During that time of contemplation, she had been pondering not only the changes that had taken place, but also what to do about it. Talitha allowed her mind to drift to the environment enveloping her.

The evening she witnessed was beautiful, warm and clear with no humidity. The thoughtful girl gazed into the dark sky, looking at the star's twinkle. She thought about the sleek, black space rock, and how it had changed her. Looking still into the sky, she wondered where it had come from. Thinking deeper, the realization came that these other points of light were essentially the same. The twinkling was only reflected light; they were not the source. In their essence, in the purest form of their being, they were in reality black stars. Funny, it was something she had never pondered before.

But then, as if somehow connected, another thought entered her mind. This one was of a more practical nature coming back to the current situation. How would she refer to herself when fulfilling her calling? She liked her name, but beyond the reality of the privacy issue, it really didn't reflect who she was or what she stood for.

She pondered that simple word, reflect. Then a name hit her as if descending from the very sky she looked into, Black Star. She wanted to reflect the light of virtue to the world around her, as well as have the impact that her star had on her. Black Star had been born.

The following day the team met together to continue planning their foray into public service. What had seemed so impossible a few short days ago now was becoming a reality.

The idea of names had been on Talitha's mind, but she didn't know how to broach the subject. After some initial discussion on other topics, the girl could stay silent no longer. "I think we need to have names for ourselves."

"What do you mean by that?" Beau asked, slightly confused by her intent.

"Well, we can't call each other by our regular names," the girl explained. "That would give away our identity. 'Hey, you' doesn't sound dignified either."

George nodded his head in agreement, "Makes sense. They would be functioning nicknames used only when M-Force was in action." Seeing Talitha vigorously nodding her head in agreement, he added, "Any suggestions?"

In truth, as the brainy teen thought about it, a name had already come to him instantly. It was a name that had been used to put him down for years, but now could be a symbol of what he stood for. No, it was a chance to reclaim something he felt had been taken from him over the years. The name might even inspire others to things greater than they thought. Yet, he was afraid to speak for fear the others would not understand, thinking him arrogant instead of thoughtful.

Tim actually spoke first with a suggestion. "That's cool. I think mine's Bulldozer. That's what I do on the football field, and that's what I'm going to do to these hoods."

The others smiled at his enthusiasm, quickly agreeing on the name.

"What about you, Talitha?" Beau asked. "Do you have any thoughts?"

The girl replied immediately, "Black Star."

The quizzical look on the faces of the three boys encouraged her to share the revelation she'd had from the previous night.

When Talitha was finished, George affirmed it, "Wow. Sounds good to me. That's some deep thinking. Black Star it is." Turning to Beau, he asked, "What about you?"

The soft-spoken teen lowered his head, as if embarrassed. "I don't know. I've never had a nickname. Besides, I'm not so good at these types of things. I've always just sort of blended in."

A broad smile lit up the face of Talitha/Black Star. "You blend in, huh?" she began. "No one seems to know you're there, but you have an impact. Unseen, but still felt. I think your name should be Grey Man."

“Grey Man,” Beau repeated enthusiastically. “ Awesome. I love it!”

Now there was only one left. All eyes turned toward George.

Talitha raising an eyebrow in inquiry, added, “Well?”

George cleared his throat awkwardly. “I do have an idea,” he began, “but before I share it, I want to explain. I don’t want you to take it the wrong way. See, it’s a name that’s been used to put me down for a long time. I’d like to see it used for good instead, maybe even show people there is a different path. But I don’t want you to think I’m stuck up by using it.”

Curious now, all wanted to know what was in the intelligent teen’s mind. It was Tim who finally said, “We won’t, George, we promise. So, what is it?”

“The Brain.”

No one spoke for a moment, reflecting on the declaration. Finally Tim broke the ice. “Works for me,” he said. “I think you’re right on.”

Talitha added, “Yes, I mean, based on what you’ve done, that sure suits you. I like it.”

George felt his eyes scratching a bit and beginning to blink involuntarily. The acceptance he’d just received from this odd group of people warmed his heart. What he’d thought of as a sacrifice only a short time ago was now becoming a source of joy for him. He would do everything in his power to bring honor to the name and to the team.

M-Force now not only had a name, but they had identities. It was time to introduce themselves to Killings-Welch.

The communications system was working great. The team had fanned out throughout downtown Kilings on Saturday, putting to the test what they’d been talking about since joining up. It was time to see if they truly could make a difference.

Earlier in the week, George and Beau had acquired, then customized their Blackberry communications tools. Beau had taken them apart, made a few modifications, then put the small devices back together. The pair was confident they had a system that would allow the team instant access. The thought was to field test it, ensuring the theory could be turned into reality.

M-Force still had no space to work out of, but that was coming soon. George had registered a company, named MF Holdings, that would act as a front for their business activities. Already he was sizing up several centrally located office locations with good street access.

Talitha and George had divided the downtown into zones that each could cover, but also allowed for them to join together swiftly. The idea was that none would advance into any kind of situation until the others had assembled. The only one of the team that seemed to struggle with this rule was Tim, who was ready to rush into any altercation head on.

The day was overcast, with intermittent showers throughout. As a result, the Saturday afternoon shopping crowd was thinner than usual. Tim, now known as the Bulldozer, had opted to stand in the archway of a building that gave a prominent view of the block he'd just traveled. Unsure of what to look for, he hoped this didn't turn into a waste of time. The idea of joining together made sense, but this waiting was a drag. He liked action, not standing around. His wish was about to come true.

The strong teen first spotted the consistent red bandanas on the four tough-looking young men. Right away he knew they were Bloods. But what was their purpose?

What are they doing downtown? Bulldozer thought to himself.

The group of wanted fugitives were trying to appear nonchalant, as if coincidentally just happening to be there. Yet something told the football player this was not the case. The fact that they were all looking in the same general direction reinforced his view that there was a specific purpose.

Then things began to happen. An attractive woman in stylish clothes came up the street toward the four men. She was carrying a bag of groceries in each hand, seeming to be without a care in the world. But the dark-haired woman became wary with the realization of the presence of the leering punks. Unfortunately, the reaction that came from the realization was too slowly. Two of them shoved her into an alley between the buildings they'd been loitering by. An attempt to scream was muffled by a rough hand clapped over her mouth.

Bulldozer quickly pulled out his Blackberry punching the button to page the whole team. Within seconds all were on the line.

"There's something going down on Duke Street near Water. A bunch of Bloods have just grabbed some woman and taken her into an alley. I'm moving in," he declared with confidence.

"Wait for the rest of us to assemble. Don't go in alone," George's voice ordered. He truly had become The Brain and the leader of M-Force.

Bulldozer didn't listen. Instead, he pulled on his mask, then went charging down the street. The few pedestrians who were out largely ignored the masked figure as he advanced on the scene of the crime. Not waiting for the rest, he charged into the alley. The foursome of Bloods was halfway down it. The woman was on her back, struggling to get free, with the muggers huddled around.

"Let her go!" Bulldozer commanded.

One of the attackers moved away from the scene to place himself between the sweatsuit clad individual and the scene of their merriment. "Get lost, punk," he ordered, "or we'll finish you off when we're done with her."

Instead, the Bulldozer swiftly stepped forward, grabbing the startled delinquent. In a feat of strength that caught the attention of the others, the criminal was picked up right off his feet, then thrown into a bunch of garbage pails. The clattering sound and the cry of pain from their colleague caused the others to ignore the woman. The remnant gathered instead to oppose this attempt at interference.

The Bloods spread out, advancing on the single, anonymous figure. Bulldozer sprang first, throwing a hard shoulder block into the midriff of the one in the middle. The punk crumpled to the ground, the wind knocked out of him. The rescuer then turned left, tackling another in mid stride. After driving his opponent to the pavement, Bulldozer was up fast as a cat. Shoving the third, the Blood flew back so hard he ended up hitting the brick wall framing the alley.

While this was going on, Bulldozer didn't notice his original foe regain his senses, then advance from the rear. Producing a wicked looking knife, the Blood was ready to plunge it into the back of the unsuspecting youth in a violent act of revenge.

The woman saw this, but was too late to gather her faculties to yell out a warning. Thus, the would-be rescuer was fatally slow to turn. The knife flashed fast as a snake seeking its mark. But at the moment of impact a blue ball of light struck the weapon and arm of the attacker, sending them both careening away.

The other attackers now saw three new masked, sweatsuit-clad figures advancing down the alley. Unwilling to experience what talents these others possessed after the encounter with the first, the Bloods ran away as fast as they could down the opposite end of the alley.

"Are you okay, ma'am?" one of the masked rescuers asked the stunned woman in a soft voice.

Badly shaken, the attractive lady stammered, "I...I think I am."

Lola Karan was still in a state of shock at the turn of events. Again, she had been mysteriously assaulted. It didn't seem like a random act, but rather a planned occurrence. Yet again she was rescued under the strangest of circumstances. She picked herself up off the ground, then straightened her clothing.

"We're glad we could help," the speaker said to her. Already her groceries were re-bagged and handed to her so she could continue on her way. "Though you won't see us, we'll make sure you get to you destination okay."

As the foursome turned to lead her out of the alley, a flash of memory caused Lola to pause. There was something about one of the masked saviors that caught her attention. It was the eyes. She had seen them before. Then it came to her. It had been at the bridge.

"Wait," she called, "you've helped me before. At least two of you have. anyway, I think. I'd…I'd like to thank you."

She could seem a gleam of pride in the one that she knew was the teenage girl from the bridge. A feminine voice replied, "We're just glad we were able to get here in time to help."

"Who are you?" the designer finally had the wherewithal to ask.

This time it was a deeper, but still young voice, coming from the tallest of the unidentified group. The only member wearing glasses, said, "We call ourselves M-Force. We've sworn to protect others from harm. But, in particular, we want to help defeat the Blood Lord and his gang of hoods."

Impressed by the bold statement of one obviously so young, Lola asked, "Is there nothing I can give you?"

"No, ma'am. Seeing you safe is reward enough for us."

The foursome turned to depart, but a brainwave hit Lola. "Wait. I can help you."

"How?" the leader asked in unveiled curiosity.

"I'm a designer. You really need something better than those old sweatsuits and balaclava masks. Let me come up with some ideas and you can see if you like them. Then I'll make up uniforms for you." Lola handed her business card to The Brain, then said, "Come by my shop tomorrow. We'll see if we can't give you something with a bit more style."

Before the team could debate the offer, the attractive woman turned and walked off with a light skip to her step. Grey Man disappeared in order to follow her and ensure she got on her way safely while the others remained.

Taking off their masks since they were now alone, George turned to Tim and exclaimed, "What do you think you were doing? I told you to wait for us."

Tim replied nonchalantly, "I know, I know. But I wasn't sure how long you guys would take, so I stepped in. Besides, the woman seemed to need help right away. I could handle it. Anyway, everything worked out."

"We have to work together. If we try to go it alone, not only may we get hurt, but so will others," George lectured. "Next time wait, okay?"

The aggressive youth nodded his head in agreement, but inside he was saying, "Whatever." To him, he had saved the day. No one was going to tell him otherwise.

George rubbed his face in frustration, hitting his glasses. *The Brain,* he thought to himself, *more like the Geek with these things on.* The teen didn't mind his glasses for the most part; he'd worn them since he was six. But in these circumstances they didn't fit. The idea of some sort of costume or uniform appealed to him, but the glasses just didn't add into the equation. He'd need to find some sort of solution to the dilemma.

Lola went immediately back to her shop. The attack was forgotten, as was the fact that it seemed like twice the Bloods had set her up. The thought of why this had happened to her was still days from coming to mind. For the time being she was consumed with the idea of coming up with something suitable for the young heroes.

Strangely, a woman who for so long had been consumed with the thought of designing something that would make its mark didn't see the connection this time. This was to be an act of service, not self-service. All that drove her was the desire to do something that would say thank you.

The next day Lola thought she heard the shop door open. Looking up from her desk, no one was there. A chill ran up her spine as the fear that she was not alone crept into mind. The place was still, yet she could feel something moving about. Suddenly, as if by magic, right before her eyes appeared one of the sweatsuit clad rescuers.

The figure went to the door, opened it, then called out, "The coast is clear. You can come on in."

Swiftly, but carefully, the other three entered the room. The shortest member kept an eye on the door. Though smaller, it was obvious that whoever it was possessed great physical power by the muscles bulging under the sweatsuit.

It was the now familiar, deeper voice that spoke. "We're here, Lola. Are you really serious about wanting to help us?"

"I'm so glad you came!" she responded enthusiastically. "I was afraid you wouldn't since I know it was kind of a strange offer."

The woman led them to the back of the shop, where she did her design work. "I know you want to keep your identities secret. That's fine with me, but can I know your names?"

There was an awkward pause, as if the mysterious figures before her didn't know what to do. Then the one with the expressive eyes, the one she had seen before, took a step forward.

"I'm Black Star," the female declared with hands on her hips.

Taking the cue another spoke. "I'm Gray Man," the disappearing artist said with a slight lisp.

"Bulldozer," was all the powerfully built member added from the door.

"And I'm called The Brain," stated the one who seemed to be the leader of the team.

"Well, I'm Lola Karan, and I'm pleased to meet you all," she declared, shaking each of their hands. "Now let me show you some of my ideas."

The team huddled around the slender woman with a growing sense of anticipation. There was a thick stack of drawings she began to show. They were all impressed by her artistic talent, but beyond that the designs were not what they thought they should be. Most looked like they belonged on a runway in New York, not fighting crime in Killings-Welch.

Lola could tell that nothing was grabbing them. She was crushed by the perceived rejection. She'd worked so hard to try to impress them, yet, in the end, they were like so many of her customers, less than awed.

Sensing her discomfort, Black Star said awkwardly, "These are all really nice, but..."

"You hate them."

"No, it's not that," the girl countered, "it's just, well, we're not that flashy."

Then it struck her, a revelation that perhaps had been coming for years, but finally came to a head at this moment. She had always been trying to impress people with her talent rather than meet their needs. This was not a design competition, but, instead, was serving real people.

Lola was afraid she'd blown her opportunity right after finally having her moment of epiphany. Holding her breath, she waited to see if the team would leave the shop.

Instead, they didn't seem to know what to do, standing there awkwardly.

This was all the opportunity she needed. With an exciting brainwave coming to mind, the designer asked, "Okay, how about this?"

Grabbing a paper and pencil, her hand virtually flew over the page. In a few minutes she had drawn four figures in costume. Then, taking some pastels, she filled in the color and tint.

"Wow," breathlessly declared the one called Grey Man who could disappear. The others shared his sentiments. What they looked at set their hearts beating in excitement.

"I think we've found our uniforms," the leader added.

What they looked at, though simple in design, possessed a certain flare.

They were forms fitting one piece body suits. Charcoal gray in color, each had hunter green panels under the arms and at the hips to allow for stretching. In the center of the chest was a lighter gray M on an oval background that was offset at an angle. Surrounding it were hunter green darts that made the M look like it was flying through space.

Each member of the team thought to themselves that the logo almost looked like a meteor flying through space. This had to be right, since none of them had ever mentioned to the designer what the M actually stood for.

In addition to the body suit, there was a cowl that covered most of the head and face. The nose was covered on the top while the mouth was open, as were the eyes.

The Brain winced to himself as he observed a cutout for glasses in his. All in all, though, it was a sleek, elegant, yet practical looking garment.

Lola's smiled radiated throughout the room. The feeling of elation at exceeding their expectations was almost intoxicating. She had looked at it from their perspective and come up with the solution. It was as if blinders had fallen from her eyes.

The Brain was silent as the others chattered excitedly among themselves. Cautiously he asked, "These look great, Ms. Karan. I know you said you wanted to help us, but what's the cost?"

George wasn't talking only about money. He wanted to know if there were other hidden costs, such as endorsements, credit or other things that might compromise their integrity.

The woman looked hurt at the question, but didn't express it. Instead, she maintained her happy disposition. "There's no charge," she confirmed, shaking her head vigorously to add emphasis. "Twice you've saved my life and I want to say thank you for it. I also won't try to profit from this. Your secret is safe with me."

Seeing smiles spread on all their faces at this generous act, she added, "And please, call me Lola."

Tirelessly the reinvigorated designer worked to create the garments for the team. She'd measured them the day the sketches had been approved; now all that was left was to make the suits.

Three days later the moment of truth arrived for the woman. *Would they approve?* Lola thought, or would she see the all too familiar look of disappointment on their faces?

It was one thing to experience this from a customer, but quite another from these people who now meant so much to her. A bond had been formed through the crucible, so their approval meant everything to the woman. Waiting alone in her shop for M-Force to arrive, the woman's heart beat hard with anticipation.

Finally the door opened and in strode the four sweatsuit-clad heroes.

Nothing was said. Instead, one took their costume, went to the dressing room and put it on while the others kept watch. Then the process was repeated with each of the other members.

The Brain was the last to enter into the change area. He took in with him a small cardboard box that caused the others to wonder about. Since the rescue of Lola in the alley George had been researching glasses on the Internet, seeking something that would fit his new role. At last he found something from an optician in Europe that even took his breath away.

Putting on the form-fitting costume, the last part was the cowl. Now it was the moment of truth. Opening the box, he took out a pair of smoky-black, futuristic looking wraparound glasses. They were his prescription, yet would darken and lighten depending on the light. The glasses were as form-fitting as his suit and seemed to be built right into his face.

Looking in the mirror after adjusting their fit, George was amazed at what he saw. The look was even better than he'd hoped for.

"Awesome," he said to himself breathlessly.

Coming out of the dressing room, George was pleased to see the nods of approval from his colleagues. The Brain had arrived.

Finally, when all were garbed M-Force stood in a circle looking at each other, no one said a word. Lola was sure they hated the costumes.

Finally, Black Star exclaimed, "These look GREAT! They're better than I even thought they would be. Thank you so much, Lola."

Gray Man added, "You're right. These sure beat our old sweatsuits."

"Yes, thank you, Lola. You've done an excellent job with these," The Brain confirmed. "They look attractive and, at least for my part, fit great. We appreciate everything you've done for us."

Lola beamed. Joy filled her, brighter than the sun that shone outside. She'd done it; she had met the challenge, even exceeding their expectations. A renewed feeling of confidence flooded in. It was a feeling she hadn't experienced since her self-assured days at design school. Savoring the sweet sensation, she knew her debt owed to M-Force had grown again.

Before anything more could be said, a scream resounded from outside on the street. M-Force sprang into action. Sprinting out of the shop, they were about to show the world their vigorous new look. No longer would the gifted teens work in anonymity. The world was about to see that a powerful force had been raised up in opposition to the tyranny offered by the Blood Lord and his gang.

Chapter 15
Successful Test

George looked with satisfaction at the run down brownstone building. He could imagine that it once had been a place of great pride sitting in a thriving part of town. But the shifting sands of economics had blown prosperity away from this location.

Market Street was off the beaten path, but still centrally located. There were few other businesses in the area and, therefore, little traffic. The rent was cheap, suiting The Brain, since money was going to be tight soon.

What would become the office of MF Holdings and the headquarters for M-Force was in a plain, average looking block of buildings. Theirs would be a two-story, flat roofed unit. The main street access was strangely via a set of stairs up to the second floor. A wooden door with thick frosted glass opened into a reception area. Once through another frosted glass door, the remainder of the floor revealed three small offices and a larger windowless room at the back. In this particular area another set of stairs travel down to a large open area on the main floor.

Since in a previous life the building had been a small shop, it possessed a roll-up door on the main floor to the street. But the critical feature was that it was only semi-attached. On one side the building flanked a deep alley. Thus, a second roll-up door led into the sheltered location with two-way street access. Overall, the place was secure, nondescript, and had good possibilities.

George knew this was perfect for their needs. He negotiated with the real estate agent representing the owner via email and phone. The contract was handled by a drop box and messenger service. Thus, the whole deal was consummated with no face to face contact.

The next phase was getting it ready for business. Phone, high speed Internet and GPS capabilities were all brought in. First the place was cleaned up. Then some basic furniture, especially in the lobby, was purchased and they were ready for business. Finally, the doors were reinforced, a sophisticated alarm system that fed into their Blackberries was constructed and an entry system was set up. M-Force had a home.

Crime was increasing exponentially it seemed in the region. Though caused mostly by the Bloods, ever since the fateful evening of the Summerfest kickoff, their leader, the Blood Lord, had not been seen. Tension was rising like a thermometer due to the continued threat. The mood wasn't helped either with the increase in heat and humidity as the dog days of summer hit the towns.

But, while crime rose, so too did the reports of an enigmatic group that kept popping up trying to stop it. Though their reported numbers varied anywhere from one to twelve, something else caused the unknown crime fighters to stick out beyond their courage at standing up to the violent threat. It was the charcoal gray costumes they wore with an M on the chest. Some thought they shouldn't be interfering in things that were not their business, but most saw them as heroes and protectors.

A little known fact about the Killings-Welch campus of State University, one that was kept a secret even from most of the faculty, was that the school had a continuing involvement with space military research. It had started in the 1980s with the "Star Wars Program" and had continued to thrive ever since. Due to the strength of the school's science and computer departments, it had been a lucrative fit for both parties. The facility produced some meaningful research for the government and some lucrative financial results for the school.

Recently, the lab had received a new specimen from the government to study with urgent instructions to do so as quickly as possible. Though none of the staff at the facility knew it, the object of curiosity was the meteorite that had landed in the region back in June.

After its recovery, NASA had studied the sleek, black space rock. But, for some reason, it was deemed by the government to need more research. Hence its trip to this facility. The scientists charged with the study were not even sure what they were looking for. No clear instructions had been given with any purpose in mind. So they began a variety of wide-ranging tests on the space stone housed in a vacuum-sealed containment unit.

The research lab was housed in a generic concrete and steel structure in an isolated corner of the campus. While it looked like any other building on campus, the only point of note was that it had its own gated entrance and a fence around it. Most who passed by figured it was part of the university's power plant. This was perfectly acceptable to those who worked there; they wished to remain anonymous. The biggest feature, for any that took the time to notice, was the presence of an armed guard at the entrance kiosk.

Terry Card was bored already. The overweight, balding security guard on the gate was only halfway through his shift, but there was nothing to do. It was an overcast day with bilious clouds hanging low in the sky. Though no rain had fallen, precipitation was thick in the air.

The guard finished the book he'd brought to read and the TV in the small office was on the fritz. The only mildly interesting thing for the retired soldier was that he'd noticed an increase in traffic lately into the research facility. That, at least, made the time go by a bit quicker. Something unusual was going on, but he wasn't paid to know details, nor did he care. It wasn't his business.

He did know that there were two other armed guards inside, one on the main door, the other patrolling within. But he didn't know what the white-coated workers inside did. It was some kind of research he figured. What he did care about was how the school's football team faired this season. Their quarterback had graduated and the replacement was an untested sophomore.

Card's thoughts were interrupted by the arrival of an unmarked cube van. The white Dodge pulled into the building entrance, stopping at the closed gate. Stepping out of the air-conditioned office, clipboard in hand, he went to see who had arrived.

Before he could even say hello, Card was slammed hard by the door, sending him tumbling to the ground. The driver was out in a flash and upon him. The guard was too stunned to offer resistance, so was swiftly beaten into unconsciousness. The passenger then dragged the prone body into the office, handcuffing him to a radiator.

The van then drove up to the main entrance, blocking its view from the road. The two men got out, going to the front door. They pushed the buzzer for admittance and the door was electronically unlocked. Less than sixty seconds later the door guard was lying motionless at his desk.

Now the side door of the van opened up and out poured ten Bloods, all armed with automatic weapons. Finally, a tall, cloaked figure strode confidently out as well, entering the building.

It was pure coincidence that Milt Shift, the third guard on duty at the research facility, found out what was happening. He was supposed to be on hall patrol, as was the regular routine, but a new pair of shoes had given him bad blisters. So, instead, he sat in the security room nursing sore feet rather than doing what he was scheduled to.

There were closed-circuit cameras posted at a variety of strategic locations throughout the building. They all tied into a bank of monitors located in the security room. It was one that gave a live feed of the front desk that caught Milt's attention.

At first he didn't believe his eyes. Nothing ever happened here. That's why he liked the job. The guard froze at the drama unfolding before him, unable to move. He'd just talked to the man who now lay prone on the floor twenty minutes before. A chill went down his spine as he watched the others enter, along with the figure who appeared to be the leader.

Though he'd paused, Milt Shift hoped it was not fatally so. First he hit the alarm button linked to the research facility triggering a lockdown of the sensitive areas. Reinforced steel doors magnetically locked, keeping everything out.

Though more scared than he'd ever been in his life, the guard's next move was to automatically pick up a red phone that gave a direct link to campus police headquarters. He didn't need to tell them who was calling, it would already come up on their computer.

"We've got armed men in the facility, lots of them. They..."

That was all Milt Shift could get out. He fell lifeless to the floor; the phone went dead.

Finding the leader, one of the intruders reported, "My master, the police have been alerted and the building is sealed. What should we do?"

The Blood Lord let out a scream of frustration. It reverberated through the room, causing his followers to cringe. The imposing figure put his fist through one of the monitors, causing a shower of sparks. "Let us prepare for their arrival. In the meantime we move quickly. But mark this, we do not leave without what we've come for," were his terse instructions.

State University campus police had sealed off the roads leading into the facility after the call. Knowing this was beyond their expertise, regional police began to stream in to assist with the situation. Ten minutes after being informed something dangerous was happening at the university, the black gun truck of the police tactical unit rolled in. The SWAT officers were already geared up, hitting the ground running. The two teams of four men each began to move into position, while the senior officer in charge updated Nate DeBeer, their commander, on the situation. It didn't look good.

George had been working for only three days on his latest project. But already he liked the professor he was assisting and hoped to stick with him. Dr. Oliver Little was an Oxford trained Englishman with a passion for science and a love of people. Ollie, as he liked to be called, was a man with a quick mind, good sense of humor and humble disposition. This character drew George to him, erasing the previous bad experiences he'd had in the internship program. So the teen tried to balance his desire to assist with not giving away the truth of his super intellect.

He first knew something was wrong when a few workers in the building went running past the lab. Next he heard the sound of sirens getting closer. Stopping one person in the hallway to see what was going on, he asked, "What's happening?"

"Some group of terrorists have taken over a building on the north part of campus!"

By now the workday was involuntarily over; everyone else in the lab was leaving to watch how things unfolded. Slipping away from the others, George pulled out his blackberry to page the other members of M-Force. Next, he pushed a few buttons that allowed him to hack into the police communications net. Beau's latest upgrade was proving useful, since it allowed the leader of the team to find out what was happening. Now fully aware of the situation, The Brain put on his uniform, then moved to the scene of the drama.

Though appearing calm on the outside, the Blood Lord was seething inside. His brilliantly laid out plan was being thwarted. The information he'd sought had come with great cost. The timetables and schedules had gone for no small sum either. Now he and his followers were unable to enter into the testing area to obtain what he wanted. Even his own considerable power could not open the door, though they were being pounded mercilessly.

Little did he know that this particular lab had also been designed for bomb testing, so could withstand even the shock of his own considerable power. Attempts to break through the walls were also met with the same lack of success. The Blood Lord's already high level of frustration boiled over. Spitting profanities and threats against the scientists cowering inside the room, he stalked away.

The criminal mastermind thought to attempt some sort of system override from the security room. Scanning the panel of monitors, he could see through the outside cameras as the police formed a cordon around the building. Now could they not only get into the lab, escape was even becoming problematic. The Blood Lord knew it was time for a display of power. Going to the window, though he knew a sniper would have a bead on him, his trusted the timidity of the authorities not to shoot.

"Command, this is position one," the black-clad police sharpshooter identified. "I have a suspect silhouetted against the windows. Orders?"

"Mark your target, one, and hold your fire," Lieutenant DeBeer responded.

"Roger that."

The Blood Lord smiled, knowing the moment was right to show something the city hadn't witnessed before. By now many eyes were on the window he stood boldly in. They saw the strange figure raise his hands in the air. Suddenly, the heavy clouds seemed to get heavier and began to drop. What started as a thin gray mist swiftly turned into a thick bank of fog. In less than ten minutes the entire building was shrouded with dark clouds, obscuring vision for everyone watching.

"Alpha Team, hold your position. Do not move in until this fog clears," their increasingly frustrated leader ordered. "Bravo Team, return to my position for night vision and thermal equipment," the radios crackled in the ears of the tactical officers who were suddenly in the dark. They could barely see each other, let alone anyone at a distance.

The Blood Lord returned to the task of trying to get into the room, satisfied he had bought more time. The latest power just demonstrated was something only recently he had discovered. His thoughts refocused on the sought after prize. He wanted the meteorite housed in the lab.

George had been watching the drama unfold from a distance. Hidden in a copse of trees, he could see the police attempt to respond to the crisis, then the fog roll in. He instinctively knew this was no ordinary crime, there was something more sinister going on. It had to be the Blood Lord's doing. When he heard the reports of the figure in the window on the tactical radio, his thoughts were confirmed.

"Where are those guys?" he said to himself, frustration growing with each tick of the clock. Surprise was on their side. If they could capture the Blood Lord, then everything would be over. Finally he felt a vibration from his communication device.

"We're on the scene, where are you?" Black Star asked.

"Lock onto my location and hurry," Brain replied with a hint of irritation in his voice.

A few minutes later the team was assembled. Rather than swing into action, The Brain let his frustration show. "Where've you been?" he asked accusingly. "I've been waiting for you for nearly an hour."

"You're The Brain, think about it, genius," Bulldozer shot back, not impressed by the leader's tone.

Black Star stepped between the two. "We got to headquarters, but had no way of getting here. We ended up having to take a taxi. Then we had to change, okay?" she explained. "That's not a real quick process. We got here as fast as we could."

"Sorry," The Brain said hurriedly, making a mental note of a logistical issue he'd not considered, "I just think we had a good chance to really take charge here, but I'm afraid it's too late."

"Well, we're here now. Let's see what we can do to help," Black Star commented tersely.

Everyone felt the tension of this first major test for them. There were multiple criminals in the building, all armed. Where they were, or what they were doing was unknown. But there were also a lot of innocent people inside. The police seemed stymied; something had to be done.

Quickly figuring out a plan of action, M-Force slipped into the fog.

"Command, this is position three. You won't believe what I just saw," the police radio reported.

"Master, someone has entered the building," one of the Bloods reported.

"Is it the police?" the Blood Lord demanded.

"I don't think so," the confused thug stated tentatively.

"What do you mean you don't think so?"

"Well, I just caught a glimpse of it on the monitor. There were four of them in some sort of costume."

"Fine," the Blood Lord sighed at this next unanticipated development. "Find them and eliminate them." The door to the research lab and the prize he sought was only minutes from being pried open. He was looking forward to teaching the researchers inside a lesson in what the cost of disobedience was.

"You saw WHAT?" Nate DeBeer responded incredulously.

"I say again, it looked like four people in some sort of dark costumes entered via a side entrance."

M-Force was inside, not knowing what to expect. This was the big time, intervention for real. Having hacked into the police communications net, they knew that a number of armed Bloods, along with the Blood Lord himself had taken over the building. This was different than rescuing women from muggers. They had graduated to the big league. There would be no mistakes allowed, this was life or death.

Yet, despite the personal anxiety of each, none wanted to show any fear, or let down the others on the team. Each was scared of being hurt, but now more scared of failing the others. They truly were a team now in more than name.

Grey Man went invisible, probing ahead. Black Star followed, prepared to put up a force field, then The Brain and Bulldozer brought up the rear, ready for action.

Heart pounding so hard he was sure everyone in the building could hear him, Beau alone entered the next room through an already open door. He could see two Bloods with HK submachine guns nervously moving their leveled weapons from side to side waiting for someone to come in. Still invisible, Beau backed out of the room. Coming back into view for the team, through hand signals he let them know what was facing them. It was moment of truth time.

Again unseen, Grey Man re-entered and moved silently to a position behind the two gunmen. He karate punched one as hard as he could, causing the thug to go sprawling back, dropping his weapon in the process. A startled cry brought the desired reaction from the second. He turned and let off a burst of bullets into the area his partner had been.

Black Star was through next. An energy ball knocked the lethal weapon out of the shooter's hands.

Bulldozer rushed through, slamming into the disoriented Blood, smashing him back into the wall.

The Brain saw that the first gunman, who Beau had hit, regaining his faculties and go for his gun. George used his telepathy to drive a metal garbage pail into the thug, knocking him sprawling. In less than a minute the two were subdued. M-Force had prevailed.

"Shots fired, we have shots fired from within." The report over the police band confirmed what the others heard as well.

Unable to wait any longer for fear a bloodbath was about to take place, the officer in charge of the situation gave the command for Nate DeBeer and SWAT to move in.

The tactical commander ordered, "Alpha team, take point, Bravo team will follow. Move in with extreme caution."

The power suddenly went off throughout the building, M-Force knew something else was happening.

The police were moving in to assault the building through the thick fog that now brought an eerie darkness to the late afternoon. Bravely entering the building, the heavily armed tactical members found the power off as well. Darkness enveloped the hallways, making their movement difficult.

Traveling silently through the lobby, the tactical teams began to move down the dark hallway toward where they knew from the building schematics the research labs were. The flashlights that were attached to their weapons played around all possible spots in the hallway lit only with battery-powered emergency lamps.

Any attempt thus far to communicate with the attackers had failed, so the purpose of occupation was still unknown. Therefore, the tactical team was going in blind. The officers were thus unsure of where in the large facility, or how many Bloods there were.

The first team was halfway down the corridor, with the second covering, when the ambush was sprung. Two doors suddenly opened on either side of the hallway. Before the police officers could respond, the bark of automatic fire had bit into two of the men. The others flattened on the tile floor, unable to return fire for fear of hitting their friends. Those behind them were in anguish at the scene, unsure what to do.

The Bloods were about to finish the first four officers off. Instead, one was slammed by a charcoal gray freight train called the Bulldozer. The shooter was hit so hard he smashed through the opposite wall. Another gunman suddenly found his weapon wrestled from his hands out of thin air. The third in the ambush party saw a tall, masked form enter in. Before he could react, a chair flew through the air and hit him hard. Trying to recover, another similarly clad form held out gloved hands, producing a light blue ball of energy. It was the last thing he remembered as he crumbled against the wall, unconscious.

In the confusion, the police were about to fire on what they thought was a new threat. Fortunately, Nate DeBeer saw what had happened from his position with the second team so barked out, "Check fire, check fire, friendlies, friendlies."

The urgent command also went over the police radio net, saving the lives of those whom had just saved theirs.

The fourth Blood who had been with the ambushers knew they were foiled, but wasn't quite sure why. All he knew was that they needed to leave, since the building was breached. Unseen in the confusion, he silently glided back to the Blood Lord at the lab door, giving his report. "Master, the police have entered the building, but they have not been stopped. What do we do"

The cloaked figure breathed heavily, saying nothing as he assessed the situation. Even with the power cut, the doors were magnetically sealed, only the people inside could unlock them. Realizing it was an exercise in futility, he ordered them to the loading bay area to escape. Several university vans were in the garage. Picking one, they waited for the opportune moment to leave.

The wounds of the police officers, though dangerous, were not life threatening. Fortunately, their body armor had saved them from more serious injury. Nonetheless, they couldn't move forward with two men down. While the second team set up a defensive perimeter, a group of officers escorted four paramedics in to rescue their injured colleagues.

In the confusion and the fog, a white State University van was able to exit through a service entrance in the fence, gliding through the police cordon on the opposite side of the sprawling building. The Blood Lord and the remnant of his gang had slipped away, though none were aware of this development as of yet, allowing the Bloods a clean getaway.

The tactical team, bolstered by a dozen other officers, swept the building, finding no other attackers beyond the ones M-Force had subdued. They were able to communicate with the researchers in the lab, so the door was opened. With the building secure, detectives swarmed in to try to make sense of what had just happened.

No one though knew what to do with the four costumed strangers found in the facility. When a pair of detectives tried to detain them, one of the tactical officers from the first team physically stepped in the man's way. "These people saved our lives in here," the SWAT member shouted, adrenaline still rushing. "Leave them alone."

The detective decided to move on.

Nate DeBeer was still trying to understand who these odd-looking characters were. While the tactical team commander had witnessed the scene and also called off the shooting in the heat of the moment, he still had questions. Coming over to the group, the burly police officer confirmed, "You did save our lives. That's the truth. Those Bloods would have cut us to ribbons. Thank you."

The tallest in the group responded, "We're glad we were able to help. I'm just sorry we weren't a little bit faster."

Now bewildered more than anything, the veteran officer asked, "Who are you guys?"

The masked speaker confidently answered, "We're called M-Force. We're here to help in the fight against the Blood Lord."

Before the startled officer could respond, or even think to try to stop them, the four slipped out a side door of the building, disappearing into the fog.

Chapter 16
Setbacks

Campus Attack! screamed the headline of *The Recorder*, detailing the assault on the research lab at State University. The police were tight-lipped about what had happened, saying only their investigation was continuing. It had been confirmed that the assault was the work of the Bloods and the Blood Lord.

No one could tell the purpose for the attack. Nor even would anyone confirm the exact nature of the research that was being done. Despite that, the fact that two police officers had been shot and three security guards were badly wounded got the public's attention. The violence of the Bloods seemed to be ratcheted up a notch.

But another piece of information had been leaked. A group known as M-Force had been on the scene and involved in the situation. With details sketchy about what had happened, the public was left to figure out the role of the unknown group. It was rumored they had aided the police, but no one could confirm this.

T.T. Tomlinson wrote a scathing editorial about vigilantes getting involved, that M-Force stood for menace. He didn't see them as providing aid. In a thinly veiled question, he wondered if there was a connection between the arrival of this unknown group and the successful escape of the Blood Lord. He presented the idea that there might even be some sort of connection. It had been alluded that they possessed some sort of strange powers as well, so the connection was natural to the crewcut wearing newspaperman.

Beyond the conjecture, to the editor, this was a new threat, every bit as big as the Bloods. He called not only for answers, but for action to stamp out the new threat. The city didn't need any more shadowy figures. When pressed, the police chief would only comment that this new development was being investigated as well.

The Blood Lord crumpled the newspaper in one hand, then threw it hard across the room, hitting a stack of boxes. He and his followers had settled into their new lair earlier in the day, so they were not entirely unpacked. With the capture of several members of his gang, it was not safe to stay at their old center of operations. He knew the young Bloods were ultimately weak, and so, would talk. Though the timeline was advanced, it was not unanticipated, contingency plans had been in place.

It was no secret the police were looking for him, so he had a series of locations ready to switch to for occasions such as this. Still, it unsettled him that his plan had been thwarted. First it had been chance getting in the way. That he could deal with. They had been close to cracking the door and securing the prize he sought. But the interference of the group he had just read about was another matter. This was not random, nor a matter of circumstance. Their intervention had been deliberate, thus calling for a response.

"Who were those clowns who meddled with me yesterday?" the Blood Lord demanded to a lieutenant standing near him.

"I don't know, master," the burly thug replied with a hint of fear in his voice.

"Find out!" the leader snarled menacingly. "I want them, and I want them punished."

The mood at M-Force headquarters was mixed. The newspaper sat on a table, the headline blaring out. The condemnation of M-Force stuck in their throats, shocking the naïve teens. They had thwarted the Blood Lord's plot, plus saved the lives of the police officers. Despite all they'd done, M-Force was being treated like criminals. Each agreed that it didn't seem fair.

The crime fighters were yet to learn the bitter lesson about the objectivity of the local press. In their case, this was magnified in the person of T.T. Tomlinson, who called most of the shots. It was he who set the course of news coverage for the region.

Despite the dark media cloud, the team was upbeat, for the most part. They had faced the Blood Lord's gang in their first violent test and come out ahead. Sobering as the escalation in violence was to them, there also was a certain exhilaration that went with it. Sitting in comfortable couches, drinking cokes from the nearby fridge, the discussion turned to the previous day's enterprise. They'd already done a debriefing, but the adrenaline from the event still pumped through them. Indeed, none had slept the previous night.

"We need to be careful, guys," Talitha cautioned. "That was a really dangerous situation. Not only could we have gotten hurt bad, but we could have gotten others hurt as well."

"Are you kidding?" Tim replied incredulously, "that was AWESOME. I say bring them on. No one can stop us."

Beau shook his head, "I don't know, Tim. The Bloods will know we're out there now and they're likely to be looking for us."

"So?" Tim retorted. "Let them come. I'd rather face these guys in a standup fight than sneak about anyway."

"But the point is," George interjected, "our enemy knows we exist. The element of surprise is gone. It's too late to turn back now, we're committed." Seeing Tim smile in satisfaction, he added, "That being said, we need to rethink how we do things. We've got to get smarter in how we approach a situation."

Then the leader of M-Force changed the focus of his analysis, "We also need to figure out what the Blood Lord's plan is. Why did he attack the lab? What was in there? That's something we need to discover." Knowing there was no answer and the others were waiting for him to give them direction, he added, "I'll try to find that out. We'll never be able to stop him unless we can anticipate what he's doing. We can never anticipate unless we understand his purpose."

"Okay, that's fine," Beau agreed. The shy teen seemed to be gaining confidence every day. Now he was beginning to freely share his thoughts. "Here's another issue. It's getting harder for us to get around. I mean, everything doesn't happen within a few blocks of this place. We've got to have a way of getting where we need to be faster than we can right now."

"What are you suggesting, Beau?" George asked, fearing where this particular conversation was heading.

"Well, since the crimes are starting to be more spread out, I think we need a vehicle."

"Cool. Let's get a Hummer!" Tim called out enthusiastically while doing pushups.

George tried to caution them. "Wait a minute. Let's not get all worked up over this. We need to think this through." Concern filled him for the implications of such a move.

"That's right," Talitha agreed, wading into the discussion, though missing the point. "We need something nondescript. It's got to be something that won't draw attention to us."

The leader of M-Force rubbed his eyes, pondering how much they had in their bank account. The suggestion made sense. Their effectiveness was compromised by a lack of mobility. But the deep-thinking teen was getting concerned as he continued to see this whole project growing into something that was way more than what he'd originally considered. Where did the future lie and how far were they prepared to go? *We're now into August and school will be starting soon,* he thought to himself. *Then what?*

The others didn't seem to be thinking that far ahead, but he was. Trying to buy time, George stalled by responding, "There's a certain logic to what you're saying. Let me ponder this a bit and get back to you with a solution."

Keith Ramsey was in a fog. Sweat rolled down the back of his thick neck, staining the silk shirt he was wearing on the muggy afternoon. Realizing this, the distraught teen considered this was yet another thing that he had no control over. His perfect life was falling apart around him. It was definite the scholarship was gone. His appeal had failed. In truth, it never even got off the ground. His mother was hardly around, and when she was, all she would do was remind him of what a loser he was. The insulated world of high school wresting champion was gone. Isolation came crowding into the void. Now he felt as though he had no identity and it seemed no future.

Then there was that snot George Alexander. The embarrassment he'd suffered weeks earlier still was grinding Keith. There was something different about the brainy teen that bugged his burly opponent even more. The more he thought about it, the more he seethed, his anger rising like the temperature on a hot day.

Not paying attention, he ran into someone walking the other way.

"Hey, watch where you're going, jerk!"

Ramsey became aware that he'd bumped into one of three Bloods coming out of a building he'd been walking past. The young tough had been sent staggering back as if hitting a wall after colliding with the solid wrestler. Now the trio was facing him threateningly.

Instead of being intimidated, face contorting with growing rage, Ramsey shot back, "Watch yourself, moron." This was an opportunity to perhaps vent some of the unreleased hostility that had been building in him like lava in a volcano.

The Bloods were about to attack the single teen before them when something started to happen to him. As he became visibly angry, it seemed as though a plate were growing out of his head. The skin was definitely stretching; his skull growing, like the earth's plates shifting. The top of his head was now starting to look like a battering ram.

Ramsey could see their stares. Now ready to strike them himself, the enraged teen screamed, "What are you butthead's looking at?"

One of the Bloods stammered, "Your...your head, man...it's...it's growing."

Shocked by the declaration, he looked at the plate glass window to his left. Catching the reflection, he could see what the others were. There was a definite protrusion, clearly square and sticking out from his head. The strangest thing was that it looked solid. He tentatively reached up a hand to touch it. The protrusion didn't hurt. In fact it felt hard as steel.

Things are going from bad to worse, Keith thought initially.

Then another, more interesting idea came to mind. Taking a couple of steps over to a brick wall that flanked a set of stairs, he braced himself. Then, with a quick jerk, he head-butted the structure. The bricks broke apart with a loud crack like Styrofoam. The wall was shattered.

The three Bloods had seen enough. They were not about to tangle with this strange guy. Backing away, they began to walk in the opposite direction.

"Wait a minute."

It was more of a command than a request. The trio froze at the words from the strange looking teen.

Keith had another, more sinister thought come into mind. It was one that caused a wicked grin to distort his handsome face.

"You guys are Bloods, right?" Ramsey asked. Seeing them nod in affirmation he told the group, "Take me to the Blood Lord. I want to meet him."

George sat alone at headquarters. The others had left since nothing seemed to be going on. He'd stayed behind to ponder the recent developments. They were beginning to make a difference in the community, despite what T.T. Tomlinson wrote. Despite the teen's initial skepticism, he'd seen the impact. They couldn't give up.

On the other side of the equation he had to agree that the need for transportation was essential. Both he and Talitha had their driver's licenses, so driving was not an issue. But the cost and expense of not only buying a vehicle but maintaining it was. He knew to the penny how much they had and he knew it wouldn't be enough to do it right. They just didn't have the capital needed to sustain operations at the level necessary to help. The headquarters was enough of an expense, plus all their technology. Would simple economics spell the ruin of M-Force?

They needed more money. But how could it be found?

"There's always poker," George breathed out in desperate frustration. But then, involuntarily recalling the faces of those he'd crushed, the answer was obvious. "I can't do that any more." Not only was it too high profile, but after what they had been doing of late, he couldn't bring himself to do that to people anymore.

Considering other options, he knew the jobs available to them would never be enough. Then there was the coming cost of college. Irritation crept in, gaining momentum. He was The Brain, he was supposed to figure it out, yet the answer escaped him. Not only that, the question was now beginning to taunt him. How to get it? The equation was out of balance; the question had no answer. Depression rose out of aggravation beginning to build, buffeting the breakwater of his confidence.

"I'm the leader," George called out aloud to the empty room. "Everyone's looking to me. I'm letting them down." Hanging his head, he felt unworthy of the calling.

For an unknown number of minutes, George Alexander sat in silent misery. No solution came to mind and the one answer he did have became stronger with every tick of the clock. Nothing seemed to it but to give up now before they got in deeper, before they started to let people down, like he had let down his friends it seemed. The thought pierced his soul.

Right at the moment they had made their breakthrough, when they'd shown what they were capable of, they had to quit because of money. "It's not right!" George yelled. But he knew right, or fair, had nothing to do with life.

The teen got up from the couch he'd been slumped on to page the others to join him. There was no sense in delaying the inevitable. It was time to give up on the dream. Economic reality spelled defeat. M-Force was no more.

George walked like a condemned man to the table where his blackberry sat. Suddenly his eyes involuntarily scanned the business section of the newspaper. Something caught hold of him, causing him to freeze in his tracks. There still might be hope.

Chapter 17
Taking It to the Next Level

George's eyes scanned the newspaper. The more he read, the more excitement built. The solution to their problems had been there all along. He just couldn't see it, but now, through a different set of lens, the answer was there. His mind began to process information, look for trends, answers. Several came out. The timing was perfect. Moving to the computer, within minutes everything would be set for their deliverance. Could it be this easy?

The Brain, George thought of the name to himself. It occurred to him that he really was. But now it wasn't some arrogant, ego thing. Rather, the thought was humbling. The power he possessed needed to be used responsibly.

He waited patiently for the computer to boot up, another new characteristic that seemed to have grown in him of late. The next step was simple. A few keystrokes, then await the response and their solution was at hand. A few more things to do and everything would be ready. Then it was done. All he needed to do was wait. But the exciting thing was the wait should not be too long if his assumptions were correct. He knew they would be—confidence had been restored.

Talitha, still wearing pink cotton pajamas, sat in her bedroom staring out the window. Cool air drifted through her open window. The maple tree outside filtered the early morning sun. It was going to be another hot day, but for now the temperature was pleasant. Rays of sunshine poked through the green canvas, causing beams of light to dance across the quilt on her bed. The captivating scene seemed to be calling, but she couldn't hear it. Instead, her mind was consumed by the future.

There had been no word from George for days. Several times she had tried to call him. Each attempt had been unsuccessful. Something was wrong, she could feel it. The last time the team was together there was tension over the transportation issue. George had been stalling, unsure of what to do. As Talitha thought more about what this meant, it only depressed her. They'd come so far, yet were still a bunch of individuals.

She was feeling a strong draw to this strange group and their calling. All of this meant something to her. Could she go back to being "ordinary?" What did that mean? She didn't want this all to end, but what could be done? Breaking the silence, as if holding out hope that there was a solution after all, her pager went off.

Tim and Beau were together, just hanging out. Despite the fact both wore matching blue jeans and white tee shirts, the pair was an odd match. Yet, the two were becoming fast friends. Though on the surface they appeared a quite different, below the veneer each had many of the same hopes and dreams. Tim had begun to interest Beau in working out, while Beau had gotten Tim into tinkering around with things and showed him some karate moves.

This early morning they were out at a junkyard looking for parts for their latest creation. Another area of agreement was that both liked the adventure of M-Force and the opportunity for action. Neither as of yet though had considered the deeper implications of their actions.

The fact that George had not called did not bother them like it did Talitha. To the pair it only meant nothing really was going on. Instead, it was a chance for them to do the things normal boys would do during the summer.

Spying the piece they were looking for, Beau signaled his discovery to Tim. The freshman had been amusing himself by bending pieces of metal with his bare hands. Before they could retrieve the prize, both of their pagers went off at the same time. Looking at each other, they grinned knowingly. Something was about to happen.

In an abandoned warehouse, now acting as headquarters for the Blood Lord, a very different appointment was about to take place. It had occupied several days of pushing for Keith Ramsey to finally get to the point of being able to meet with the leader of the Bloods. Only now had he begun to ponder its implications. The thoughts swimming through his head made the burly teen a bit hesitant. While the idea of connecting with the crime lord appealed to him, there was a certain degree of apprehension that went with it. What did this really mean and where was it leading? Plus, the changes that had occurred in him were unsettling. The powers he had displayed earlier in the week had not been a fluke.

The brute his mother called a boyfriend had called him a loser the previous day and, in his rage, Keith had sent him crashing through a door. His mother's rant was stopped mid sentence by a look that caused her to quake in fear. Since then she avoided him. Strangely, something that should have been upsetting was exhilarating. He was gaining power. The thought of submitting it to some unknown character didn't appeal to him.

Traveling through a large open area that used to be a production facility, he was unimpressed by the number and look of the Bloods assembled there. They in turn looked at him with a mixture of curiosity and hostility.

Ramsey was led through this area to a metal door, which opened into a smaller room. It had once been an office so still had some pieces of furniture within. That was only the backdrop though. Dominating the room was a person sitting in a chair wearing a black cloak, his face shrouded by a hood. The imposing figure stood up, looking at the one before him. Ramsey felt a chill running down his spine, as if his very soul was being examined.

"Why did you come here and, more importantly, why should I let you leave?" the figure said in a strange voice.

Oddly, the voice and stance of the character was vaguely familiar to Keith Ramsey. He just couldn't place it. Suddenly, he also felt something that had been gone for many years, intimidation. Now he was uncertain of what he wanted to do. Perhaps there was another way for him, another path. Perhaps he could make his mark through hard work and effort. But then those thoughts were pushed away by a rawer, baser desire. Why work for something you can take?

"I want to join your crew," the youth declared, confidence restored.

"Do you now, Mr. Ramsey?" the Blood Lord asked, an edge to his voice. "Why would you want to do that?"

Keith was startled that the shadowy character before him knew his name. Pushing the thought out, he replied, "I'm tired of not getting what I want."

"And what might that be?" the Blood Lord coyly questioned.

"Power."

The Blood Lord laughed, long and sinister. The sound of it made Keith Ramsey's blood turn cold. It was a laugh of pure evil.

"You are an ambitious one, Mr. Ramsey. But you are also one different from the others I keep around me. You understand that the material things you may desire are obtained by a deeper desire. Power will give you all you seek. Show me what you can do."

Ramsey smiled. He'd been practicing his newfound skill since its discovery. Now it was show time. Quickly concentrating, he built up the rage that boiled within him. Then, with a jerk, he brought his head down on a three-drawer metal filing cabinet in the room. The sturdy piece of furniture was crushed down like a tin pop can.

"Very impressive, Mr. Ramsey, but I have a demonstration of my own." Raising his hand toward Keith, the wrestler suddenly felt intense pressure all around him. It was as if he were now being crushed like the filing cabinet. Panic set in at the inability to move. Then, just as quickly, the Blood Lord released him and it was finished.

Ramsey recovered swiftly. In a rage, he charged at his attacker, not thinking of anything other than showing him some pain as well. But partway there the hand came up and another wave of pressure hit the burly teen. This one was even worse than the first. Wave after wave of pain smashed into him like a sledgehammer. Involuntarily, he fell to his knees, unable to stand. Cries of anguish attempted to come from his purple, twisted face but nothing but an open mouth happened.

The Blood Lord, arm still extended, cloak swishing in the silent room walked up to him saying, "You understand power, Mr. Ramsey, and have the ambition to seek it. But also understand submission. Do that and you will go far and achieve much." Then he released the wrestler from the grip he'd had him in.

Ramsey was on his hands and knees, breathing deeply but listening intently.

"Yes, it will be given. But if you ever decide to take, well," the Blood Lord chuckled, "let us hope you never get that ambitious."

Ramsey looked up, a mixture of hatred and fear in his eyes. Yet, he also in that moment decided where his destiny lay.

"Good...good. That is what I like to see. You will go far and serve me well. From now on, you'll be known as 'The Ram.'" The Blood Lord sized him up. Satisfied with what he saw, the sinister figure added, "I have something I'd like you to do."

M-Force assembled at their headquarters after being paged. The three sat on couches waiting for George to come upstairs. He had warmly greeted them on arrival but asked that they wait for him in the lounge. The three lightly chatted among themselves, genuinely enjoying each other's company.

George confidently strode into the room, then stood before them with a lopsided grin on his face. He waited to ensure he had their attention before speaking. In truth, giving the jovial look the others had never witnessed before was enough to catch their attention. "Lately I've been pondering our future and wondering how we could continue in our current form," the leader of M-Force began. The casual look turned to concern. "The thorny issue has been that of transportation. We need to get around and cover a wider range, but that's impossible on foot. Therefore, we need a vehicle of our own or risk becoming irrelevant in the growing tension in the city."

The others were with him on this, but not sure where he was going.

George adjusted his glasses and continued, "I pondered this in the reality of the cash we had. I want to show you what I came up with as a solution."

Bidding them follow him downstairs, George led the others to the abandoned shop on the main floor of the building. Sitting on the concrete pad was a brand new, sparkling white GMC Savana van.

Tim let out a low whistle.

Talitha gasped. "Where did this come from?" she exclaimed. "You didn't..."

"Steal it?" George answered her question. "No, I bought it."

"But how? With what?" she replied.

"Well, as I said, I was wondering what we could do." He was now enjoying stretching the story out for dramatic effect. "Then I came upon the solution to our money woes."

"You went back to poker?" Beau piped up.

"No, that chapter of my life is closed."

"Then what?" an exasperated Talitha asked.

"Internet stock trading." George could see the two younger members were a bit confused by the statement so he explained, "I saw an ad in the newspaper for trading on the stock market using the Internet. I decided to do some research and found some good buys. So I opened an account on-line for MF Holdings, took the money we had left and started to invest."

"That sounds like gambling!" Talitha exclaimed.

"Not if you do your research," George countered, "it's investing. Anyway, several paid off big time, so I had enough to buy this van."

"Awesome!" Tim cried out.

Seeing Beau circling the vehicle, the leader of M-Force said to him, "So what do you think? We need someone who can camouflage this thing. Do you know anyone who could do it?"

A wide smile came across the sophomore's face. "I think I can come up with something," he responded enthusiastically.

For the next week Beau Joseph really let his talent shine. He began work on the van with a fervor. With the help of Tim, first he set up the interior of the vehicle with a variety of electronic equipment, plus seats for them to sit in. But that was only the beginning.

The issue of stealth kept coming up for him. M-Force needed to be able to move around unseen. They needed to blend into the surroundings. How could they do it with a van that everyone would be able to eventually recognize?

Then, like a light bulb being turned on it came to him. He thought of the chameleon that could change color to adapt to its surroundings. That's what he'd do with the van. With a sense of purpose, fueled by his passion to contribute, the quiet sophomore threw himself into bringing to reality the idea that had come to him.

In the end, he was able to develop a cloaking technology for the vehicle. On the dashboard panel he installed a number of buttons and switches. Some would activate panels that would pop up a large variety of company logos like 'Keith Electric' or 'Able Plumbing' on the side. Also, even the license plate number could be changed.

But that was only the beginning. He also came up with a technology that would allow them to change the color of the exterior shell at the flip of a switch. Working with George, they developed a special heat-sensitive paint to coat the van with. Then coils were mounted between the exterior and interior wall that would allow for activation. Wiring it back then to the main panel, it was ready to go. The result was the vehicle could be turned blue, green, gray or a variety of colors in seconds.

There was one final act to perform. With it the team would be able to go anywhere without being detected. Using Tim's muscles, he also cut a new garage door into the bay, this one opening into the alley. But once it was installed he had it covered to blend in with the brick wall so that if someone walked past they'd never know it was a door.

In a little more than a week and half, M-Force was mobile.

The quietest member of the team called everyone together to show them what had been accomplished. A brief demonstration of the van's capabilities had them in awe of the humble teen.

"Beau, what you did was incredible," Talitha gushed.

George added, awe showing for the first time, "I agree. It really is amazing. I don't know what to say." Walking around the van, taking in every detail, the leader of M-Force added, "This is way more than I had even hoped for. The van is going to be perfect."

Beau smiled, but lowered his head in embarrassment. "I'm just happy I could do something to contribute," he modestly answered. "All of you can do so much, I just want to be able to do what I can."

Tim was already in the van, pushing buttons and pulling levers. "Hey, let's take it out for a test drive!" he called enthusiastically.

They pilled into the vehicle and went cruising. The machine handled well and the electronic equipment installed worked perfectly. This definitely balanced the equation with the Blood Lord.

The ability to drive anywhere stimulated animated conversation among the new friends. After a while though Tim asked, "What do think we should call this?"

"What do you mean?" Talitha replied in confusion.

"I mean we've got to have a name for it." Beau and George were enthusiastic for the suggestion. Talitha rolled her eyes, saying only, "Men."

"How about Forcemobile?" Tim offered. That was met with groans.

"Force buggy?" he added, again with no positive response.

Beau said softly "What about the Equalizer? I mean it balances things out with the Blood Lord and his gang."

"I like it," Talitha replied before Tim could come up with another suggestion. "It's simple, but to the point. Besides, you really had the vision and did the work, so you should be able to name it. Are we agreed?"

The name Equalizer was enthusiastically endorsed by all.

"Speaking of the Blood Lord," George broke into the revelry, "let's take a cruise over to the university. I'd like to see if we could get some information on why he broke into that lab. I have a hunch there was something unique that he was searching for."

It was a short drive to State University. Arriving on the campus, George parked well away from the main traffic areas. He and Talitha decided they alone would poke around.

"Hey, why can't I go along?" Tim interjected. "I want into the action."

"A crowd would attract attention," George explained. "You and Beau stay here and watch the van."

"You're not my mom, you can't order me around," the muscular freshman belligerently replied.

"No, but I AM telling you that you're staying," the leader of M-Force ordered.

Though Tim was visibly unhappy, the pair set off. Coming shortly to the lab complex, they could see security had been tightened up. Armed guards patrolled around the perimeter fence, plus closed circuit cameras had also been strategically placed.

"We're not going to get anywhere here," George observed dejectedly. Pondering the situation for a moment he came up with an alternative. "Let's go to the lab I work at and see if anyone there knows about it. We can play dumb and ask questions."

While the others searched, Tim was getting bored waiting. Gazing out the van window the aggressive football player perked up. "Look," he observed, "there's a bunch of Bloods. Let's find out what they're up to."

Beau responded with caution. "I don't know. We were told to stay here. Plus, there's four of them and only two of us." It also seemed strange to him that they would be casually walking around such a high profile public place. The thought didn't sit right, so he added, "Plus, it seems strange they'd just be walking around flying their colors."

"Don't be such a wimp," Tim retorted. "We can take them."

Reluctantly Beau agreed, since in reality he had little choice. Donning their M-Force costumes and becoming the Bulldozer and Grey Man the pair slipped out, beginning to trail the hoods. Initially they kept their distance, content to observe. The thugs seemed to have no purpose for being on campus, moving about randomly. But experience told the pair that nothing about the Bloods was random. If they were in public and wearing their colors there was a reason.

Again, the Bulldozer chaffed at the lack of action, so they began to push closer and closer. Grey Man tried to hold him back, but couldn't. Finally they were spotted.

"See, the boss said that if we went trolling long enough we'd find some fish!" one of the group exclaimed.

As if on cue, a fifth person came out of the late afternoon shadows, joining the group. This one had an even more sinister look than the others. He wore a red mask, yet to Grey Man there was something familiar about him.

They had been set up. Bulldozer hesitated, not knowing what to do. Grey Man grabbed his pager and signaled the others to assemble. As the Bloods advanced, he said to the Bulldozer, "This is more than we can handle. We need to get out of here."

The powerful freshman wasn't sure what to do, but would never stand down from a fight. "The Bulldozer doesn't back down," he responded, and charged ahead.

At the science building, the other half of M-Force was not having much luck. They had subtly asked some people what the building that had been attacked housed, but none seemed to know. The pagers worn by Talitha and George began to beep at the same time. Startled, both grabbed them to see what was happening. George stared at the locator, then exclaimed, "This is weird. It's Beau pager but he's away from the van. I wonder what's going on." Then realizing further discussion was of no use, exclaimed, "It's not far from here. Let's go."

Bulldozer was pleased so far. He'd knocked one Blood down and was toying with another. Grey Man had gone invisible and been able to get another. *Maybe we can do this after all*, he thought.

Then the newest Blood, the one with the mask, stepped in. He ran toward Bulldozer, lowered his shoulder, then smashed into him. A sharp *crack* was heard as the muscular member of M-Force, along with the one he'd been holding were sent flying. Hitting the ground, the pair went down hard.

Standing with hands on hips, the powerful antagonist called out, "You're messing with The Ram now punk. I'm going to have fun busting you up."

Bulldozer slowly got back to his feet. Though a bit stunned, he was in a rage. Charging back, he engaged the formidable foe.

The two grappled like mythological warriors. In the ensuing carnage, nothing was able to stand in their way. Signs were knocked over, cars slammed into and turf dug up. It was a war. Bulldozer picked up a mailbox and threw it. He missed, but the projectile crashed through the window of an adjoining building. His opponent attacked, missed and destroyed an ornate column holding up an awning out front of another building. The result was the whole thing came crashing down.

Bulldozer was tiring from the constant exertion, plus the new foe had caught him off guard. Try as he might, he couldn't overcome the strength aligned against him. The guy was hard as steel and nothing he could do seemed to dent it. Grey Man was hard pressed with the other Bloods and in over his head. The risk that the pair would be overwhelmed came to a bitter reality for the aggressive teen. Something needed to be done.

Desperately the Bulldozer tried one last charge, but missed. The Ram grabbed him, then swiftly drove him to the ground by letting loose a deadly head butt.

The hard-hitting member of M-Force was stunned by the blow, so could offer no resistance. The attacker picked him off the now mangled lawn by the throat, beginning to squeeze away all life from the boy. Blackness began to enter in. But just as quickly as he'd been caught, he was released.

Falling to the ground, gasping for breath, the Bulldozer turned his head to see that The Ram had Grey Man in his arms. His friend had engaged the attacker despite his own battle with the other Bloods in an attempt to save him.

The Ram contemptuously took the slender boy and threw him like a rag doll against a brick wall. Grey Man crumpled into a heap, not moving. The Ram turned back toward Bulldozer, a wicked grin showing through the mask. He raised his foot to stomp on the groggy victim's head, but was hit by a flying trash bin, followed by a blast of energy. The other Bloods instinctively fled from this new threat, leaving their colleague behind. He stood his ground for a moment. Realized there was no profit in a continued engagement, The Ram trotted off, confident he'd made his presence felt.

Bulldozer got to his feet, bruised and sore. Shaking his head as if to regain his thoughts, he looked over at Grey Man. His friend was not moving. Black Star and The Brain were kneeling at the fourth member of the team's side, examining him. Black Star screamed, "He's hurt bad. We need to get him to the hospital. Get the van."

The Brain ran off and in a few minutes was back with the Equalizer.

A crowd had gathered, keeping a distance. The group of university students silently watched what was going on. Stunned by the violence of the scene they'd just witnessed, none could do anything more.

Gingerly Grey Man was taken into the van and it sped off.

With cowls off so they could gasp for air easier, M-Force now became four upset teenagers. Talitha sat with Beau's head on her lap. He wasn't moving and barely breathing. She demanded, "What happened?"

Tim was stunned. His body seemed to be able to recover quickly, so already the physical pain from his fight with The Ram was gone and he felt ready to go again. But instead of the hard-charger, a more subdued and almost vulnerable looking boy sat in his place. A greater pain than he'd ever experienced entered in, coursing through his body. It was guilt. "I…I," he stammered, "I wanted us to go after some Bloods. But there was a new one, a tough one. He…I…" Tears fell down Tim's cheeks as he began to cry.

"What did you do?" Talitha berated the guilt-ridden youth.

"Talitha, leave it alone for now," George instructed from the front. "There'll be time for that later. For now we need to look after Beau."

"What are we going to do?" Talitha asked, weeping now at the sight of their unconscious friend.

George was concentrating on the road, a grim look on his face. "Leave that to me. I'll do the talking when we get there, but get his costume off." While he was saying that, he pulled into a side street, flipped some switches to change the van and continued on to the hospital. They'd come this far; an invisible line had been crossed. There was no going back now.

Chapter 18
Dark Days

The Equalizer pulled up to the well-lit emergency entrance of the hospital. A gurney and pair of orderlies was waiting to spring into action. One quickly opened the door, then the pair lifted the still unconscious Beau, now wearing jeans and a blue and red stripped shirt, out of the front seat. Wheeling him into the main building of K-W General Hospital, a cry was heard as the youth's parents arrived on the scene. George followed along behind them trying not to get in the way. After the hustle and bustle, everything was again quiet in the driveway.

Talitha came out from behind the curtain that was closed to shield the back of the van. Hopping into the driver's seat, she pulled out and away from the hospital, unsure what the future held for their friend or for M-Force. Talitha was loath to leave Beau without knowing his condition. But she knew if they'd all come in it would have attracted attention

As they'd driven to the hospital, George had called Beau's parents on a cell phone to let them know their son was hurt. His next call was to the hospital to inform them that he was bringing in an unconscious teen. Finally, he told the others to stay in the back out of sight. He would deal with things at the hospital, then find his own way home. The remainder of M-Force was too stunned to do anything other than woodenly comply.

Beau was quickly wheeled into an examining room where he was hooked up to several monitors. A doctor began to examine him to determine the state of his injuries. While all this was going on George took a seat with Beau's parent's just outside. In order to obtain background information for the doctors, an admitting nurse arrived and began to ask some questions. The distraught parents listened on, eager to find out what had happened to their son.

"What are you able to tell me about the nature of the accident?" the nurse asked.

"Well," George began, "I was at Victory Park for a walk when I came across this guy from school named Beau. Anyway, he was climbing a tree and pretty high up. I was actually kind of impressed with how far he'd gotten. So we chatted for a bit, then I turned to leave. Next thing I knew I heard him cry out. He must have slipped because when I turned around there he was falling."

George prayed that they would believe his story. The nurse nodded and kept writing. Beau's mother began to cry. No one questioned it, so he concluded, "I was parked close by, so instead of calling an ambulance I grabbed my vehicle and brought him here right away."

"Thank you," the nurse replied. "Please stay around for a while in case the doctor needs to ask you anything."

"Yes, thank you," Beau's mother added, "for looking after our son."

The comment stabbed George in the heart. He was already feeling guilty about what had happened. He was the leader. He was supposed to look after things. Instead, he'd failed

Guilt was also bombarding Tim as Talitha drove silently back to headquarters. Beau could be dead and it would be his fault. He had gone after the Bloods. He had ignored his friend's call to pull back. He had stupidly rushed in without waiting. The guilt was like acid eating through metal.

"Tim…Tim?"

The youth snapped out of the fog, realizing Talitha was speaking to him. "What?" he numbly responded.

"I asked you what happened," she said.

He opened his mouth to reply an excuse all ready. But something changed in Tim David that moment. It was as if he'd passed through a door. The time had come to grow up and take responsibility.

"It was my fault."

"What?" Talitha exclaimed.

"I wanted to go after the Bloods, but Beau said we should stay put. Then I pushed it and they spotted us. He wanted to back off, but I charged in. Then, when I got into trouble, Beau jumped in and saved me." Tears began to roll down Tim's face. "He got hurt looking after me." No longer able to hold back his emotions, face twisted in anguish, the boy began to cry, adding, "He sacrificed himself for me."

Talitha was stunned by the admission, but not surprised. Rather than speak, she continued to drive silently. Instead of comforting the distraught youth, she kept him in silent purgatory, allowing her own anger to overcome better judgement.

The doctor examining Beau was in fact an intern. At the end of a particularly difficult twelve-hour shift, he was tired. Glancing at the monitors hooked up to the boy in order to check his vital signs, the results caused him to do a double take. Pondering the results for a moment finally he decided to call for the other doctor on duty.

"There's something wrong with this kid's vitals doctor," the intern reported.

Instead of paying close attention to his colleague, the experienced physician was thinking about his upcoming golf vacation. "What's wrong with them?" he casually asked.

"Well, nothing really. They just seem off. First off, his metabolic rate is way up. Also the brain patterns are in the high end of the band and his white cell count is huge."

"So?" the senior member of the emergency medical team questioned.

"So the guy's got a head injury." Showing the distracted physician the chart, he added, "Okay, so dismiss the other items. Why would his white count be this high? There's no infection. I don't think that should be happening," the intern stated. "This guy shouldn't be showing these signs."

"I think you're reading too much into this. Set the kid up, then move him along."

The intern wouldn't back down. "We should bring one of the specialists in, or, at the very least, be running more tests to figure out what's going on."

"Do you see the backup in Emergency?" the doctor retorted. "We don't have time for all this." Seeing the look of disappointment, he tried to sooth his young colleague's conscience. "Listen, I know the vitals seem off. But I'm sure this can happen when a body is shocked during trauma. Don't worry about it. Stabilize him and send him upstairs."

"That's another thing, he's already stable."

Instead of being shocked, the other was relieved. Now they could pass him off to someone else and he could get back to more pleasant thoughts. What one missed due to inexperience, the other missed because of inattentiveness. Beau's body was healing itself. By the time he was transferred to the trauma unit his eyes were open.

"Where am I?" Beau asked.

The trauma unit admitting nurse almost dropped her chart in surprise at the patient speaking to her. Taking a quick look at the chart on the end of the bed, she replied, "At the hospital."

"What happened?"

"You fell out of a tree and were brought here by a friend," the nurse answered, still unsure what to make of this development with the patient.

Leaving Beau alone, the now perturbed woman went to find a doctor to look at this new case. She wondered why someone who was not hurt that bad had been misdirected to already overworked floor. She missed looking at the early part of the chart that showed what condition he'd been brought in. Instead, the nurse was more concerned with the perceived administrative screwup that had caused someone who didn't belong to be sent to them.

Beau closed his eyes. It all came back to him. Whoever had given that story was covering. He had tried to take on Tim's attacker and failed. Desperately did he want to know what had happened to his friend, but couldn't contradict the story. Looking around the room, Beau could see only hospital staff. Then a burst of pain caused him to wince and lie still. Tim could be dead for all he knew. He'd let him down. He had failed. The only company the youth was left with was misery.

"Tell me again what happened."

"We went to the campus as you instructed, master. As you'd predicted the meddlers were there," The Ram began to report to the Blood Lord. "Two tried to stop us, but we handled them easily. We'd almost finished them except another two showed up and jumped us. I think we still could have destroyed them, but the guys with me fled." Keith Ramsey gave the other Bloods in the room a withering look before he continued. "I don't think there are any others, but I can't guarantee it. They've got some strange powers though. One is pretty strong. But they're nothing we can't handle. Or I can't handle anyway."

"Tell me more about these powers," their leader prodded. He too suspected something was different about their new opponent, but hadn't been able to pinpoint it yet.

Ramsey paused as if ensuring what he was about to say would be accurate. "Okay, it may sound weird, but this is what I saw. One of them seems to be able to disappear when he wants. Another can move objects. A third, it looked like a girl to me, can shoot energy."

The Blood Lord was pleased by the report. He had sent his newest member out to see what he was made of. That had been a success in his estimation, despite the lack of courage shown by the others. He'd not only flushed out this new threat, but also had some idea of what they could do. Both plans had worked well.

A question arose for the Blood Lord though: who were these meddlers and where did they come from? Each seemed to possess powers similar to his. How could that be? He would need to ponder this.

Regardless, the criminal mastermind knew what he was up against. Now it was simply a matter of finding out who they were. Confident that could be accomplished in short order, the sinister figure called over one of his lackeys. "I have an assignment for you."

Several hours after being rushed to the hospital Beau was walking around and felt fine. Despite this dramatic change in health, it was decided to keep him overnight for observations though he was well enough to leave.

In the end, it was decided that he hadn't been hurt as bad as initially thought. So, first thing in the morning, the youth was discharged. Due to his rapid recovery, no one had looked at the youth's x-rays since there seemed little point to it. If someone had taken the time to do this they would have gotten a different picture. They would have seen a young man with several fractures, and also severe internal damage from the impact. Instead of being hailed as a miraculous recovery, it was being chalked up to overreaction.

Beau Joseph walked out of K-W General Hospital without anyone knowing they were in the presence of one with a unique physiology.

New Threat called out the headline of the morning edition of *The Recorder*. Full coverage of the battle at State University, plus the damage done on the campus was detailed. A witness had taken several pictures with a cell phone camera, so one of Bulldozer and The Ram fighting was on the front cover. T.T. Tomlinson's editorial was scathing. To him, M-Force stood for menace and he let everyone know it. They were vigilantes and would eventually get someone killed by their foolish intervention the publisher contended in the paper.

As knowledge of the group grew throughout the community, so did the discussion about them. Debate was underway throughout Kilings-Welch on the value of this group. Despite *The Recorder's* point of view, there were others who saw the value of the team. To them, M-Force meant magnificent.

Two of the local radio stations both held call-in sessions with the majority of people commending the courage of M-Force at standing up to the Blood Lord. But there was also a significant number who chided them for a variety of reasons. For some, it was the fact they hid their identify and were not accountable. Others felt the group was taking the law into their own hands. Some thought they should mind their own business and let the police take care of the situation.

None of this was lost on the team. Already there was tension over Beau's injury, an uncertainty of how to proceed. The Blood Lord's latest recruit also was a cause for concern. While Beau had been released from hospital, his mother was keeping him at home to be sure he was okay. Again a dark cloud hung over the foursome. Once more, when things looked up, something happened to give them pause for thought.

The tension began to affect each of their outside lives as well.

"You missed a key input, George. We have to start the experiment all over again."

Face turning red with embarrassment, George hung his head. "I'm sorry, Doctor Little. I guess I wasn't paying attention," he sheepishly replied.

The professor shook his head, shaggy salt and pepper hair waving as if emphasizing the point. "I don't know what to make of you, lad," he said in his thick English accent. "There are genuine flashes of brilliance you've shown, but you also miss too much. You don't pay attention and don't seem to apply yourself. That mind of yours is being wasted."

The man genuinely liked his assistant and knew he was helping him tremendously, yet there was this problem of inconsistency. Rubbing his creased temples, he concluded, "Take the rest of the day off. Consider our conversation and where you're going. I had thought to keep you on come fall since there have been times you've really helped me. But now I'm not so sure."

George left the lab, his heart heavier than it had ever been. The pressure of what he was going through with M-Force was enough, but now he was failing in the lab.

The problem was he'd lost his confidence and now wasn't sure how much to do. The experiments Doctor Little was conducting were not overly complex, but he just didn't know how far to go with his help. Always the threat of detection was on his mind.

George was also hurt by the words, since he really liked the older man. They had worked well together. The professor had a quiet confidence about him and was not afraid to allow others to shine. There was no ego with the man, only a genuine desire to help mankind through his work. Plus, his work was in the area of biophysics, which he thought might even be able to help him with his condition. No, this recent turn of events was a disaster for George Alexander.

Tim missed another tackle in scrimmage. After the whistle blew, the defensive coordinator yelled, "David, get your head in the game! Pay attention!"

Try as he could, the image of his friend lying motionless on the ground haunted him. He couldn't rid himself of it. *Beau's injury is my fault,* he thought to himself. His aggression may have ruined everything.

Again the play was run, again Tim David missed the tackle. In addition, he was knocked to the ground by a hard block.

"That does it!" the coach exclaimed. "David, go sit on the bench. You're of no use to us."

He was of no use to the team. He was no use to M-Force. He felt like he really was useless.

Once practice was over, the distracted youth was called into the head coach's office. Tom Jeffries silently looked empathetically at the player before him. The observant middle-aged man could see there was no fire in the player's eyes, no passion like there'd been before. Something was wrong. "What's the matter Tim?" he asked quietly. "You used to be a tiger out there. Now, there's no life. What's changed?"

Tim didn't know what to say. "I don't know, Coach," he stammered, "I just don't feel well, I guess. I'll get better. I won't let you down."

"I hope so, because lately I've been questioning my decision to bring you onto the squad. You have shown real promise, but you need to apply yourself. If you don't, you'll be of no use to anyone."

Walking home, Tim David looked like a man carrying a heavy burden. Shoulders slumped, head down, he plodded along, bearing the load of guilt he felt.

Talitha was having a decent day relative to her friends. She loved being around kids. They always perked her up. Despite Beau's recovery, the sensitive girl was still seriously questioning what they were doing. *I'm only a teenager going into university in a few weeks,* she thought. *What am I doing running around pretending to be some sort of superhero?* Pondering the question further, it also became obvious that no one had asked her to do it. Even worse, few seemed to care, let alone appreciate if she did.

Tommy always made her smile; he was so full of life. Seeing the slender, mop-headed boy clambering over the climbing structure in the park couldn't help but make her smile. He'd come so far during the summer. He listened, was attentive, and eager to please. She hoped they would peraps be able to see each other on occasion during the fall. No, he was very different.

Talitha watched as he stood on the highest point beyond where he should be, balancing himself. She could see it coming, as if it were happening in slow motion. Standing to warn the exuberant boy, it was too late. The look of fear on his face cut her to the core as he stumbled and began to fall. She was about to extend her hand and use her powers to catch him, but there was a large crowd around. Not wanting to be detected, the sensitive girl became sick to her stomach as she watched him fall.

With a dull thud, Tommy hit hard. Like Beau Joseph only a few days before, the boy lay motionless. Talitha ran to him, in near hysterics. She couldn't think, didn't know what to do.

The teen's mind condemned her decision. *You could have stopped it, but you didn't, you let him fall*, she chastised herself.

The playground supervisor pushed Talitha aside since she was doing nothing other than sob and began to examine the boy. Thankfully, his eyes fluttered then opened. Moaning in pain, he began to cry.

In the end, Tommy broke his arm in the fall. He likely wouldn't be back to the camp for the rest of the summer. Talitha Beck cried herself to sleep that night.

Beau lay in bed, not because he was tired or hurt, but because his mother had ordered him there to rest. He didn't want to, instead wishing to see his friends. Interrupting these thoughts, his mother entered the room with a tray of food.

"Hello, dear, are you feeling better?" she cheerfully asked.

Beau tried not to let his irritation show through, "I was feeling fine the last time you asked. I'm okay, all right? I want to do something."

"You've had a nasty fall and we need to make sure that you're well."

"Have any of my friends called?" he asked hopefully.

"No, you've not had any calls since you got home from the hospital," his mother lied. In fact, all of M-Force had called to see how he was, but she wouldn't put the calls through. She distrusted the trio, thinking they were a bad influence on him. The woman loved her son deeply, not wanting to let go of her little boy. The call about the fall had been as if her worst nightmare had come true. She would double her efforts to keep him safe.

Beau rolled over in exasperation, wanting the conversation to end. His mother took the hint and left.

Alone again with his thoughts, he was hurt by the idea the others wouldn't check in on him. He didn't feel like he fit in. Sure, he could build things, but he wasn't tough and brave like Tim. He also wasn't decisive like Talitha and George. Beginning to analyze what had happened the other day, what he came up with only made him feel worse. He thought, *Why do I always want to back down all the time?* Tim was so confident, with no fear. Yet Beau had fear, hesitation. *Am I a coward?* Beau thought to himself. In a state of confusion and agitated emotions the youth began to wonder if he were.

Even the power he had as Grey Man made him wonder. The power to disappear. What was that? The ability to hide and be safe. Condemnation flooded in.

"I really am a coward," Beau whispered to himself, hot tears beginning to soak his pillow. "The others think so, that's why they hadn't called. I really didn't belong."

There would be no rest for Beau Joseph this evening.

Four people, brought together by circumstance, given unique powers, were now seeing the down side or consequence of those powers. They were beginning to realize that nothing of value comes without a cost. The only question now remaining for the four was, were they willing to pay it?

Chapter 19
Answers

Crime continued to rise in lockstep with the stifling humidity in the mid-part of August causing a boiling irritation within the community.

A new figure had risen within the ranks of the Bloods. A powerful force calling himself The Ram emerged as an even greater threat. Video coverage of this notable character bowling over a group of police officers, then destroying their car, had played over and over again. The fear within the law enforcement community was evident. If something was not done soon to restore order the area might slip into anarchy.

Some were beginning to ask where M-Force was. Others implored their help. One media outlet, radio station WKW, was particularly vocal in encouraging the team. "The voice of Kilings-Welch" as they called themselves, encouraged the foursome to stand up against this threat. But, as of yet, there had only been silence in response. The twin cities stood on the brink.

Unable to ignore circumstances any longer, George called the team together to discuss their future. Talitha and Tim showed up, displaying no life. Both were still obviously downcast about their circumstances. The sight of the energetic pair so dejected only furthered George's own dark thoughts. Beau was late arriving. Head down, he entered the room, but wouldn't look at anybody. The foursome, who for the last several weeks had gotten along so freely, now faced awkward silence. George tried to start a conversation, but for some reason no one wanted to speak. There was something creating a barrier.

Tim David, the Bulldozer, the hard charger, was the one who turned the course M-Force was heading on. Though feeling awkward and embarrassed, he went over to Beau, humbly saying, "I'm sorry you got hurt. It was my fault. I should have listened to you. I'll try to use more common sense in the future."

Beau had a shocked look on his face. "What?" he replied in confusion. "I let you guys down. I don't think I fit in. That's why you didn't call or visit me when I was hurt."

Now it was Talitha's turn to be confused. "What do you mean? All of us called and tried to see you. I know I called every day and came by your house three times. Each time your mother told us you were sleeping, or else you didn't want to see anybody."

Shocked by the declaration, Beau wasn't sure what to think. The realization of what had happened hadn't sunk in yet. "I thought you guys didn't want me around anymore."

Talitha sat beside the slumping youth and put her arm around his shoulder. "No. You have done so much for this team. We can't do it without you."

Tim came over and added, "For sure. It's not only just your building either. Who else is going to be our scout and make sure I don't get myself into a jam?"

Talitha looked at him, commenting, "We also need you on the team as well, Tim."

The youth understood the thrust of her statement. Nodding his head in agreement, he somberly replied, "I've learned my lesson. I'll do what I need to be a team player from now on."

Revelry was renewed, but only for a moment. George had been silent throughout the initial conversation. He had been analyzing the situation over and over in his mind every day since Beau had gotten hurt. Despite the renewed optimism of the others, only one conclusion kept coming to him. They were in over their heads. Not only that, he felt that the teenagers were fooling themselves about the potential difference they could be made by their actions.

"Are we kidding ourselves?" George asked. "I mean, are we playing superhero here? Tomlinson calls us a menace. Beau nearly gets killed. Should we quit before we do some real damage?"

There was a long pause as each reflected on the question. It was a thought each had been trying to keep in the back of their minds rather than dealing with. Now The Brain had brought the issue to the forefront. They needed to deal with it.

Should they continue? The logical conclusion was obvious. It was a no-brainer. Everything said no. They were in no position to make a difference, felt unqualified, were outmatched and feeling unappreciated. It was only for the youths to figure that out and walk away. Why shouldn't they? That was the example of the society around them that did the same thing. When things got tough, others would pack it in or pay someone else to deal with it. Who did they think they were? Different from the norm? Able to make a difference? It sure didn't seem like it.

"Why are we here?" Talitha asked, breaking the silence.

"To stop the Blood Lord," Tim replied.

"No," Talitha shook her head, "I don't think it is. Yes, that's part of it, but it's more the result. Think of what happened to us in the first place. Think of how we came together. Have we used it for our own good?" she asked. "For our own gain? No. We want to help people. That's our calling." The next question caught the others off guard. "Does it matter if we succeed?"

"Well, I think it does," George responded.

"I don't," she countered. "I think what matters is we care enough to try. We do our best. It's not about success. It's about effort. Our powers are a gift. Our joining together is a testimony." Growing in enthusiasm, she continued, "Think about it. How unusual is this group? I mean, none of us have anything in common other than our powers. But is that true? I don't think so. We also have in common our desire to help. That's worth something! Besides, if we show we care, maybe others will begin to do the same thing. No, we can't give up."

The others were hit hard by the speech. Even Talitha herself was impacted by it. She wasn't even sure where the thoughts had come from. They had just popped into her head.

Individually, at first, each came to a new, deeper realization. What Talitha had said was true. What they were doing was not only about stopping the Blood Lord. The bigger purpose was using the gifts they had been given for society's better good. The action is a consequence of the attitude. If M-Force exists only to counter this evil, then they are like seeds planted in shallow soil. They will grow quickly, but when heat and drought come will wither up due to their shallow roots. But if rooted in deep soil, the soil of love for their fellow man and desire for the betterment of all, they could withstand any adversity.

These individual thoughts, as if driven by some unseen force, began to mesh together. Smiling with relief, and also a renewed sense of purpose, the four, having learned this lesson, now were about to sink their roots deeper.

They had crossed the divide and there was no turning back. Half-measures and less than a full effort was no longer acceptable. It was time for M-Force to move to the next level, but how?

Talitha looked affectionately at the others she now thought of as brothers, and asked, "So what now?"

George pulled out his cell phone. With a twinkle in his eyes, he replied, "I have an idea."

"WKW News Room, Dave Snider."

The man who answered to that name was, in fact, the news director of the local radio station. He was not having a good week. Some recent data showed the station had lately slipped to number three in the ratings. This had caused great concern for the owners who'd prided themselves on being number one. Each director was being pressured to retake the top spot. In the future, this particular phone call was to be viewed as an answer to prayer.

"I'm the leader of M-Force," the confident voice declared. "I would like to give some perspective on what's been happening. Are you interested in an interview?"

Startled by the boldness of the statement, Snider spilled his mug of coffee in surprise. Stifling an oath, along with his enthusiasm, he cautiously replied, "Yes, I'm very interested. But how do I know you're legit?"

The caller went on to describe in intimate detail what had happened during the attack on the lab at the university. Only one who was there would have known the details.

"Okay, you've convinced me" the news director confirmed. He then eagerly asked, "When would you like to come in?"

The time was set for two days later. This would allow the radio station to adequately publicize the exclusive interview. Dave Snider rubbed his hands together in glee, anticipating the bonus he was going to receive for pulling this off. No one needed to know all he did was say yes to the request.

Interest grew in the community as the announcement got out to the general public. In fact, it became the talk of the town. The hope of most was that they could find out more about this unknown, but exciting group.

There was another keenly interested in the event as well. The Blood Lord had been alerted to the coming interview, so decided to take advantage of the situation. Gathering several of his gang leaders, he instructed, "Get over to the station and give the people a lesson. Ram, you lead. Deal with the meddlers as you see fit."

The Ram smirked evilly, "With pleasure."

The appointed day arrived. The Equalizer parked a short distance from the location of the station in an alley behind a strip mall. It was only a few minutes from the appointed hour. With WKW located on the top floor of a tall building at the edge of downtown Kilings, it would only take minutes to get there. While the destination may only be minutes away the results of what would happen would last a lifetime. No longer would the teens be an anonymous entity, they would be in the public eye. It was the moment of truth for M-Force. There was no turning back after this.

Though each was committed to their future course of action, the others still had concerns about what their leader was proposing to do. Talitha asked for the third time, "Are you sure you want to go in alone? That's still seems pretty risky to me."

"Yea," Beau chorused, his confidence brimming, "I could go grey and stay with you."

"No," George responded, shaking his head for emphasis, "I don't want too many people to see us all yet. We still have some element of surprise left."

"All right," Talitha said, "but if you need us, just shout."

George chuckled, "Will do. See you in a bit."

He slipped out of the van and moved into the building. A short time later, the leader of M-Force walked through the plate glass door of the radio station on the top floor of the Midland Bank building. The receptionist, and the others in the modernly appointed waiting room, stared at the costumed figure with a mixture of awe and curiosity.

Dave Snider appeared and introduced himself, "Hi, I'm Dave, the news director here. Welcome to the station. We have a few minutes, can I show you around?"

Everywhere the pair went work stopped. George was acutely aware of how public he now was. Almost immediately he became uncomfortable with the stares. Though no one said a word other than the chatty news director, he could feel people sizing him up.

Finally they arrived in the broadcast booth and it was time to get ready for the interview. A sound engineer clipped a microphone to his costume and an assistant gave him a bottle of water. The general manager of the station arrived, beginning to chat with him too. The buzz of activity relaxed George. He looked over the series of questions that was going to be asked, preparing responses in his mind.

Then he and the announcer were alone in the booth. The sound engineer was doing a countdown and George realized he hadn't even caught the man's name.

"This is Dak Leery and you're listening to 'Talk Back' on WKW, the voice of Kilings-Welch," the announcer smoothly began. "As promised, we have live and in person the leader of the new group in the area everyone is talking about, M-Force. Welcome."

"Thank you," George replied shakily.

"So first off, what's your name?"

"I'm called The Brain."

"Cool handle, makes sense for the leader of the group," Leery replied. "I can figure out by your costume that you want to keep your true identity private. I can respect that, so I won't ask you anything that would compromise it."

The Brain nodded his head in agreement, still a bit tense in the surroundings.

The interviewer pointed at his lips and mouthed, "This is radio!"

The realization made him chuckle, chasing away the nervousness. "Thanks, I appreciate that," he answered.

"Okay, so then I will ask, what's up with you guys? Why are you doing what you're doing? I mean, you've come out of nowhere and done what others can't. You've been creating quite the buzz by checking the Blood Lord and his gang. What's your secret?"

Over his initial jitters, The Brain confidently stated, "We're just doing our part. Remember, two months ago no one had heard of the Blood Lord and we weren't having problems of this scale. There was no need for M-Force. But sadly, this criminal seems to be the tip of the iceberg. I've watched this area sink lower and lower for some time now, so I guess it's no surprise that this is where we end up." Gaining momentum, he boldly declared, "I don't believe this is how we want to live. We just seem to have drifted a bit from our values. M-Force was born to try to help those who need it. We'd like to turn the iceberg into ice cubes."

Leery chuckled at the clever imagery. But the cynic in him was having difficulty believing what he was hearing, "Yea, but why? Why put yourself at risk? What reward are you hoping to get from this?"

"Seeing people happy and free from fear," The Brain shot back. Then he tried to explain from their perspective, "We're not looking for anything. We have some abilities, so want to use them to help people. Is that so hard to understand? We just want to do what we can, so right now that means stopping the Blood Lord and his gang."

Catching the point, the interviewer pressed in, "So you're telling me you're here to stay?"

"You better believe it, Mr. Leery," The Brain emphatically responded. "As long as needed."

The others were excitedly listening to the broadcast from the van. George sounded so mature, answering the questions expertly. Then there was a crash in the background, as if something were breaking. A sound of commotion followed, causing George and Dak Leery to stop talking in distraction.

Someone called out, "What's going on here?"

A wicked sounding voice responded, "We're here to create a little balance in the interview."

Then pandemonium broke loose as the sound of shouting and fighting broke out.

"I recognize that voice," Tim yelled from back in the van, "that's the Blood I tangled with. Come on, we have to help George."

The impetuous youth grabbed for the door handle, but Talitha cautioned him, "Wait, we need to work together."

Tim paused, though his impatience was evident.

Slipping Black Star's mask over her face, Talitha continued, "I'll use my speed to get there as fast as I can. You and Beau follow as quickly as you can. Work together to find George and I in the broadcast area. Let's show these creeps what M-Force can do!"

Black Star stepped out, and after the first step, was almost a blur. Slowing to enter the building, others parted the way at the sight, oblivious to what was going on above them. Figuring the elevator would be too slow, Black Star took to the stairs charging up two at time. Within moments she was at the WKW office. There was no need to ask directions from the receptionist who cowered below the desk; the girl could hear where the action was.

The Brain had been caught off guard by the intrusion of the attackers being bowled over in the initial assault. Regaining his composure, he began to fight back. There were numerous Bloods swarming over the area, causing all form of damage, while attacking the radio staff. He had to help them. Levitating a variety of items, he hurled them at the foes. Then he noticed a new opponent. This one's features were hidden by a red mask, but The Brain recognized him from the campus attack. The grotesquely distorted head gave him away.

Anything thrown at this character just bounced off of him. It was as if he were made of steel. In return, The Ram slammed into the leader of M-Force, sending him hard into a wall. Stunned by the force of the blow, The Brain couldn't respond.

The Ram picked the limp form up with one hand, propping him up against the wall like some sort of target. Then the raging bull prepared to strike again, finishing the job.

At the last moment The Brain regained his faculties. A new thought entered his mind, one that he'd been toying with for some time. The moment was right to test his theory. Jumping up, the teen was able to levitate himself, holding a position near the ceiling. The Ram, like a run away freight train, was not able to stop, slamming instead into the wall. The result was smashed drywall and mangled steel studs.

Outmatched against the stronger opponent, The Brain wasn't sure what to do. Unable to hold the elevated position, he dropped to the carpeted floor. Immediately the thug grabbed the head of M-Force, then held him tight so levitation was no longer an option.

He could also sense the leader of the attackers was about to head butt him, something he knew would be trouble, considering the anvil-like protrusion on his head. The other attackers paused from their destruction to cheer on their leader. The Brain closed his eyes in anticipation of the strike.

Instead, a surge of energy caused The Ram to drop his opponent involuntarily. All eyes turned to the source.

Standing in the doorway was Black Star. "Do I need a reservation for this party?" she playfully asked. Then getting deadly serious, the girl sent another energy blast into The Ram.

The other Bloods got back into the action. Forgetting the station employees, they concentrated on M-Force. The Brain and Black Star fought off the attackers as best they could, but were outnumbered and beginning to tire. Again it seemed as if the followers of the dark force would triumph.

But then, with a yell, the Bulldozer entered the fray. Crashing into a pair of Bloods, he knocked them senseless.

Meanwhile, two more had worked their way behind Talitha. One had a section of steel pipe and was about to bash her on the head. Before they could reach the unprepared girl, both stumbled over something unseen, falling hard to the ground. Black Star whirled around at the sound, realizing how close she'd come to serious injury, only to see a grinning Grey Man standing over the pair. Two swift karate kicks from him stunned them as well.

With M-Force now fully assembled, the odds were evened, yet the Bloods would still not back down. With Black star leading the way using energy blasts, and Grey Man, along with Bulldozer working together, they were turning the tide. There was a change in the attitude and confidence of the young heroes. Using his martial arts skills, Grey man was holding his own, causing an incredible feeling of redemption within the shy member. Meanwhile, Bulldozer was holding his ground, resisting the desire to go off on his own. They could now truly call themselves a team. The result for the Bloods was devastating.

Initially shocked by the boldness of the attack, Dak Leery hid from sight, hoping the Bloods would not see him. With the arrival of the other members of M-Force, the station personnel were left alone. His broadcaster's mind and sense of flare took over. Sneaking over to a control panel, he was able to see that the channel was still open and broadcasting. Leery grabbed a microphone, then began giving a commentary on what was happening like some play-by-play sports announcer. In particular, he eloquently described the individual powers M-Force was displaying. With the words flowing smoothly, it was an electrifying moment for him.

Throughout Kilings-Welch and into the wider area the station covered, people listening were transfixed by the drama. Some thought it was set up, but others realized they were participating in a rare moment of spontaneous drama, a once in a lifetime experience. Cell phone calls, text messages and pager announcements soon brought thousands of others into the WKW spectacle.

The police were slow to respond, unsure of how to act. Eventually, the tactical unit was brought in, formed up, and began to move up the stairs to the top of the building.

The Ram knew it was over. He was furious, and his rage called him to stay. But his cunning told him to get out while they still could, then seek another opportunity to overcome their nemesis.

Grabbing the cowering female broadcast assistant, he dragged her over to the floor to ceiling window in the booth. Smashing it, he dangled her with one arm outside. "Hey, do-gooders," he called out. "Let's see how heroic you are now!" Then he let her drop.

Black Star and The Brain immediately disengaged from the Bloods they were beating. Black Star was there in a millisecond, again using her speed. Putting out her hands, she caught the screaming woman tumbling down to the pavement below in an energy net. Straining to hold the girl in the air, the girl realized The Brain was now beside her. Using his powers of levitation, he raised the screaming assistant back to the broken window.

Bulldozer desperately wanted to go after The Ram. He saw the opponent he desperately wanted to face off with again gathering his minions and preparing to flee. Preparing to move to intercept them, he also saw Grey Man beginning to assist some of the station employees. Instead of leaving on his own, he joined his friend and began to help as well.

Back inside the building, the blond-haired girl was sobbing, clutching both The Brain and Black Star. By the time everything was settled down, The Ram and the rest of the Bloods has disappeared down the emergency steps, missing the SWAT officers who had come up the main staircase.

The black clad police burst into the broadcast area, automatic weapons at the ready.

"On the ground now!" they ordered, but no one moved. The tension mounted as both M-Force and the employees of WKW didn't know how to respond.

Lieutenant Nate DeBeer entered moments later with a second team. Realizing what was going on, he barked out, "Stand down, boys. These aren't the bad guys. Alpha team, sweep the floor for Bloods, Bravo team check the back stairs." Then, talking into his walkie-talkie, he reported, "Tac Lead to command. The Bloods are gone and everything is under control."

The muscular police officer removed his helmet, then ran a thick hand through his close-cropped brown hair. Looking at M-Force, he remembered how this odd group had saved his life and the life of his men recently. While those wounded were still recovering in hospital, they were at least alive. Uncertain what to do, he said instead, "We meet again."

The station manager stated decisively, "These people saved our lives," stepping between the police and M-Force for emphasis. "Leave them alone."

The leader of the tactical unit shook his head at the unusual display of loyalty, and chuckled, "Relax. It's okay, they've helped us too."

The Brain wasn't sure what to do either. He was still breathing heavy from the exertion of the fight. Plus, with the adrenaline from saving the young lady still coursing through his veins, he had trouble thinking. There would be no slipping away into the fog this time. In a way, they were trapped. He hadn't thought of this contingency. What could they do?

It was Grey Man that instead stepped forward, bringing things into focus. Boldly he asked the SWAT officer, "So what happens now?"

The lieutenant chuckled again, replying, "I'm not sure, but I've got an idea." Grabbing his walkie-talkie once more he said, "This is DeBeer, get me a patch through to Deputy Chief Gonzalez."

Ten minutes later a plan was in place. The SWAT team had found nothing but destruction on the floor, so re-formed to leave. As M-Force left the broadcast area, Dak Leery called out, "Hey, guys, pretty awesome powers! Thanks for the great interview, Brain! We'll have to do it again sometime."

The leader of M-Force shot back to the DJ, "Anytime!"

The Brain did a quick survey of the surroundings, processing the memories of what had happened. One chapter in their journey seemed to end in the broadcast booth and another was beginning. He still didn't know where it would all end, but the new emotion of quiet pride felt great. They'd shown they were here to stay. No, he didn't know what the future held but was excited by the prospect.

Riding down the elevator to the lobby, they chatted with the lieutenant, asking about his wounded men, unsure of what they would find on the ground floor. The lobby was deserted, but as they moved toward the revolving doors into the building they could see the street out front was blocked off and filled with people. TV cameras were evident, as were photographers.

M-Force headed to the steps of the building, becoming overwhelmed by what they saw. Flanked by armor clad tactical officers, the spontaneous pose they struck was like something out of a movie.

The crowd exploded in response to their new heroes. "*Yea, M-Force*!" was the roar. The four were stunned by the response. Police had to hold the crowd back from surging toward the team. They stopped dead in their tracks, unsure of how to deal with the outpouring of affection. Suddenly shy, and acutely aware of the attention they were receiving, the foursome stood like deer in the headlights of an oncoming vehicle.

Lieutenant DeBeer could see how uneasy M-Force was. The contrast struck him like a hammer on the head. There was no doubt this brave group was powerful, yet they possessed a naïve innocence that made them even more charming. Kilings-Welch needed M-Force he decided, and he would do what he could to help. Things needed to change. Maybe these were the ones to do it.

Moving over to the group, the tough police officer said, "The people love you guys." Then, with eyes welling up with tears, he added, "So do I."

That broke the ice. M-Force waved to the crowd, bringing a cry of approval. They then went to the people shaking hands, high-fiving, connecting with a community desperate for something to believe in.

Lola Karan watched a live feed of the spectacle on the television in her shop. The attractive designer could not help but smile at the scene. She thought of the publicity she could get and money she could make by selling her story, letting people know Lola Karan was the "exclusive designer" of M-Force would finally put her on the map.

Yet, there was an innocent delight in watching the foursome interact with the crowd. She thought back with affection on her times with the group and hoped to see them again. No, this was not about cashing in. This was about something deeper, about a cause bigger than self. This was about character.

No, she would keep the secret. In doing so, something began to change in the jaded woman. The hardness of her heart began to melt. In the end, she received something far more valuable than a monetary reward. She was filled with an almost overwhelming joy. *The uniforms did look good though*, she thought.

Chapter 20
Progress on Several Fronts

The celebration in front of the Midland Bank Building went on for longer than the four young crime fighters expected. There was a releasing of emotion and a purging of tension by the people of the area, with the young crime fighters the focal point. While danger arises from an attitude of indifference, there is a separate challenge with putting people up on an unrealistic pedestal. M-Force was not mature enough to see the shift, instead soaking up the attention of the crowd.

After M-Force had their moment of fame with the enthusiastic crowd, it was time to move. Lieutenant DeBeer led them to one of the black SWAT trucks, then they drove off with a police escort. A number of vehicles attempted to follow them, but were discouraged by the heavy law enforcement presence.

Finally able to shake the pursuers, they traveled to a secluded parking lot in Victory Park. Passing a police cordon, the entourage drove in. There was a single beige sedan in the parking lot with a lone figure standing beside it. The tactical unit stopped and the four members of M-Force got out to meet their reception committee.

Deputy Chief Santiago Gonzalez was a success story in his own right. A career police officer, his ambition was to be chief of a large metropolitan force some day.

He'd been born in the poor slums of Mexico City, then later moved to California as an illegal immigrant whose parents picked fruit. The door of opportunity had opened when he gained U.S. citizenship through an amnesty program.

The young boy became singularly ambitious throughout high school, then after earning a degree in psychology at UCLA, joined the LAPD. The enthusiastic police officer worked hard there, becoming an outspoken opponent of racism and discrimination. Officer Gonzalez gained not only notice, but also notoriety through his efforts. Yet, despite all society's progress, it was still hard for a Hispanic to get promoted.

Stuck at the rank of lieutenant, he found he needed to move twice to other cities in order to get to his current rank. Finally, the hard-working man ended up in Kilings-Welch. The experience had left him somewhat cynical and a bit jaded. On the surface, though, he was a handsome, late forties professional. With dark, slicked back hair and stylish goatee, he looked every part the success he was.

Sizing up the four costumed figures being led toward him by the SWAT commander, he couldn't believe he'd agreed to the meeting. Yet something intrigued him about this enigmatic group.

"Deputy Chief Gonzalez, this is M-Force," Nate DeBeer introduced.

He nodded in acknowledgment, but didn't say anything initially. Doubting what the tactical leader had proposed, he responded, "May I have a word with you, Lieutenant?"

The two went out of earshot to begin a conversation.

"Well, that doesn't look too good," Bulldozer commented.

"Just wait," The Brain said. "Let the guy get his bearings. This is definitely going to require some out of the box thinking."

Santiago Gonzalez was a forward thinker. Not one to rest on convention, this situation was even a bit much for him. Wanting to ensure he understood the proposal, he cautiously asked his subordinate, "Just so we're on the same page, explain to me again what you think should be done."

"I know this sounds crazy, sir," DeBeer replied confidently, "but think about it. M-Force has helped us out of more than one jam. Why not work with them instead of against them? They're on our side."

"There's no way we could deputize them. We'd be laughing stocks, let alone lose our credibility as enforcers of the law."

"No, that's not what I mean. Instead, we have a working relationship and mutual co-operation. We share information and work with them when necessary. Also, I think we should use these kids for PR as well. The people love them, and they could help with our image."

Gonzalez was about to ask about liability issues, but checked the thought. He was already tired of insurance companies running the world. The idea was beginning to gel in his mind. "Okay, so if I did buy into this and agreed to sell it to the chief, we'd need a liaison officer to interact with them. Any idea who that would be?"

DeBeer smiled in response, causing the Deputy Chief to laugh. "You got all the angles covered don't you, Lieutenant?"

"I wouldn't be a good tactical commander if I didn't."

"All right. You've convinced me," Gonzalez said. "Let's go talk to these guys and see what they think."

The two law enforcement officers rejoined M-Force. They had an animated conversation about the proposal. Gonzalez was surprised at how articulate and well spoken the members were. Though their identities were hidden, it was obvious these were likely a group of teenagers. The more he spoke with them, the more comfortable he became with the idea. It was time for them to pool their resources and stop this threat.

After the meeting concluded, the team was driven back to the Equalizer in the tactical truck. Saying goodbye tp Lieutenant DeBeer and the other SWAT officers, a satisfied M-Force piled into the van and drove off. None noticed a figure hidden nearby observing the whole scene.

Back at the Blood Lord's hideout, the leader of the criminal gang was in a fury. He was raging against the latest developments. In particular, the leader was incensed at the negative publicity his gang had received during the battle at the radio station. This could only help but bolster the confidence of an area he was trying to bring to its knees. A new lesson was needed to show the city who was in charge.

"I'm tired of these clowns interfering with my plans. I want them found and eliminated at once," the Blood Lord screamed.

The Ram wanted to suggest that their leader actually go out and do something himself rather than make others do it for him. But the pragmatic powerhouse realized that wasn't going to help. The grappler was steadily climbing the ranks of this group and had ambitions beyond where he stood. Just like wrestling a tough opponent, this took tactics and patience. He saw his objective, so was willing to wait for the opportunity.

Several Bloods entered into the main area, then whispered to one of the leaders. The Blood Lord ignored the exchange, continuing his outburst.

The one who received the report was tired of the rapid ascension of The

Ram. He didn't like the fact that the other was the favorite of their leader, a position he sought. Seeing the opportunity to change the situation, the man boldly stepped forward, interrupting the volcanic leader. "Excuse me, my lord, but we have some information for you. I had several of our men staking the building out after everything happened. One caught sight of M-Force returning and saw their vehicle. It was a Heritage Heating van. He also got the license plate number."

"Well done," the Blood Lord enthusiastically said, "that was excellent thinking. Boot up the computer."

The Ram sat in silent rage at what he perceived was the other's blatant attempt to usurp him. That was okay, he could deal with more than M-Force as well.

Professor Oliver Little sat quietly at his desk fiddling unconsciously with the lapels on the tweed sports jacket he wore underneath his white lab coat. The usually active scientist instead was deep in thought. Then, closing the laptop computer he'd been working on, he turned to his assistant. "George," he began, "I want to apologize for something. I've been overly hard on you and that's wrong. You've been an excellent assistant, and if you want to stay on once classes start I'd be happy to have you."

George was overjoyed at the offer. "I'd love to stay," he enthusiastically responded, not needing to think of his reply.

The professor seemed pleased by the answer and relaxed a little. Changing the subject, he asked, "So what do you think of M-Force?"

The youth turned pale at the mention, stumbling through a response.

The trained observer could not help but notice the change in his assistant. "For my part, I think what they're doing is admirable. I also agree with their leader that the problem of the Bloods is only an indication of a broader problem."

Then an interesting thought entered the analytical mind. Looking right at George, he added, "Their leader seems to be unusually intelligent. He also seems very young. It's a curious combination, don't you think, Mr. Alexander?"

Again George was on the spot. Stumbling to find words, all he could say was, "Ah...well...I haven't really given it a lot of thought to be quite honest."

The shaggy haired academic looked intently at the young man for several minutes, not saying a word. George was terrified the professor had figured him out. Anxiety grew. The professor had a thought, but would not articulate it. The idea seemed too preposterous. This needed more consideration. Instead of talking further on the subject, he stated, "We're meeting some guests this afternoon, Mr. Alexander. I think you'll find them quite fascinating."

The leader of the Bloods loomed over his computer operator, waiting for a reply. An expert hacker, he'd been able to tap into the State Department of Transportation database in order to obtain license plate information. Bringing up that particular part of the database, he then punched in the license information that had been given. A puzzled look crossed the face of the bespectacled hacker who then re-entered the information.

"What's the problem?" the Blood Lord impatiently demanded.

Fearful of the wrath of his employer, the computer expert hesitantly stated, "It's coming up as a negative match. They must have written down the wrong plate number."

Whirling over to the one who had provided the information, he challenged, "So?" raising his hand as if to strike.

Rather than cower in anticipation of the blow, the tattooed, yet mature man in his twenties stood his ground. "No way," he vigorously stated, "it was copied down exactly."

"Well, then what's the problem? Why doesn't it come up?"

The Blood thought about it for a minute. On a hunch, he grabbed a nearby phone book. Obtaining the information he required, the man flipped open his cell phone and dialed.

"Heritage Heating."

"Good afternoon," the criminal said politely, mimicking an elderly voice. "I don't want to be a bother, but I wanted to report one of your vans driving recklessly today."

The voice on the other end became concerned, so asked, "Would you be able to give me the license plate or vehicle number?"

The Blood related the number they had discovered, then waited for a reply. There was a long pause until the person on the other end of the line asked, "Are you sure that was the number? We don't have any vehicles with a tag even close to that one. Perhaps you got our van mixed up with one from another company."

"Thank you for your help. I'm sorry to have bothered you." After hanging up, the thug looked at their leader and said in his normal voice, "They're using a phony plate."

The Blood Lord screamed in frustration. They still were no closer to the information they needed. He would need to consider their options and come up with a solution.

Dr. Little had asked George to come along with him to a meeting he was going to. Few other details were given, but instead of staying in the learned professor's office, they had left, going to another part of the university. George's heart began to pound as they walked through the campus to what more and more seemed like a particular destination of interest. Travelling to the northern part of the school, they seemed to be heading in a direction that was almost a dream come true. In a few seemingly long minutes the youth's thoughts were confirmed. They were heading to the restricted building the Blood Lord had attacked, and he so desperately wanted to find out what it held.

The armed guard at the gate first checked the professor's ID, then the assistant's. George was surprised to find he was already on the approved list for entry.

His boss guessed the thought and stated in his English accent, "I knew that if you were to stay with me eventually we'd end up here, so I went ahead and got you clearance. You see, some of my research is actually tied in with had happens at this facility."

There was an intense, strange look of curiosity on the young assistant's face, but he said nothing. Little noted it, and added, "They do a lot of space and space system research here mainly for the government. There, you now know State's wee secret."

George was happy to be acquainted with the information, but it still didn't answer the question of why the Blood Lord was interested in this particular building.

Walking through the hallway, the teen was having flashbacks of their fight against the criminal mastermind's gang at the facility a few short weeks ago. Any signs of the violence that had taken place were removed, so someone coming in would have never known what a desperate fight had taken place.

The secret leader of M-Force thought about their first contact with Lieutenant DeBeer and how the SWAT team leader now seemed to be a big supporter. The tacit endorsement of the Deputy Chief would be very helpful in their work as well. While T.T. Tomlinson and *The Recorder* was still a thorn in their flesh, his influence thankfully was waning.

After the battle at the radio station, the newspaper editor again decried M-Force for their "interference" in the affairs of the area. He called for them to be disbanded. But, increasingly, his was a voice that was becoming isolated.

The radio coverage of the battle at WKW had been syndicated and sent throughout the country. The other media outlets were now desperate to have the team interact in hopes of generating similar excitement, while general public opinion was upbeat.

"George…George?"

The accented voice of Professor Little snapped the youth out of his thoughts. Before him were two distinctly different looking middle-aged men in white lab coats.

"I'd like to introduce you to these gentlemen. They are from NASA and are here to check on the progress of research going on here," Little explained. "As with the research you help me with, I have to tell you again how confidential this is. Do you understand?"

George nodded in agreement.

"Excellent. Let me introduce then you to Dr. Larry Storm, a senior researcher, and Eric Brunner who is a program manager at Cape Canaveral."

They all shook hands, and Storm said to George, "Ollie says you've really helped him with elements of his space research. It's good to see a young man with such confidence and interest in these things."

George was flattered by the recognition. "I try to do what I can. I'm just happy to be able to work with Dr. Little," he humbly added.

The leader of M-Force observed that while Dr. Storm seemed to fit his role, Brunner appeared out of place. He looked tougher than a program manager should. There was something about him that made the youth believe the man could handle himself in a fight. Also, the heavyset man's eyes had a penetrating feature that seemed more intent on sweeping up information then guiding a project. Putting the uneasy thought out of his head, he concentrated on the conversation.

But all the while there was something vaguely familiar about the intense executive. It was as if they'd met before. Then it hit him like a brick. The man called Brunner had been at Great Pine State Park as part of the investigation when the meteorite landed. In fact, he seemed to have been in charge. *What could he be doing here and what does he want?* George thought apprehensively to himself.

After a brief discussion, Brunner, who seemed to be the leader of the pair, punched a series of numbers into the keypad beside a door leading into another chamber. With a hiss, the magnetically sealed door opened.

"We do a variety of space related research at this facility and most of it is funded by NASA," Professor Little explained to George. "Recently, though, we've been looking at an interesting object. NASA and the federal government were good enough to allow us to take possession of it to see what we can learn."

The party entered the chamber. The room was a research lab. It was extremely clean, almost everything, including the equipment, was colored white. Giving it an almost futuristic look, the colorless room found contrast through a set of polished stainless steel furniture.

Each new arriver immediately observed that prominently in the center of the room, in a sealed container was...

The meteorite! George thought to himself in shock. It was the same one he had been exposed to causing his mutation and that of the others. The connection smacked him like a hammer as he stared dumbfounded at it.

George caught Brunner looking inquisitively at him, so he tried to check his surprise. Nonchalantly, the youth asked, "Why is this particular one of interest?"

"Because it had a collision in space with a man-made object, changing its trajectory," Dr. Storm answered. "That incident not only caused us to delay a space shuttle launch, but also brought it to earth. We're researching the results of the crash and its impact on the environment."

The youth nodded his head in understanding. On the surface he appeared calm, but underneath his heart was racing. *This was no ordinary meteorite,* he thought to himself. Then the connection was made, like a high-speed download. *The Blood Lord had been after this! He had to have been.* The revelation was exciting to the youth. Then, the next natural question was, *But why and how did he know about it?* Something else was trying to make a connection in his mind, but this one was more like a dial-up connection that was having trouble linking up. The pieces were still trying to join together.

The group examined some readouts and data on the meteorite, then discussed a few different scenarios. After a half-hour the meeting ended, so George and the professor left the high-security lab to return to their own work.

Once the pair from State University had left, the two men from NASA sat down to talk.

"What do you think?" Brunner asked.

"I'm not sure," the scientist responded. "I'd like to get some readings off the kid, but how?"

"Good catch, Larry, on connecting Little and the kid," the program manager congratulated his colleague.

The researcher replied, "It wasn't hard. I knew this area was a priority for us. So I kept an eye on the reports coming out of the academic community here. When I saw this kid's name come up, I made the match."

The bald executive said, "Well, it's the first thing we have to go on. It's pretty thin, but a starting point."

"Was it wise to tell the kid about the meteorite?" Storm queried.

"I think he knows more than he's letting on," Brunner answered. "No, we need to flesh this story out, and the only way to do that is shaking the bushes a bit."

Storm suggested, "We could bring Little into the picture."

"Absolutely not!" Brunner ordered. "This has national security implications. No one finds out why we're really here. Now, if you'll excuse me, I have a call to make."

The doctor went to speak to the other researchers in the room, allowing his colleague the privacy he'd requested. Brunner flipped open his phone and punched in a number from memory. "I'm in and have made contact," he reported.

Eric Brunner had left out several key pieces of information in his discussion with the pair from State University. He had failed to share that the meteorite had collided in space with an old Soviet satellite. Further research, and a little help from some operatives in the Russian government, had discovered the piece of space junk was actually a failed attempt by the former communist regime at a space weapons program. The satellite was to have been a weapon and, as such, was equipped in that fashion. Also, the environmental impact he'd mentioned to George was on the human environment. That information was "need to know" and this youth didn't need to know.

There was also a bit of personal information on the man that even Dr. Storm didn't know. Brunner not only worked for NASA, but, more importantly, he doubled as a CIA agent. Though skilled in the space field, his first duty was with the Agency. While not a sleeper agent in the sense that he was inactive waiting for a specific call, his cover was deep.

Primarily, the man was tasked with keeping an eye on NASA for any spying going on there. But his position also allowed him to travel around the world on space-related business, thus having a more active role. As a result, he was regularly able to participate in covert operations for the CIA as well. Therefore, as a field agent, he also was part of the national security group. The bald, non-descript, though powerfully built man was, in fact, an important agent in the spy community.

The program manager had seen the reports on the news about the strange things going on in Kilings-Welch this summer. He'd heard of a shadowy crime lord, but his interest was perked up when found out about this group called M-Force that seemed to possess superhuman powers. There could be no coincidence that this had happened after the crash of the meteorite he had originally checked. From then on the area was his priority assignment.

After the report on the WKW incident, he'd immediately flown with his researcher to the area to investigate. *There has to be a connection,* the CIA agent thought to himself, *but what is it?*

Brunner opened his dossier to the list of students that had been examined in the impact area of the meteor. The name George Alexander was prominent on the list. He'd need to keep an eye on this one since he had a hunch there was more to this youth than met the eye.

While the Blood Lord raged at his followers about their incompetence, Keith Ramsey was on a different track. He had downloaded the WKW interview from their website onto his ipod and was listening to it intently. There was something about the leader of M-Force that was not sitting right with him.

There were two different facets of the brute's life trying to link up, but they seemed so outrageous his arrogance wouldn't allow them to gel together. He listened angrily to the confidence of the leader of this group who dared to defy them. But then, as if a cloud momentarily opened to reveal the sun, a thought hit him. The name and the voice; there was something to it. *The Brain... The Brain,* the aggressive youth kept rolling around the name around in his mind, seeking a connection.

Then it all clicked. With a smile of satisfaction, he went to see the Blood Lord.

Chapter 21
Point of Intersection

After the anxiety of the questions from Dr. Little and tension of seeing the meteorite, George began to settle down and think. While he was concerned about confrontation with Dr. Little, he knew he could deflect any inquiry. Instead, meeting Eric Brunner unsettled him. He didn't like the way the NASA man had looked at him. There was something about the bureaucrat that didn't make sense. Unfortunately, the agitation of seeing the object that had so dramatically altered his life kept him from thinking clearly. Looking at his watch, he knew he had to meet the others at headquarters. For the time being the thought was shelved.

Tim and Beau were walking together, reflecting on the last few days.

"Wasn't that awesome how all those people were there at the radio station cheering for us?" Tim exclaimed.

"Yea," Beau agreed, "it was pretty cool. It's hard to believe how things are turning out. Now, with the police on our side, we really can make a difference."

Tim looked whimsically, "That is all good news, but it's a drag sometimes to stay hidden. I mean, there were some pretty cute girls in the crowd. I bet even you wouldn't have a problem getting a date if people knew." Then he became frustrated. "I don't know why we have to sneak around like this. What would be the big deal if people knew?

Beau became serious, "No way, Tim! Think about it. We'd lose our freedom. We wouldn't be able to move around without attracting attention.

Plus, our enemies might come after our families. No, there's no way we could go public with our identities."

"You're right," Tim agreed, though downcast at the thought. "It's just too bad we have to stay anonymous."

Then something caught the eye of the young football player. They could see several youths breaking into a home. With a twinkle in his eye, he said to Beau, "Let's get in some exercise."

His friend replied, "I'm right behind you!"

The pair slipped into a clump of bushes, changed quickly into the costumes each carried in backpacks and sprung into action. They moved silently to the home, then found the point of entry. Grey Man went invisible and entered in. He circled behind the gang that was ransacking the home, then became visible. The young burglars were so startled they ran for their place of original entry. Unfortunately for them, they ran into a brick wall called the Bulldozer.

"Sorry, boys, your shopping spree is over," he said. "I think you need to take a break and catch your breath." With that the Bulldozer slammed into the trio, knocking them sprawling. Grey Man was there with some rope he'd found to tie them tightly up.

"Well, that was fun," Bulldozer observed.

Grey Man agreed, "Yea, it was. Let's call it in."

Taking out a phone, he called a special number they had been given by Lieutenant DeBeer to report their activity. After giving the dispatcher the information and location, they waited for the police to arrive. Several people in the neighborhood had heard the commotion, so they came over to investigate. Seeing two members of M-Force set off a frenzy of excitement.

Two police cruisers showed up within minutes, and the officers took the burglars into custody. The pair from M-Force was enjoying their congratulations when a scream broke the revelry. Leaving the prisoners with two of the officers, Bulldozer and Grey Man rushed over to where the sound had originated, followed by the other police. They found several doors down a woman sitting on her front porch. She was crying while holding a handkerchief to a bleeding nose. The two young members of M-Force didn't know what to do, so the police officers stepped forward and began to question the woman.

The middle age woman reported that she'd been watching the activity down the road when suddenly two young men came out of nowhere. First, they robbed her of a purse and jewelry, then when she tried to resist one had punched her in the nose. Afterward, they had snuck away in the opposite direction of where the activity was going on. Regaining her composure, the woman's tone suddenly turned to one of anger. Grabbing Bulldozer by the costume, she demanded, "Why didn't you guys stop them? Why did I have to get robbed when you were around?"

Bulldozer had no clue of what to do. He stammered that they didn't know anything was happening at her home, then apologized for what had gone on.

The woman continued her offensive. "What were you guys doing?" she complained. "While you were showing off over there, I get robbed and beat up. What good are you guys if you won't do your job?"

The pair of police officers looked away sheepishly at the verbal assault, happy it wasn't directed at them.

Then she made a comment that cut deeply. "You know, T.T. Tomlinson is right. You guys are no good. We'd be better off without you. Why don't you just get lost?"

While the police officers tried to get some information from the woman, as well as calm her down, Bulldozer and Grey Man were dumbfounded by the accusations. Instead of basking in their moment of triumph, they slunk away in embarrassment.

Talitha walked alone to headquarters, contemplating what had happening in her life lately. While the events at WKW had been exciting and the response afterward a bit overwhelming, there was something else on her mind. When would this end with the Blood Lord? In a few weeks, summer would be over and school beginning. She was looking forward to becoming a freshman at State University and the others would be doing their own thing as well. Could they go to school and maintain their presence as M-Force?

Despite the very practical question, she was satisfied with the acceptance they were getting in the community. Talitha had read the articles and heard the interviews with people praising their actions. Admittedly, it felt good to be, not only recognized, but also affirmed for what they were doing. The compassionate girl had even seen Tommy and he was doing well. Life seemed to be finally shining on her. She was happy.

Lola looked at the wedding dress that had just been completed with satisfaction. For some strange reason during the last month or so her design work and sewing had improved. The quality of product had noticeably increased as well, with the effect that more business had come in. The designer was almost to the point where she couldn't handle the work and would need help. A smile of satisfaction crossed her attractive face at the thought.

Her eyes drifted to the picture of M-Force on the wall she'd clipped from the newspaper. Things had changed since she'd met the group of remarkable teens. A joyful spirit had been resurrected, and for the first time in years she had an optimistic view of the future.

"You look beautiful, Lola."

The designer let out a gasp of surprise at the sound of the deep bass voice. Standing before her was Ulysses Hammerman.

"How did you get in here without me knowing?" she asked with apprehension.

"I'm a man of many talents," her former boyfriend answered. "I'd like you to let me show you all I can do. That may change your opinion of me." His thoughts seemed to drift. "I know in the past I didn't have much to offer you. An ordinary teacher in some hick town is not much to recommend a man to a woman of your background. But there's more to me than you know." Then he followed her gaze to the picture of M-Force on the wall. As quickly as his thoughts had drifted, they came back into sharp focus. "M-Force really is a remarkable group, aren't they?"

She made no reply. Fear was instinctively creeping into her mind and she didn't know what to do.

"I've seen them up close...know them in a way, though I wouldn't call them friends. But I, like so many others, wonder who they are. Then I look at their costumes and think, 'who else but Lola could make something so elegant?'"

Suddenly his even tone turned harsh. Grabbing her savagely by the arm, he demanded, "Who are they, Lola? I know you made their costumes. Who are they?" he screamed.

"Ow, you're hurting me. Why are you doing this, Ulysses?"

Face red with rage, he shouted, "You're not answering my question! I want to know who M-Force is!"

"I don't know," she honestly answered, then finding a vein of courage defiantly added, "and even if I did, I wouldn't tell you."

Hammerman calmed down, his face returning to normal, though he didn't relax his grip. He gave the woman a long stare, as if measuring something. She was transfixed by the gaze, frozen in time.

Finally he said, "So be it." Without emotion or feeling, he added, "If you will not embrace me by one name, then you will bow to me by another." Without another word he swatted her on the head like a fly, causing the woman to sink into unconsciousness.

The members of M-Force gathered to, not only review events of late, but to look at the future too. While Talitha was upbeat, the two younger boys were a bit down from their incident on the way to the meeting. George tried to listen intently to the others chat away, but he seemed distracted. Once the others had spoken, their leader finally shared with them his thoughts.

"I saw the meteorite," George quietly reported.

"What?" Talitha exclaimed.

"In fact, I saw it in the building the Blood Lord attacked on campus. It turns out the place is some sort of secret space research facility. I'm not sure when they brought the meteorite there, but I saw it."

"But you saw the meteorite?" she confirmed. "It's still in the area?"

George nodded his head in acknowledgment, sending a shudder up the spines of the others. The other teens involuntarily shivered at the thought of the item that had so dramatically altered their lives. The room fell silent for a few minutes as the group pondering the implications of the statement.

Talitha finally broke the quiet. "That must have been what the Blood Lord was after. But how did he know about it and why does he want it?"

"I don't know," George answered candidly, a tinge of frustration in his voice. "There also were a couple of guys from NASA at the lab to look at it as well. One of them gave me a real weird feeling." The leader of the team then added, "There's something going on here, but I just can't put my finger on it."

Each member of M-Force again went into silent thought, pondering what was going on. The air seemed thick with anticipation of what it all meant. The near trance-like state was shattered by the sound of George's phone ringing. Startled out of his thoughts, he answered.

"This is Nate DeBeer. We have a situation we need your help with."

The Bloods were not subtle in their approach this time. A number of vans pulled up to the curb in downtown Kilings, revealing them to be filled with the gang. Brazenly, the hoods entered several banks and jewelry stores, beginning to take what they wanted. But this time they were not alone. The final members who stepped out of the vehicles were The Ram and the Blood Lord himself.

Instead of participating in the robberies, they waited for the response. In less that two minutes a pair of squad cars came roaring up to the scene with sirens blaring. The first was knocked over like a tin can by an energy blast from the Blood Lord, stunning the occupants. The Ram, his head protrusion prominent, battered the other, knocking the police officers inside around like rag dolls.

The pair was satisfied they'd made their presence felt and would not likely be opposed for some time. The Blood Lord signaled for the others to join him. His objective was the Recorder Building, home of the newspaper that bore its name. While a contingent of armed Bloods stood guard outside, the others went in. There was no petty thievery or destruction this time. Instead, the contingent moved steadily to the upper floor to find their objective.

While T.T. Tomlinson could be accused of many things, being a coward was not one of them. Receiving a warning call of the Blood Lord's entry, he resisted the entreaties of his personal assistant to flee the scene while it was still possible. Part of it was defiance, but another part was his journalist's curiosity to find out what was going on. Within minutes, the Blood Lord, flanked by The Ram and several other Bloods burst into his opulent office.

Tomlinson boldly stood his ground. But the true mood of the man was displayed by the visibly shaking knees at the formidable sight of the tall, cloaked figure before him.

The Blood Lord strode over and, in his distorted voice, said, "Mr. Tomlinson, it is a pleasure to finally meet you. Long have I desired this opportunity. I would like to sit and discuss with you several of the errors in your paper, but, sadly, time does not allow. Instead I come on a matter of business."

Picking up a sculpture and examining it closely, the crime lord seemed to be lost in himself for a moment. Then, carefully replacing the delicate item on the desk, he made his demand. "At the university in a secret research lab, the same one I visited several weeks ago I might add, is a certain item. It's a meteorite. I want it and I want it delivered to me. You will take my demand to the necessary authorities."

"I'm nobody's messenger boy." Tomlinson spontaneously retorted.

"Oh, but I insist," the Blood Lord replied. To emphasize his point he raised his hand and sent a burst of energy that brought the man painfully to his knees.

Gasping for air, the newspaper publisher could only say, "Okay. Whatever you want."

"Excellent. I knew you'd see it my way. Now ensure the message is promptly delivered and I might even have a story for you."

"But what if they don't?" Tomlinson stammered. "Well, let us say they don't want to take that option."

"That would be a mistake with severe consequences."

To emphasize his point, the crime leader went over to the large office window overlooking the main street. With a wave of his hand, the glass exploded outward, letting the warm summer air in. Taking a few more steps to the broken window, he then lifted his arms and looked across the street. Raising them higher in the air, the lights began to flicker as if the power was being drained from the room. Bringing his hands together, a visible pulse wave of energy exploded from the Blood Lord, directed at the building across the street. As if hit by a bomb, the upper story of the building collapsed onto the floor it sat on, showering the street below with debris.

Tomlinson stood in stunned silence, his mouth open at the display of power. The Blood Lord looked at him, ensuring he had the man's attention. Confident his point had been made, he stated, "I want the meteorite delivered to a place of my choosing within forty-eight hours. Twenty-four hours from now I will call you and tell you where that is. If it is not delivered, or if anyone tries to interfere, I take this town apart."

Signaling to The Ram, then the others, the Blood Lord and his followers left the publisher's large office. Moving at a leisurely pace, they left the Recorder building and returned to their vehicles. Passing through the lobby and onto the street, the gang was surprised by the sight greeting them.

Standing in the middle of the street were four lone figures blocking the way. The Bloods left on guard were either unconscious and tied up, or had run away. M-Force had arrived.

Though his face could not been seen, the Blood Lord took a stance that showed irritation toward his followers. The few that remained with him were unsure how to proceed, seeing the state of their colleagues.

One member of M-Force stepped forward to confront the threat to the region. It was their leader. The Brain confidently called out, "It's over, Blood Lord. Give up and come in quietly."

The laughter that came in response to the challenge from the shrouded figure echoed up and down the street. "You young whelps have interfered in my plans for the last time," he dryly responded.

"Oh really?" The Brain questioned. "We'll see."

He moved closer, then levitated a garbage bin, directing it toward his target. The Blood Lord raised a hand and seemed to catch the flying object in the air. Then, raising his fingers in the air, the criminal boss sent the item spinning back toward where it had originally come from. It happened so fast that The Brain had no time to respond. The can slammed into him, knocking the leader of M-Force to the pavement.

"My turn!" Bulldozer shouted and charged forward.

Again, extending one hand only, the Blood Lord caught the charging attacker in mid-stride with an energy blast. The force of it caused the strong youth to be pushed right off his feet and sent flying back until he crashed into the brick wall of a store across the street.

"Wait guys!" Black Star called out in desperation. "We need to work together."

But Grey Man had already disappeared and she was standing alone. The girl could see he had reappeared to the rear of the Blood Lord, about to strike. But The Ram was there to instead grab the youth and toss him helter-skelter away

Bulldozer was up again. Another stronger burst of energy sent him smashing once more into the wall, causing bricks to crumble and break.

Grey Man was on his hands and knees, trying to recover from the force of the toss he'd endured. But, instead, The Ram strode over, dealing the prone youth several swift kicks in succession to his midsection. The force was such that it caused him to flip over onto his back. The youth lay motionless.

The Brain could see how badly things were going, so he tried to counterattack. His head was foggy, though, due to the force of the initial shot he'd taken. Nonetheless, he attempted to levitate and throw a mailbox. Derisive laughter echoed down the street from his opponent as the object was sent back at him. This time the intelligent youth anticipated the move, so was able to get out of the way. But the youth wasn't prepared for the fact that the Blood Lord raised his other hand and sent an energy blast directly toward him. It caught The Brain squarely in the chest, knocking him head over heels. The attacker then swept his hand toward a light fixture beside the street, causing it to snap in half. The heavy metal pole fell toward the prone figure, threatening to crush him. But, before impact, it was caught in mid-air, hanging instead above him.

Black Star had witnessed the scene and as the pole came falling toward her friend was able to put out an energy shield to protect him. But, right as the girl pushed it away from her colleague, she herself was smashed hard and knocked sprawling to the pavement.

The Ram had been looking for an objective, so seeing the lone remaining figure of the crime fighting team standing, had charged after her, catching the girl off guard. Black Star, for her part, had needed to intently concentrate to save her friend, so did not see the attack coming on. She lay there, grimacing in pain.

The successful attacker came over to see what state the fallen Black Star was in. "Sorry, sweetheart," the grinning figure said, looking down at her. "Ladies first."

No member of M-Force was left standing. They had been defeated.

The Blood Lord surveyed the scene with unbridled enthusiasm. He'd faced the last serious threat and easily overcome it. The city was his. He could see a crowd of people a distance away that had watched the drama unfold before them. It would be simple to crush the life out of those who had dared defy him. Instead, he preferred the pleasure of crushing their spirit through this act of humiliation. Moving into the middle of the street, he called out, "M-Force? Ha! M-Farce is more like it."

Satisfied his work was done, the crime boss knew it was time to leave. The police in view retreated, leaving him alone to free his captured followers and load up into the van their stolen goods at leisure.

The Ram stood over the prostrate form of The Brain. With one foot, he pressed down on the youth like one would squash a bug. Removing his mask the wicked grin of Keith Ramsey was revealed. The Brain was shocked by the discovery, but didn't have time to think about it.

"Hello, George," Ramsey said. He laughed at the visible shock evident in his defeated opponent at the realization of recognition. Then his merry mood turned serious. "I better not see you or any of these other losers anymore. Just disappear, or retire. I don't care. If I do see you again, the next time none of you walk away from this alive. That also goes for your family, too. The only reason I'm letting you go now is for all your fans to see what a true champion is. See ya."

Tears welled up in George's eyes. They were not tears of pain though. Rather it was the realization of discovery. Now what could they do?

Chapter 22
Decisions

The Blood Lord and his crew left unmolested from the downtown area. Afterward, stunned observers of the earlier mayhem began to filter back into the zone of destruction. In response, a feeble attempt was made by the police to cordon off the area to keep that from happening. But they too were in a state of shock at what had happened, so enforced it with little vigor.

None of M-Force was seriously hurt. They gathered together to take stock. No one could make eye contact with any of the others, let alone look at the crowd that had gathered. Silence hung over the onlookers like a dark mist matching the storm clouds that a growing wind had brought in to blanket the city.

There was no repetition of the outpouring of emotion as there had been at WKW. No one cheered or cried out for autographs. This time the people were mutely staggered over what they had just witnessed. The incredible power of the Blood Lord and the failure of M-Force to stop him were a sobering combination.

The Brain looked around. The words of The Ram were still echoing in his ears. Knowing this was not the place to reveal his news, nor were any of the others prepared to hear it, he ordered, "Let's get out of here."

The others stiffly responded, as shocked as the crowd by the turn of events. The four teens slunk away. This time no one followed after them.

Back at headquarters, it was time to share the bad news.

"The Ram is Keith Ramsey," George reported.

"What?" Talitha gasped in disbelief. "You can't be right."

"I am. He took off his mask to show me. He also knows who I am."

Talitha turned white at the news, "No. He can't."

"He does. He also said if we don't quit that he'll go after not only us, but my family."

"What are we going to do?" Tim blurted out, the first hint of fear in his voice that any had ever heard.

"I don't know. I'll need to think about this," George answered despondently. But then he changed focus, saying, "Does it even matter? I mean, can we even do anything to stop this madman? We did our best, but he took us apart. Should we just give up? Would our sticking with it even make a difference?"

"It has to," Talitha desperately declared. "Look at everything we've done so far."

"Sure, but if we can't take the Blood Lord, then what's the point?"

"Well, let's look at what happened this afternoon," she said.

"We got our butts handed to us," Tim replied in frustration.

Visibly angry, Talitha declared, "No, I'll tell you what happened. We didn't work together. All we did was charge in by ourselves looking for our own glory."

There was a moment of silence as the others considered the girl's statement.

"You mean the three of us went charging in on our own?" George said to the lone female member of the team. "You held your ground and likely saved my life."

"We're in this together, glory or shame," she replied. "So we need to make sure we really are working together against the Blood Lord. We just can't pay lip service to it, then do our own thing when we feel like it. I think if we combined our powers we could not only match him, we could beat him." Then Talitha became quiet. "But that would be up to you, George. You're the one whose family has been threatened."

"I'll think about that, but you've given us something to consider. The thing that gets me, though, is how did Ramsey get his powers?"

Beau had been thinking of that for the whole time after the identity of The Ram had been identified. Then it clicked. "The field trip!" he declared.

The others intently looked at him after the revelation.

"Think about it. How did we get our powers? It had to be from getting close to the meteorite. Remember? He'd gotten as close to it as any of us did. He's had the same reaction."

"Good thinking, Beau," George acknowledged. "So then, if that's the case, let's take it the next logical step. Who else might be out there with these powers? Also, the Blood Lord didn't surface until after the meteorite as well. Just because he's tied in with the Bloods doesn't mean he hasn't just come onto the scene. Could he be someone from the trip, or else someone that got exposed during the investigation? It's obvious he was after it when he attacked the lab, but why does he want it?"

Talitha had a disturbing thought come to mind during George's discourse. *If it happened during the field trip and Keith has figured George out, it's only a matter of time before he connects the rest of us to M-Force too. We're all in danger, and so are our families. Are we prepared to continue with that in mind?*

Lola had lost track of time. When the designer had regained consciousness, she found herself bound and blindfolded. She was sitting in a hard, straight-backed chair. Trying to stand up, it was discovered her hands were behind her back and attached to an object that felt like a pipe. The woman didn't know where she was, but could hear voices not far away. Lola suspected she was in some sort of separate, closed room, since the conversations were muffled. Hunger and thirst ate away at the designer more than fear. But the shock of her former boyfriend's actions kept her distracted from those thoughts.

She heard voices coming closer, one of which seemed vaguely familiar. Then a door opened and closed. Though she could hear nothing, a distinct, evil presence could be felt in the room. Uneasiness grew to an unnerving level. Someone was looking at her, she could feel it. Then the idea was confirmed as hot breath massaged her neck and face. The thought of someone leering at her was repulsive. Trying to recoil, Lola found she couldn't move.

Then she heard a laugh. It was soft, but close. The sound was playful, yet a wicked overtone enveloped any joy that was part of it. This was more like that of someone enjoying the torment of a caged animal.

For Lola, blind panic began to set in. She thrashed about saying, "Who are you? Where is Ulysses Hammerman? Tell me, or I'll scream!"

"Go ahead, scream all you want. In fact, I'd like that," the strange voice replied.

Lola stopped. She knew resistance was futile. "What do you want with me?" she cried out.

"Many things, my beautiful, but misguided young lady."

She felt the blindfold being removed. Blinking her eyes as they adjusted to the neon light in the room, Lola could see she was in some sort of nondescript factory office. Who had been speaking to her became clear as well. Recognition was instant. The woman knew it was the Blood Lord from pictures she had seen before. Realization of who was behind the shroud, though, was a bit slower. The hooded figure before her laughed again, as if reading her mind.

"You still don't get it, do you, my dear Lola?"

She started at the hearing of her name, but also at the familiarity of the voice. Bile began to rise up in her stomach at the growing awareness of who was speaking to her. But before her brain would connect all the parts together, the Blood Lord removed his hood.

"Ulysses!" she gasped. "You're the Blood Lord? How can that be?"

The man stood before her, grinning. "Yes, I can believe that you wouldn't think me capable of rising to such greatness. But see? You've gotten me wrong over the past year. I'm more than what you've seen. Now that you know what I'm capable of, I think your attitude will change."

"What attitude?" the woman asked, still in shock over the realization of who stood before her. "I just don't get it. What do you want from me?"

"I want you, Lola. I want you to be part of my life," the teacher stated.

With a shudder, she declared, "We dated for less than two months, Ulysses, and most of that time the relationship wasn't even any good. We were a bad fit."

"No, you're wrong. It's because I wasn't successful. It was because you didn't really know me," Hammerman belligerently countered.

"You don't get it, do you? I don't like you! I tried, but you're not my type. It doesn't matter what you have, or what you do." Then a bit of stubbornness overcame her fear. "You were obnoxious and overbearing. I could never feel for you the way you wanted me to. Now look at you. You're a criminal and you've killed people. Do you think that would make me love you?"

He snorted in reply, "What do you know about love? You're so mixed up you wouldn't know it even if you were."

"You've changed. At least before you had compassion, you cared about things other than yourself. What happened to you?"

"I opened my eyes," Hammerman responded coldly. "I saw what I was capable of and finally had the capacity to get what I deserve." Taking a deep breath, the man explained, "I came into contact with a meteorite one day and the blinders came off my eye. The giant within was awakened. Plus I found the ability to do this." He lifted his hand toward a filing cabinet and sent an energy blast towards it, crushing the object.

"Let me help you, Ulysses," Lola pleaded with the man. "Untie me, we can find doctors who can help with this problem."

"Problem!" he shrieked. "I have been liberated! Once I have possession of the meteorite, I will expose the members of my gang and see what powers they will achieve. If their response is anything like The Ram, they will be unstoppable. I will own this town. Then I will recruit more and more. The state will be next, then who knows? As others flock to the Blood Lord's banner, perhaps the country, perhaps the whole world in the end. Who's to stop me?"

"You're crazy!" Lola declared.

"Crazy am I?" Hammerman screamed in her face. "We'll see what you think after you have been exposed to the meteorite yourself. You will change as I have. You will think as I do. Yes, once you gaze into this object, you'll see it my way and rule at my side."

Repulsed at the thought, Lola instinctively tried to recoil from the man. Bound as she was, the effort was fruitless other than to amuse her captor.

Instead of compassion for the trapped woman, smiling lustfully, he walked over and began to stroke her hair. She tried to resist, but he grabbed her by the throat, continuing the caress. "No," he said, "you'll change your mind one way or the other." Releasing her, his tone changed. "Now, let's talk about M-Force."

Word of the Blood Lord's demand spread quickly through the area. *The Recorder* detailed the meeting of T.T. Tomlinson with the crime lord. They also showed pictures and had several articles on the criminal boss's defeat of M-Force. *M-Farce* had been the headline. The publisher put himself forward as one wanting to help the city. He would be an intermediary. He would broker a compromise solution. T.T. Tomlinson would personally work for a peaceful resolution to the conflict as he called it, which had been plaguing the region. Yet, nowhere was there any condemnation of the blind ambition of one bent on controlling those around him.

The twin cities were on edge, waiting for the next move of the powerful foe that threatened to wreak more destruction on the area, wondering where it would all end.

The Brain sat with Nate DeBeer and Deputy Chief Gonzalez. He had called the law enforcement officers asking to meet. With all that had gone on, it proved to be a very hard call to make. The youth was still embarrassed by their failure the day before. But he also knew about the Blood Lord's ultimatum, so time didn't allow for hurt feelings.

Neither of the two leaders in the police force asked any questions about what had happened. They seemed to have more confidence in him than he had in himself.

Knowing the clock was ticking, George got right to the point. "You can't let that meteorite fall into the hands of the Blood Lord. If you think things are bad now, they'll only get worse if this happens. It has to be destroyed for everyone's protection."

Santiago Gonzalez suspiciously asked, "Why do you think this?"

The Brain had anticipated the question. "There has to be something powerful about it for this madman to want it. This is the only answer." The Brain hoped his lie was convincing enough. To tell the truth could lead to even more people connecting him to George Alexander. He already didn't know how to deal with Keith Ramsey, so he didn't want to have the police on him as well.

The Deputy Chief looked hard at him for a moment, eyes boring unnervingly into the teen. Seemingly satisfied by what he saw, the man replied, "I agree with you. I'm not entirely convinced of the destruction part, but I also think we can't let this maniac get a hold of it either."

"So what happens now?" a relieved Brain asked.

"I'm meeting shortly with the NASA people to discuss the matter. Hopefully, we can find some common ground and deal with this situation. We also may be able to trap the Blood Lord in the process."

The Brain was moved by the trust the senior officer displayed by sharing such thoughts with him. Concern for the man flooded in. Something within, like an alarm bell, was calling to him, telling him it wouldn't be that simple. But the youth was still overwhelmed with all that had happened in the last twenty-four hours, so could only say, "That sounds risky."

"We've got to do what we've got to do," Gonzalez countered. Then, turning the tables on The Brain, he asked, "Can we count on M-Force?"

The leader of the team wavered. Logical and reasonable thoughts of why to say no filled his mind. He pictured all the bad things that could happen. The reasons to hedge or back down were conjured up. *Besides, it wasn't the teens' problem really,* he thought. *Hadn't they had tried their best? Wasn't it time to find some experts instead to deal with the threat? Sure they wanted to help but shouldn't there be conditions?* All these ideas and questions gnawed into the mind of the deep-thinking teen.

But then resolution crashed in. He would not allow the threat to divert him or M-Force from what they knew to be the right thing to do. As far as the risk was concerned, they would cross that other bridge when they got to it.

"You bet," The Brain answered. The last vestige of the old, scared George Alexander was gone. A new, hard as steel man had replaced him. "We won't let you down again."

With time running out before the instructions for delivery of the meteorite would come in from the Blood Lord, the principle players got together to figure out how to respond. Eric Brunner and Dr. Storm met with Deputy Chief Gonzalez at the lab.

The police officer explained the situation from the local authority's standpoint. "We have a difficult dilemma," he began. "We've seen this guy's power, so we know his threat is for real. Why he wants this space rock I don't know, but it can't be for any good. I think we should destroy it and try to take the gang down."

Brunner snapped, "I don't care what you do with the Blood Lord. That's none of my concern. Then the NASA man declared, "You will not allow this item to fall into that madman's hands, nor will you destroy it."

"So what do you propose we do?" Gonzalez asked suspiciously.

"The only option is for it to be moved from this town to a new and safer location."

"Where might that be?" the Deputy Chief asked. "Besides, how does that serve any purpose? He'll just find it again," the man declared. "And what about the threat to the city? What are we supposed to do about that?"

"That's your problem. Just make the move happen," Brunner ordered.

"Well, I don't think that's your call, Mr. Brunner," Gonzalez coldly replied.

"We'll see," the NASA man replied. Picking up his phone, he punched in some numbers. Once connected, he said, "We're having some difficulties with cooperation from the local authorities. Make the call." Satisfied with the exchange, he closed his phone and waited.

Within two minutes Gonzalez's own phone went off. Looking at the number, he was surprised to see it was the chief who was calling. "Yes sir?" he answered. A dark look crossed the man's handsome face. "But, Chief..." he tried to argue. Then, as if given no room for discussion, he responded coldly, "Understood," and hung up. With restrained emotion, he said to the man before him, "We'll do whatever you want."

The Blood Lord's telephone instructions came into the office of T.T. Tomlinson at 5:00 p.m. Several detectives were present to try to trace the call, and also discover the details of the conversation. The discussion was short and to the point. The meteorite was to be delivered to a location in the warehouse district of Kilings at 6:00 a.m. in an unmarked cube van, one driver only, no escort within four blocks. The call ended with a reminder of the consequences of not fulfilling the demand. No trace was possible; the call had not lasted long enough.

The time for discussion was ended; it was time for action. The senior command of the police met and a plan of action was put together, along with the team that would make it happen. The idea was simple, but to the point. A decoy vehicle would meet the Blood Lord, at which time the police tactical team would arrest him and his followers. The meteorite would be transported under heavy escort during that time period out of state to a new location.

Commander Jake Austen, a slender, red-faced career officer, was placed in overall control of the operation. He was to be assisted by Nate DeBeer, who would be in charge of the arrest of the Blood Lord, and Lieutenant Don Graves, a hawk-nosed middle-aged patrol division supervisor. His role was command of the transport and security of the space rock.

The three men sat in a briefing room at police headquarters detailing the process to move the meteorite. Eric Brunner sat in on the meeting to ensure things met with his satisfaction. While none of the law enforcement personnel liked having him there, they had little choice. The order to cooperate had come directly from the chief.

Everything was set and it seemed like an airtight plan. The cube van would leave at 5:45 a.m. with a visible police escort, since it was determined it would take about fifteen minutes to get to the rendezvous point. The escort would peel off four blocks away from the meeting point. The lone vehicle, filled with SWAT officers, would proceed to the meet and spring the trap.

The meteorite would leave at 6:01 a.m. from another loading dock with an unmarked escort of three vehicles. It was figured the Blood Lord would have someone watching the lab, so leaving just after the meeting time should mean the trap would be sprung before departure. Even if something went wrong, the package could still get away in time. The plan was airtight and couldn't fail.

Lieutenant DeBeer had listened carefully to the briefing, but was uneasy with the arrangements. When it was time for comments, he said, "The timetable and transport arrangements seem fine. I'm also convinced we can handle the Bloods at our end." Then he observed, "But we're missing something."

"Oh, what's that?" Commander Austen asked.

"We should have M-Force in on this. If anything goes wrong, we'll need their help."

Graves snorted. “We don’t need a bunch of cop wannabes hanging around,” he declared. “I know you seem taken by these freaks, but I’d just as soon have them as far away as I can. Besides, look how they handled the situation yesterday. They’re a joke.”

Tension was already high over the situation, so it took little to push things over the top. DeBeer aggressively countered his peer’s assertion, bringing a strong rebuke in response. The two began arguing until Commander Austen stepped in.

The phone in the briefing room rang, breaking up the disagreement. The senior officer moved away from his subordinates to pick up the receiver. In an irritated tone he barked out, “Austen.” Though not able to hear the conversation, the two other leaders could tell by the expression on the Commander’s face that the news wasn’t good.

The slender man ended the conversation, then slammed the telephone down. “Plans have changed. T.T. Tomlinson has been kidnapped and the Blood Lord has moved the drop up to 3:00 a.m. There’s no more time for debate. Nate, we don’t need any outside help with this, and it’s about time the KWPD took charge of things. I’m tired of people thinking we need help doing our job.”

Seeing the continued look of concern on the SWAT commander’s face, he admitted, “Listen, I know we’ve had out troubles with these Bloods. I’m not that naïve to say we haven’t. But that was on their terms and their timetable. This time we’re adequately prepared and we’re ready. This shift in timing means nothing. It’s a ploy by this clown to rattle us. Not this time. No, we can handle it.” Then, with further pointless discussion, he announced, “Both of you, get your troops ready, we move in an hour.”

At M-Force headquarters, the team waited for a phone call or page from the police to signal it was time to face off again against the Blood Lord. Each felt the same resolution that George did. No threat was going to stop them from doing what needed to be done. Their past difficulties and failures, indecision and apprehension, had now all been channeled into steely resolve, drawing them closer together as a team. Sorely did they want the opportunity to face their nemesis again and show what they had learned.

M-Force was aware the time for the crime boss’s call was well past, so know the next stage was about to transpire. They had come too far to back down now, even with the personal threat from Ramsey. Each knew that the only way for any of them to be safe was by stopping the Blood Lord and his gang once and for all. They'd learned from their mistakes the previous day. None would make the same ones again. Motivated and ready, they waited for notification to spring into action.

Unfortunately, they were waiting for a call that wasn't going to come.

At 2:45 a.m. a plain white cube van pulled out of the lab at State University. Two police squad cars took up position in front and behind to see there was no impediment to their progress to the meeting point.

Before 2:00 a.m. the entire tactical unit of the KWPD was deployed around the target location. Snipers were in position, covering the whole area, while other assault members were in the shadows ready to strike. Things were quiet around the warehouse, nothing moved.

The place chosen by the Blood Lord was a large aluminum sided building with six loading docks surrounded by a chain link fence. A large double gate permitted entry into the parking lot. Where once there had been lights, none worked anymore. A half moon was out, so the location was dimly lit by the natural glow of the night.

Tension grew as the clock moved closer to 3:00 a.m. The remaining four members of the tactical team were in the back of the cube van that was supposed to be carrying the meteorite. All were armed with night vision gear, ready to spring the trap. Two blocks away, a command post was set up with additional police. All were under the steady command of Lieutenant DeBeer.

The main center for the operation was back at police headquarters. All radio communications was feeding into it. In addition, each of the main vehicles was equipped with small, dashboard mounted, fiber optic cameras. This allowed for a live video feed from, not only the decoy vehicle, but also the van with the package.

Commander Austen wished he'd had a helicopter as well, but there was no time to put that together. Regardless, the veteran officer was confident everything would go according to plan.

High on a nearby building, nestled in the shadows, spotters scanned the area looking for movement. One position picked up the cube van moving into position.

"This is Survey One, decoy is inbound."

Nate DeBeer asked, "This is Tac Lead Survey One, any other movement?"

"Negative Lead, nothing."

"This is Survey Two, confirm package and nothing else." Then something caught his eye. "Wait, one. We have movement at seven o'clock heading to RV. I make it three panel vans inbound."

"This is Tac Lead to all stations, it's game time. No one moves until the package is in play." Then, changing focus, DeBeer asked another group, "Decoy One, you all set?"

From the van heading to the moment of destiny, the team leader answered, "Roger that, Tac Lead, we're one minute out." The four heavily armed tactical officers checked their body armor, adjusted helmets, then took the safeties off their automatic weapons. They were the most skilled officers on the squad. All had served in the military, and all had seen combat in the Gulf. They knew it might come down to life or death. Each pledged it wouldn't be theirs.

The driver pulled up to the rendezvous point and stopped, shutting off the engine. Getting out of the van, the lone police officer waited to see what was happening. Then, at the stroke of 3:00, three vans pulled up, parking beside each other. Quickly the drivers got out with AK47 assault rifles drawn. Looking around, once confident of what they saw, each opened the back of their vans. Joining the three and moving forward was a tall, cloaked figure.

"Do you have it?" the voice of the Blood Lord asked, distinctive and chilling in the cool night air.

"Yes, it's in the van just as you ordered," the nervous officer replied.

"Stay where you are," the voice demanded in a clipped tone.

The Bloods kept their guns trained on the driver while the Blood Lord moved closer to the van. Reaching the rear of the vehicle, a gloved hand grabbed hold of the door handle, then turned it. The door flew open and out poured the SWAT members. Four large floodlights came on from above, turning the night into day. From all directions other heavily armed tactical officers came pouring out.

"Police, freeze! Police, freeze!"

"On the ground! On the ground!"

The frenzy of rapid activity allowed no opportunity for the Bloods to respond. Unable to react to the lightning fast assault, all they could do was stare in shock and awe. Each was swiftly handcuffed, then pushed hard against the van. While this was happening, other SWAT members were converging on the three vans, ready for action. Three flash bang grenades were lobbed into the darkened backs, followed by the police charging in. Instead of finding other Bloods, all the vans were empty. Save the three drivers and the Blood Lord there were no other gang members present.

The leader of the Tactical Team was instantly suspicious. Grabbing the Blood Lord's hood, he pulled it down to see that instead of the crime leader they found T.T. Tomlinson, with duct tape over his mouth and a voice activated device strapped to his chest.

One of the Bloods called out to the newspaper publisher, "See, we told you you'd have a story."

The police on the scene swiftly got sick feelings in their stomachs. It had not gone as anticipated

"This is Decoy One, we are buster. Repeat, we are buster."

The pre-arranged signal went out that the mission had failed. Nate DeBeer swore, pounding his fist onto the table that held their communications equipment.

Back at the operations center, Commander Austen could hear the same information, plus see the video feed of the failure to capture the Blood Lord.

Immediately, Austen took the radio that was on the frequency for the meteorite convoy and called out, "Escort Lead this is Ops Center, decoy is buster, I say again, decoy is buster. Acknowledge."

"Ops Center this is Escort Lead, roger that. We are..."

Before the statement could be completed a sound like an inbound missile overwhelmed the airwaves, then the radio went dead. The video feed was lost as well.

"Escort Lead, come in! Escort one or two, come in!" Austen yelled into the radio.

The silence was deafening.

Hands shaking, the leader of the operation switched frequencies to the regular dispatch channel, fearing things were going badly wrong. "This is Commander Austen. I want all available units to converge on State University."

The van moving the meteorite was escorted by three unmarked Chevy Suburbans. There were four police officers in the first; in the second was Lieutenant Graves, along with Eric Brunner and a driver. The cube van with the meteorite had a driver and escort, while the last vehicle held another team of four men. Though not SWAT members, they were all highly experienced and capable of handling themselves. The convoy had departed at 3:01 a.m. and began to drive north, away from the campus. They had just turned onto the main road off of the school's property when the call came in that the mission to capture the Blood Lord had failed.

Before there was an opportunity for discussion on what to do next after the distress call, an energy blast had slammed into the lead vehicle. The electric force caused by it knocked out all communications.

Three more blasts and the convoy was a shambles. All the vehicles were disabled. No one in the convoy moved. Then, out of the shadows on the side of the road, a lone figure walked toward the vehicles. Motioning into the darkness, several vans pulled up and out piled heavily armed Bloods. Though ready for action, it was unnecessary. There was no response from the police vehicles. The occupants were down. All were too hurt or unconscious.

Swiftly, the police cube van was opened and a sealed container holding the cargo was removed to an awaiting vehicle. Though sirens could be heard in the distance, they were too far away for concern.

The Ram moved to the side of his leader, a look of genuine respect on his face. "You sure called this one right," he acknowledged.

"I was aware the fools would never willingly give me what I wanted," the Blood Lord answered. "But I also know my demand was the best way to achieve the desired reaction. I knew it would be easier to take it this way then to try to obtain it again from the lab."

Motioning to the twisted police vehicles, The Ram asked, "What do we do with them?"

"Leave them. They are of no consequence. Besides, I want survivors who will tell of what I've done."

"Makes sense," the young thug acknowledged. "But what do we do now? The fact is, they did try to double cross you, and that means the others have likely been arrested."

"There will be a suitable response, my friend," the Blood Lord answered. "For now, we will move to the new headquarters I've already established. The other has already been abandoned."

The Ram reacted with surprise, "You mean you expected all this?"

"Of course. Everything is going as planned. In forty-eight hours these cities will be mine."

Chapter 23
Convergence

Beep, beep, beep...

The sound was shrill and piercing, disturbing every recess of the young man's slumber. But it was a wail that penetrated his mind, almost like a cry for help.

George tried to ignore the sound of the pager. He rolled over, groaning when his clock radio revealed it was not even 4:00 a.m. But then the fog of sleep enveloping his mind lifted, so he sat bolt upright, grabbing the pager. The number on it caused his heartbeat to quicken. Fumbling to turn on his cell phone, the youth knew something important was up. He placed a return call to the number that was logged, impatiently waiting for the person who had beckoned to pick up. Finally the connection was made.

"This is The Brain. You called."

On the other end of the line was Nate DeBeer. "We need M-Force right now. Something has happened."

In less than an hour the team had assembled and was driving to meet the police officer near State University. Passing to the north end of the campus, they could see flashing lights ahead of them. It was a police cordon blocking the road. A gentle rain had briefly fallen, causing the now wet black asphalt to reflect back the fact that something unusual was up.

What little traffic there was at this time of morning was being ordered back. When the Equalizer pulled up, the officers on the barricade saw who it was, so they waved them on. All the members of M-Force were in the front of the van, eager to see what the commotion was about. Nearing a cluster of emergency vehicles, they could see the twisted remains of several heavy trucks.

There had been little discussion in the rush to assemble, then move to the location DeBeer had given them. Each was preparing for the attempt to stop the Blood Lord from grabbing the meteorite. They were aware of the 6:00 a.m. deadline, but not the change in plans.

Traveling to the university, their hope rose that they would be involved in the plan. But seeing the destroyed convoy a new, unexpected truth came to light. They were being called in to help after the fact.

Pulling up to where the team could see the SWAT Lieutenant waiting, M-Force swiftly joined him. He was standing with a pair of officers, one holding a bandage to a bloodied head. It was obvious, even from a distance, that the unknown pair didn't seem overly thrilled to see the team.

"Thanks for coming, guys," DeBeer greeted them. "This is Commander Austen and Lieutenant Don Graves. We need your help. This convoy was taking the meteorite out of town. The Blood Lord ambushed it and got what he was after. Thankfully, no one was killed, but several officers are in the hospital with serious injuries."

"Why move it? Why not destroy it like I suggested?" The Brain questioned. Irritation etched his voice at not only being called in after things had gone wrong, but also not being listened to in the first place.

Out of the shadow of the early morning dawn came the reply. "Because I ordered it moved. That's why."

Behind his mask, George Alexander was startled to see Eric Brunner walk toward them with Santiago Gonzalez. The others didn't know who the man with the Deputy Chief was, but could tell from their leader's reaction that he wasn't a friend.

The Brain knew the risk they were facing with the Blood Lord and was willing to do it. But he felt as if M-Force wasn't really wanted. They seemed to be treated like some sort of add on commodity. But that was only one issue processing through the youth's quick mind.

Seeing the NASA man there confirmed the fact he was more than a researcher. The whole thing was beginning to stink and The Brain didn't like it. The others weren't sure how to proceed, so he responded for them. "Why should we? You obviously didn't want us around in the first place. What good can we do now?"

It was Gonzalez who spoke for the rest. "We should have called you in to help out, but we didn't. That was a tactical decision. That's the past. We need you now to get it back and bring this guy down once and for all. Are you up for it?"

Once again the pang of conscience overruled emotion. The Brain desperately wanted to tell them to stuff it. But seeing the situation and instinctively knowing the risk to the area, he held his emotions in check. The youth silently cursed the character that had risen within, not allowing him to take the easy course.

But then The Brain saw something that caused him to pause. There was a look of desperation on the faces of these powerful men around him. Even those who didn't seem supportive of M-Force knew they had nowhere else to turn. This was an opportunity to show a graciousness that thus far had not been extended to them. Not just that, but they could also demonstrate the power that comes from commitment and character. All processed through the computer-like brain of George Alexander. There could only be one answer.

"Yes, we'll help," The Brain softly answered.

"You bet we will!" the Bulldozer called out, pounding his hand into his fist.

"We're ready for them," Black Star added, standing with hands on her hips.

Grey Man nodded his head vigorously in agreement.

M-Force was in.

"Okay, so how are we going to find him? The Blood Lord and the meteorite could be anywhere by now," The Brain declared.

It was Eric Brunner who answered. "We know exactly where they are. I installed a tracking device onto the meteorite's case in the event something like this happened."

Opening a briefcase, he took out a handheld device that looked like a GPS unit. Turning it on, a display reading came out right away.

"Who are you?" The Brain asked, attempting to mask the reality of his knowledge of the mysterious agent.

"Eric Brunner. I'm a program manager with NASA." Shaking hands with the costumed leader of M-Force, he added, "Have we met before?"

Face turning slightly red at the recognition, The Brain changed the subject. "Program manager, huh? I think there is more to you than you're letting on, Mr. Brunner."

Brunner laughed. "Let's just say I'm involved in a few other sideline projects."

The NASA man impressed The Brain for the first time since they'd met. "Okay, how do you want to play this?"

DeBeer answered, "M-Force goes in first. You handle the Blood Lord and Ram. My guys follow and bag the Bloods. We only have one shot at this. If we mess it up, who knows what happens."

Within minutes they were following an unmarked police vehicle in the Equalizer.

Alone and able to discuss the upcoming mission for the first time, Bulldozer asked, "So how is this going to be different from last time?"

"Because it has to," The Brain responded. "There's too much riding on it."

Grey Man jumped in, "Yes, but we need a plan."

"I think the key is to isolate The Ram from the Blood Lord," Black Star observed. "Don't let them work together. Plus, we have the element of surprise this time."

They began to discuss for the remainder of the drive how they would deal with the situation. The police vehicle took them to where the original command post had been set up. As it turned out, the real lair of the Blood Lord was not far from where the attempt to capture the fugitive had taken place.

A blueprint of the building was laid out on a table, along with a 3D image on a computer screen. Several video monitors from hidden cameras were also showing a variety of images from the outside of the building. All seemed quiet and peaceful. Before the final briefing, each member of M-Force was issued with a black tactical vest in order to hold a walkie-talkie and other items useful for the assault.

Gathering all the key players together, Nate DeBeer laid out the plan. "Okay, M-Force, you go in quietly and locate the package. The best Brunner can determine from GPS is that it's likely here," he pointed to a large room in the center of the labyrinth-like building. "Once you've got eyes on, report back any Blood activity, then we'll move in. Once we make contact, the building will be sealed off and no one will be able to slip away." He looked at Commander Austen, who nodded his head in agreement. "Any questions?" Seeing none he concluded, "We move in five minutes."

Moving like ghosts, M-Force silently entered the building after finding an unlocked door. Once inside, they slipped through the dark shadows of the halls in search of the target. Time was important, since dawn had already turned the inky darkness of night into a dull gray. Two Bloods patrolling an outer corridor were quietly rendered unconscious shortly after entry.

"We're in," The Brain whispered into the communicator hanging from his ear, linking them with the police. "Proceeding to objective."

Grey Man disappeared, going ahead of the others. He would lead the way.

Bulldozer brought up the rear to ensure no one came at them from the back. They quietly passed two rooms that were filled with Bloods laughing and joking. The team had hoped to find them asleep, but that was a matter for SWAT. The Brain marked each room with a laser designator that would give the police the location on an electronic map at the command post.

Without a sound, M-Force continued deeper into the building in search of the item that had brought them together in the first place. Finally they moved toward the center, seeking the expected container with the meteorite. Grey Man saw a guard at a door leading to the room he knew from the blueprint was the central storage area. Without waiting for the others to come up, he took care of the Blood himself with a swift karate chop.

For a moment the quiet teen pondered the changes in his life the past few months, changes that had given rise to the confidence to do such things. The others soon joined him. Bulldozer smiled and gave a thumbs up sign at the sight of the prostrate Blood.

The Brain took some lubricant from his tactical vest, spraying the door handle and hinges to ensure no noise would give them away. Carefully opening the door, it swung without a sound, revealing the room to be empty. In the center was a rectangular metal box with NASA markings on it. Fanning out, M-Force scanned all parts of the plain room and looked up at the balcony overhead to ensure no one was there.

The Brain whispered into his communicator, "Package in sight and secure. Move in."

Suddenly the lights in the room came on. Before the leader of the group could react, a painful energy blast hit him, forcing the communicator from his ear. Bloods carrying a variety of automatic weapons and handguns burst into the room, leveling them at M-Force. The team instinctively moved into a defensive circle, but it was no use, they were outnumbered and outgunned.

A strange chuckling sound came from the shadows of the room. The Blood Lord, followed by The Ram came sauntering out. He stepped on the communicator, crushing it, in the process of moving toward the trapped teens.

"We have been expecting you," the Blood Lord said. Surprise was evident on the faces of each member of M-Force, despite their masks. "Do you think I'm so foolish as to not search for a tracking device?" Reveling in his triumph, he then added, "I wondered who would come. I have to admit to being surprised to see you. After your performance the other day I thought you'd have given up. Your tenacity impresses me. But then, for a group of bright students from KW High, I should expect no less."

The shock of the revelation was like a balloon being burst. The foursome was visibly deflated by the acknowledgment. The Blood Lord laughed again, enjoying the scene. "Yes, my friend The Ram informed me of who you are. Noble intentions, but you should have joined me instead. Sadly, we all have to make choices, don't we?" The cloaked figure seemed to ponder the thought for a moment, then moved on. "Now we can finish you once and for all, along with the pathetic police presence. One final move and the city is mine."

Black Star, trying to buy time for the police to converge, called out, "Why are you doing this? Don't you care about the people you're hurting?"

"And did anyone care about me when I was being hurt? When I was being denied what I deserved? NO! No one cared. But now that I have the power to claim what I deserve, everyone cares. I'm not doing anything that anyone else in my place wouldn't. I'm grabbing hold of the American dream, I'm being all I can be."

Totally unafraid and repulsed at the twisted view, the teen girl shot back, "You're wrong. There are lots of decent people who work hard for what they've got. They don't take something that's not theirs and they don't destroy lives in the process. What you're talking about is not a dream, it's a nightmare."

"Nightmare is it?" the Blood Lord shrieked, on the edge of hysterics at the boldness of opposition he faced. "Well, then here is someone to share it with you."

An attractive dark-haired woman, instantly recognized by M-Force, was dragged into the room.

"Lola!" they gasped.

"Yes, Lola," the Blood Lord confirmed with contempt in his voice. "I love what she did with the costumes. I'll have to get her to make me one when I'm finished here. My new position will be worthy of more than a mere cloak and hood." Seeing the look of dismay on The Brain's face, he added, "Oh, don't think she betrayed you in any way. She has been loyal to the end. I like that quality in a woman."

A Blood moved into the conversation, reporting, "Master, the SWAT team has entered the building and are about to enter the ambush spot."

"Excellent. Have the rest of our men join you in welcoming our guests." Then a hard edge replaced the previous jovial tone, "Kill them all. I want no survivors this time."

The Blood turned, signaling a number of the other gangsters in the room to follow him.

The help M-Force had hoped for was not going to make it. In fact, they were about to be slaughtered. Not a word was spoken, not even a look was exchanged. Yet, each knew what to do. There was an almost psychic connection between the four. They truly had become a team.

With one step, Black Star ran and was a blur of speed, heading in the direction of Lieutenant DeBeer and his team. Grey Man disappeared and moved away from the room. Bulldozer crashed through a wall to free himself. The Brain levitated up to the balcony so was able to escape.

The Blood Lord screamed in frustration. Too late, a burst of automatic weapon fire not only missed the mark, but signaled the police something was going on.

Black Star made it to the SWAT leader within seconds. Nate DeBeer saw the dark streak coming toward them. Something in his instincts told him it was a friend, so had his men hold their fire.

"It's an ambush. The Bloods knew we were coming," the girl panted, not from fatigue, but from the anxiety of the moment.

DeBeer asked, "What should we do?"

"Turn the tables, make them come to you," Black Star encouraged. "The original plan still holds, you take care of the Bloods, we take care of the Blood Lord and Ram."

As the tactical team members regrouped, preparing to move to a new position, the other members of M-Force arrived as well.

The Brain reported, "The Bloods are right behind us. We'll make our way back to where the meteorite is and meet you there."

M-Force slipped out into an adjacent hallway. The Brain had already calculated another way to get to the main room based on his perfect recollection of the blueprint.

This time, Bulldozer led the way and he smashed aside Bloods like Moses parting the Red Sea. A half dozen went down under his charge as they moved against the flow of their opponents. Just as suddenly they were alone and heading through the halls.

The other Bloods faired no better. Their ambush broken, instead, they tried to charge the new position with guns blazing. The SWAT officers were in protected positions and responded with a flurry of flash bang and stun grenades. When the smoke cleared, the Bloods lay on the concrete floor in groaning piles, unable to put up any resistance. Lieutenant DeBeer signaled for support officers to come in take the criminals into custody. Without waiting, he led his men toward their objective.

M-Force got there first, catching the few remaining Bloods and their leader off guard. Several energy balls from Black Star disarmed them, so it came down to the Blood Lord and Ram against the foursome.

The Ram charged, but before making contact, he found himself raised a foot off the ground and his progress stopped by The Brain. Before the powerful criminal could react, he was slammed hard to the floor, hit by a runaway freight train called the Bulldozer.

"That's for yesterday," the strong youth called out. "And here's a little something extra for keeping me up past my bedtime tonight." Grabbing The Ram, he threw the stunned opponent with a thud into a wall.

The Blood Lord responded with an energy blast toward the Bulldozer, but Black Star blocked it. Then the criminal leader toppled over when hit by a flying piece of machinery. Grey Man appeared out of nowhere on all fours to provide the lever to knock him over after The Brain levitated the object. Getting up, he was hit first by an energy ball from Black Star, then slammed to the ground by Bulldozer.

The SWAT team burst into the room, weapons at the ready, swiftly taking the stunned Bloods into custody. They put up no resistance. The unbelief at seeing their leader bested caused them to not know how to react.

The four members of M-Force could not believe it; they had beaten their opponent. Elation filled them, but it was premature.

Lola had remained in the room the whole time. The Blood Lord grabbed the designer, holding her in front of him. The petrified woman acted as a shield from the police and from any further attack by M-Force. He motioned The Ram to join him. Moving back, he headed toward the metal box containing the meteorite. No one moved against him, since he held the woman by the throat in a vise-like grip.

"Let her go!" Lieutenant DeBeer commanded.

Reaching the box, the Blood Lord tossed Lola aside like a rag doll, then threw off the lid exposing himself and The Ram to its contents.

Laughing hysterically, he shrieked, "Now we will have more power, the power to obliterate you, your families, this city!"

They both bent over the box and grabbed hold of the space rock. A glow came over their faces. A smile of satisfaction was evident.

"Yes, I can feel it surging through me."

Unsure what to expect, the police fell back into a defensive position in the corner of the cavernous room, as if seeking shelter from some expected assault. But M-Force held their ground in the center of the room, not moving. The Blood Lord raised his hands to unleash a massive energy blast. Black Star braced herself to try to receive it and protect her friends, but nothing happened. No energy came out.

The Ram let out a cry of rage and raced toward Bulldozer, intent on driving him into the opposite wall. He didn't let up, hitting the youth in full stride. Bulldozer didn't move, instead, The Ram bounced off him like he'd hit a brick wall.

Both had lost their powers.

Neither could accept the reality of what had happened when they re-exposed themselves. The Blood Lord, then The Ram, surged forward, attempting to batter the members of M-Force down. It was a sad display by the once powerful pair. Both were swiftly swatted down like pesky flies, their strength seeming to have drained away.

M-Force moved in closer to check on the criminals. The Blood Lord lay unconscious on the cold floor. The Ram was in a stupor, unable to speak, barely able to raise his arms. Exhausted, he too slipped into a state of oblivion. Both were quickly handcuffed, but under the current circumstances that seemed like overkill. A stretcher was brought in for the Blood Lord, while The Ram was dragged out to an awaiting police van.

Curiosity, and a desire for closure, filled the commander of the tactical team. Going over to the prostrate criminal mastermind, he said, "Well now, let's see who we have here."

Pulling the deep hood back, a face familiar to the four teens was revealed.

"Mr. Hammerman!" Black Star involuntarily exclaimed, unable to hide her emotions.

"You know this guy?" Nate DeBeer questioned. "How's that possible?"

Each member of M-Force looked at the others. It was a moment of truth. They had won, but what was the cost going to be? In the intensity of all that had been transpiring, it seemed that none had thought that far along. But now it was finally time.

"Can we please have a moment to discuss this with each other?" The Brain asked.

Eric Brunner, who had joined the group in the room, hesitated, but Lieutenant DeBeer replied, "Sure. Take as much time as you need. We have some loose ends to tie up anyway." Moving toward the distraught Lola, they began to speak with her.

Alone in a corner of the room, the four friends looked at each other with a combination of joy and relief. But then a sense of decision, perhaps the biggest of their lives, overcame the feeling.

"Those two will figure out who we are. Our identities will be revealed," The Brain stated. "I knew it would come to this, though. I'd figured that was who the Blood Lord was," the leader of M-Force announced. "Once Keith Ramsey identified himself, the conclusion was obvious." But then the gifted teen became more reflective. "I knew it, but I didn't want to believe it."

Black Star added, "Well, it doesn't matter any more whether they know or not. Once Mr. Hammerman and Keith come to, they'll tell anyone who'll listen who we are. Our identity will come out."

"Well, if that's the case, why don't we re-expose ourselves like they did and get rid of our powers?" The Brain asked. "At least then we can go back to normal."

Deep emotion registered on Black Star's face. "Is that what you want? Is that what any of you want?"

Looking around the room, M-Force saw it was empty. Lieutenant DeBeer and Eric Brunner had left with Lola. Taking their masks off, the teens looked at each other as they truly were. This was a decision that had to be made unshrouded and in the open.

There was a long awkward silence. Each thought about the time they'd had together and what they'd been able to do. Each weighed it against the comfort of going back to normal lives.

Beau spoke first. "I don't want to. I like being Grey Man and I like helping people."

"I'm willing to take my chances with this," Tim added. "I think I understand now how to keep everything in balance. I'd like the chance to use my powers to help others, rather than myself."

Talitha declared, "I'm with you guys. Black Star is part of me and I never would have discovered this if it hadn't happened. Plus, I wouldn't have my new brothers. I'm not going to let any of this go lightly."

The three of them looked at George, who was still in silent reflection. The leader of M-Force seemed uncertain of what to do.

"We're not going to do this without you, George. It's all or none for us," Talitha declared.

"This is bigger than me," the intelligent teen admitted. "I can't not be The Brain and live with myself. If we're all in agreement, then let's go and take our chances."

Becoming M-Force again, not a bunch of teens, they invited the police officer and man from NASA back into the room. It was time to answer the original question posed to them.

"Okay, we're ready to answer your question," The Brain began. "I'm sure you'll find it out soon enough, but his name is Ulysses Hammerman. He was our high school geography teacher. The Ram is one of our classmates named Keith Ramsey. We all received our powers after being exposed to the meteorite when it landed while on a field trip. Our names are…"

Nate DeBeer cut him off before the leader of M-Force could finish, "That's all we need to know."

As it became evident the SWAT officer had nothing further to say on the matter, surprise was evident on the faces of the foursome. In seconds, that look turned to relief, followed swiftly by concern.

The Brain stated, "Then you know why this needs to be destroyed. Look what it did to us. You can't risk someone like Hammerman or Ramsey being exposed to it and turning out how they did."

The head of the tactical team thought about the statement for a moment, then said, "You have a point." Then, nodding his head, added, "No, you're right."

Eric Brunner swiftly pulled a Glock 9mm pistol from his belt, leveling it at the team. "I can't let that happen."

"Put the gun down, Brunner," DeBeer ordered.

"No way. I'm taking charge of this operation. You know I have the authority. Don't stand in my way."

Several SWAT members who had drifted onto the periphery of the conversation instinctively brought their weapons up to protect their leader. Fearlessly, the man raised a hand for them to lower their weapons.

Black Star stepped between the two groups. The NASA man's gun pointed right at her stomach. "You have to destroy it," she said passionately. "No one can control how someone is going to respond. The risk is too great."

Brunner didn't know what to do. He held the automatic, but he felt out of control. "I have my orders."

"But do they include destroying the lives of people?" the girl quietly responded.

"She's right, Eric," Lieutenant DeBeer added. "This thing is dangerous. It's too dangerous. We need to get rid of it before the thing can be used for the wrong reasons again. If the meteorite leaves from here, who knows where it'll go and what it'll be used for"

The masked foursome and SWAT leader's argument was logical. Brunner's common sense said they were right. But he had his orders. This had nothing to do with NASA. It had everything to do with bringing into his real superiors a powerful weapon, more powerful than any had imagined. The prestige and reward for him through doing this would be significant. Yet, his conscience stirred, saying it was wrong. The four youths in the charcoal gray costumes had resurrected something in him he'd thought was long gone. Once he'd believed he could make a difference. Perhaps it was time to believe again. He'd been trained well. Too well it seemed, for in the end the independent element of his character won out over the practical.

Placing the pistol back into his holster, he declared, "Okay, you win. We destroy it."

Instead of any sense of triumph, The Brain responded, "No, Mr. Brunner, it's not about you against us. The winner here is humanity. You made the right decision."

The undercover CIA operative looked at the slender figure before him. Though he couldn't tell what the youth looked like, behind the costume he knew there was someone who cared.

M-Force moved carefully, replacing the lid to close the containment unit. "Last chance," The Brain quietly said to his friends. Each looked at the others, knowing the answer already. Grey Man spoke for the rest when he responded, "Seal it up."

Four tactical team members carried the box away under escort of the rest of them. All that was left were M-Force, Lieutenant DeBeer and Eric Brunner. The four costumed crime fighters seemed to hesitate when it came time to leave, as if unsure what they would find when they walked out of the room.

"Come on guys," Nate DeBeer called out, "what are you waiting for?"

"So now what happens?" Black Star asked nervously. "You know who we are. Is M-Force finished?"

"No," the police officer responded without hesitation. "We owe you a debt that no one could ever repay. We also need M-Force. Who knows what other problems may come up that need your particular talents. Your secret is safe with me."

The five turned and looked accusingly at Eric Brunner.

"Hey, I'm not the bad guy here," he responded. "I know how to keep secrets, trust me. I'll keep this one."

"With what strings attached?" The Brain suspiciously asked.

"I like you, kid," Brunner smiled. "You get straight to the point. No strings attached, it's just the right thing to do."

"So we're in agreement, the meteorite gets destroyed," Black Star confirmed. "How do we do it?"

"Leave that to me," DeBeer stated.

The meteorite was driven to a quarry on the outskirts of town. The two demolition experts from the tactical team rigged up a charge of C4 explosives to the case. It was time for the drama to end.

Nodding his head, Brunner gave the signal to DeBeer. "Do it."

"Fire in the hole!"

The sharp blast echoed throughout the open pit like a bell tolling the last watch of the day. Once the dust had settled, a front-end loader buried the area in slag. The meteorite was gone, the destinies of four unrelated teenagers were now unbreakably locked together, signaling the potential of new destinies to come.

Chapter 24
Tying Up Loose Ends

Sparkling and bright, the sun rose over Kilings-Welch. The air was fresh, with a hint of fall in it. A new day had dawned and with it a new chapter in the region.

The media converged on the area where the Blood Lord had been captured, reporting on the destruction of the super criminal and his gang. Deputy Chief Gonzalez held a news conference along with M-Force and Lieutenant DeBeer to explain what had happened. Unfortunately, few details could be released at this point due to the ongoing investigation. What was made clear, though, was that the threat to the region had ended. The criminal's reign of terror had been put to an end due to the joint efforts of the police and M-Force. After the formal presentation, the gathering was thrown open to questions.

"Is this the last we'll see of M-Force?" one reporter called out.

"Yes, what's next for you after this?" another added.

The questions caught the foursome off guard. They hadn't thought about the future, let alone discussed it. The Brain looked at the others, then stepped forward. "We'll be around if you need us. Until then, well, we'll be watching. We're happy to do our part, just like the police are, but it's not just up to us. Everyone in these cities has a part to play. We all need to stand up and do what we can. Let's all of us ensure what caused this to happen never happens again."

Journalists are often accused of being cynical and unfeeling. Yet, the honest truth of the statement caused the group at the news conference to break into spontaneous applause. It was a glorious moment for the teenagers who had struggled so hard with the same statement. It appeared that perhaps Kilings-Welch would be okay after all.

Later that day, four nondescript teenagers walked together through Victory Park. No one paid attention to them as life quickly got back to normal.

"Did we do the right thing?" Talitha asked. "I mean, by not re-exposing ourselves. We could have gone back to normal lives."

"Are you having second thoughts?" George responded.

"You know what? I'm not. I'm at peace with who I am. And actually I kind of like Black Star. No, she and M-Force are part of me."

As they enjoyed the peace of the beautiful day, an angry cloud still hung over their collected spirits. The issue of what would happen when Ulysses Hammerman and Keith Ramsey were able to speak weighed heavily on each. Though the pair may no longer possessed the physical power to destroy, they did have the power to destroy M-Force through revelation.

George decided that instead of waiting for it to happen he would go and see what destiny would dictate. Taking his phone, he called Nate DeBeer. "I'd like to see the Blood Lord and Ram if I could."

"Sure. I can arrange that through Deputy Chief Gonzalez. Meet me at the hospital."

An hour later, The Brain met the SWAT leader and followed him to an area under heavy security on the fourth floor of the hospital. Wherever they walked, curious onlookers stared in awe at the pair. Several children even stopped the leader of M-Force, asking for his autograph. While the full story had yet to be widely released, M-Force's defeat of the Blood Lord was getting around enough that people knew who the new heroes in town were.

Traveling past the police officers guarding the isolated block of rooms, the pair entered. The first room they went into was that of the Blood Lord. Instead of the intimidating character George remembered, he saw, instead, his geography teacher lying strapped down to a white hospital bed. The man seemed entirely passive, restraints unnecessary. Though immobile, his eyes did dart over to the entrance as the pair entered in.

Hammerman looked up from the bed, confusion in his eyes, "Who are you?" he asked The Brain. "Are you a performer from the Children's Ward?"

"Don't you know me?" The Brain responded, unable to believe what he was hearing.

Though the look of non-recognition from the teacher was genuine, his response was incredible. "No, I don't. I don't even know why I'm here. I keep asking, but no one will tell me. Did I have an accident? I feel fine. I just don't know why I'm here."

The Brain was stunned by the response. Was it true? Did he not know M-Force, or was this some ruse by the Blood Lord to escape? Moving across the hall, he went to see the other member of the sinister gang.

Though more belligerent, Keith Ramsey seemed to be equally confused. "Nice Halloween costume," he cynically called out. Then becoming agitated, not only at his surroundings, but visitors as well, he added, "What are you staring at butthead? And why am I here? What's going on? I want to know what's going on!"

"Don't you know me, Keith?" George asked. "It's me, The Brain."

"Brain?" he snorted, "More like the Clown if you ask me. Why would I know some loser like you? Get out of here unless you can give me some answers."

Though irritated by the verbal abuse, The Brain was exhilarated by the possibility of what seemed to be happening. Daring not even to hope, he and Nate DeBeer visited with the lead doctor in charge of care for the patients to receive an assessment.

"Neither patient exhibits any signs of extraordinary power," the middle-aged, bespectacled doctor reported. "Their brain waves are stable and physical signs are fine as well. The only thing is they have no recollection of events for the past several months. In fact, the only common memory between them was of a geography field trip prior to the end of the school year." Then the physician added, "We're not certain if it's some form of amnesia, or post-traumatic stress disorder. But we've run a battery of tests and the memory loss seems genuine, not a ruse."

The Brain left the hospital shortly after that. They were free! Hammerman and Ramsey had no recollection of their past, or who they'd tangled with. M-Force was still anonymous. There was almost a skip in his stride as he walked away to his now continuing destiny.

Then another thought entered in, one that caused the tall youth to stop dead in his tracks. What would have happened if he, or any of the other members of M-Force, had re-exposed themselves to the meteorite? It was clear they likely would have lost their powers first off. But not only that, it appeared all memory going back to the initial exposure would have been erased as well.

He thought of the love he had for the other members of M-Force. He thought about how his life had been changed by the events over the past several months. The idea that this would be denied him and he would go back, literally, to the person he was before, took his breath away. George said a silent prayer of thanksgiving for the choice he and the others had made. He was The Brain, and M-Force lived.

Lola sat in the back room of her shop, sipping a mug of herbal tea. The attractive designer looked with affection at the costumed figure before her. The woman's new assistant was busy taking orders in the front, and her recently hired seamstress was steadily working away on a new creation. She'd never had so much work.

"I have an offer from a design house in New York to go and work with them. It's a dream come true in many ways," the pretty woman shared, pushing a wisp of tinted blond hair out of her eyes.

"So you're leaving Kilings-Welch?" Black Star asked, a hint of disappointment in her voice.

A smile lit up Lola's radiant face, "No, I decided to turn it down. I've discovered the bright lights and big city aren't for me. This is my home and I don't want to leave it."

Black Star smiled as well at the announcement.

Lola, happier than she'd felt in years, added, "Besides, I have some people here who are important to me, who've stuck by me. I wouldn't leave them for anything. Now, let's talk about some ideas I have for upgrading your costumes…"

The whistle blew signaling the end of the game. It was the final contest of the summer season and Tim David had dominated on the field. Not only did he play tough, but he also played smart, position football, making no mental errors. George, Talitha and Beau had sat together in the stands cheering their friend on. In turn, he happily waved to them while leaving the field for the locker room after the game. Once showered and changed, he was asked to meet with Coach Jeffrey.

"You wanted to see me, Coach?"

"You played a great game, Tim. Your best all summer, in fact. I have to admit that I can't figure you out. You've been all over the map in terms of your play and focus. But I wanted to tell you that the last week I've noticed a difference. There's a new maturity to you I like to see. Something's happened and it's made a big improvement. You had power before, but now you've got smarts. Both are needed to succeed in this game."

Gary Jeffrey then smiled broadly. Standing up, he clapped the solid youth on the shoulders and ordered, "Enjoy your week off, but next week I want to see you on the field trying out for the KW High varsity squad. I think we've got a place for you."

Tim left the office and jumped in the air for joy. The dream was still alive.

Beau sat in his back yard and sighed with satisfaction. The night air was crisp, the sky clear. Crickets serenaded him and peace filled his spirit. He looked up at the stars, wondering if there were any other meteors like the one that had changed his life. Looking at the stars had once made him feel small in the vastness of the universe. Now he felt unique, specially created for a higher purpose. Part of the youth wished there were hundreds of similar meteors so everyone could feel the joy that surged through him. Then one bright star shone, dominating the others, as if answering the thought. Perhaps in the end there was one for all.

Earlier in the day Beau had fixed, then upgraded a motorized wheelchair for one of his neighbors. The elderly man had joked that with the improvements he was ready for the NASCAR circuit. The quiet teen liked being able to help people. To him, the circumstance didn't matter. He also looked forward to getting back to school. There were a couple of improvements he wanted to try out on the robot he'd built in the spring. He'd planned on joining the robotics team. They'd likely win the state competition this year.

The call The Brain had received earlier in the evening sent a chill down his spine. He wasn't sure how to deal with it. The head of M-Force was now alone, and for the first time it bothered him. He'd been used to having the other members of the team around, but the instructions had been specific. Come alone. Now The Brain stood waiting in the north parking lot of State University.

"I'm glad you decided to come," the bass voice announced out of the darkness.

The Brain was startled slightly as Eric Brunner appeared out of the inky black of night. The man definitely had the ability to blend into the surroundings. In a clipped tone, the teen replied, "I'm here, so let's talk."

"Why don't we take a walk?" the NASA man suggested casually. "I'd like to stretch my legs."

At this particular hour the campus was deserted, so the odd pair didn't attract attention. They walked toward where the convoy carrying the meteorite had been ambushed. Though the site was now cleaned up, there were still scorch marks on the road from where the vehicles had been torched. The Brain was reminded of the awesome power the Blood Lord had once possessed. It truly had only been teamwork that got them through.

"You know, a lot changed the other night when we got attacked," Brunner said reflectively. "I was sure of so many things. Now I'm not so sure."

The Brain watched the man carefully, wondering what game he was playing. Yet, the man was exuding a genuine spirit of contemplation. The mysterious operative seemed torn.

"Do you know what this is?" Brunner asked, holding up a file folder.

The Brain shook his head no.

He was becoming more nervous as the conversation went on. The call earlier that had brought him to this unexpected meeting had told him the man from NASA possessed some interesting information on a teen named George Alexander. That got his attention like a shock of electricity.

"It's a file on a student named George Alexander started the day a certain meteorite crashed in this area. It has medical readings from the day, field reports...a lot of good stuff. It shows an intelligent young man who has gone through a remarkable change, all tracing back to this event."

"What do you want from me?" The Brain shot back, fists clenched.

"I've seen you in action," Brunner responded casually, "and I'm impressed by what you and your friends can do. I'd like to call on you from time to time to help me out."

Panic overwhelmed The Brain. He could feel a chain of control being put around his neck. "Who are you, really?" the teen asked.

"Well, you know that I'm no simple NASA program manager. You're smart enough to figure that one out. Okay, confession-time for me. I'm a CIA agent. I work in high-level national security situations." Suddenly the man seemed even more dangerous. Then, offhandedly, Brunner added, "Well, that's not entirely true either. I am actually a program manager too, but that's a cover. My point is, that situations arise with CIA where I think you're unique skills could really help me out."

"And so you plan on holding this folder over me to get me to cooperate," The Brain spat out.

The agent shook his head, a look of sadness crossing the man's hard face. "You still have me all wrong."

Taking a lighter out of his pocket, he lit a corner of the file and watched it catch on fire. Dropping the flaming bundle of paper to the ground, the pair watched it burn. Stomping on the embers to ensure there was no more flames, Brunner declared, "George Alexander no longer exists in the world of CIA or NASA. The computer data banks have been wiped clean, too. This file was all the information left anyone had. This young man is now anonymous again."

The Brain stammered, "Then why…why ask for my help?"

"Because I'd like to think you'd want to do the right thing. My hope is that you'd want to help your country."

"Why just me? Why not the whole team?" the leader of M-Force asked.

"Oh, I'm hoping you'll all help."

"Why then not have us all here?"

"Because you're the leader," Brunner answered. "They trust you and will follow you. Plus, yours was the only file that existed."

The truth out in the open, George Alexander finally spoke, rather than The Brain. Speaking bluntly, the youth declared, "You know my secret. What's to keep you from using it against me later?"

The CIA agent shook his head in disbelief. "For such a smart guy, there's a lot you still don't get. We all have secrets, son. It's only a matter of degrees. They don't necessarily have to be a prison, though. Instead, they can also set a person free to rise above the things they think they're capable of. Besides, you know the truth of who I am too. I'd say that makes us even."

George began to understand, but was still having difficulty seeing the vision of the man before him. "What could I do?" he honestly asked. "I'm a student starting university in a week. I mean, what happened here was one thing, but what you're talking about is huge."

"Why not you?" Brunner patiently questioned. "If not you, then who? Do you think there is some sort of national security factory? Some place where those willing to defend their country are produced on some assembly line? No. It's ordinary people doing what they can with their God-given abilities, who care about freedom and stopping evil." The man then added, "What I saw you do was remarkable. You and your friends are very special people. If I didn't think you could make a difference I'd already be on my way back to Canaveral with my cooked up story about how the meteorite got destroyed."

"I'm…I'm not sure. I need to think about this," George responded. But in truth he already knew what they would do.

"Go ahead," Brunner responded, understanding evident on his face. Handing The Brain a business card, he said, "Here's my number. It's direct to me alone. Talk to your friends, then give me a call if you want to see what a real difference you can make."

Extending his hand, he shook The Brain's, then disappeared into the blackness of the evening.

George Alexander, The Brain, the leader of M-Force, was left standing alone in the silence of the night. It seemed like the destinies of the four young adventurers were about to head into a new direction.